"Hope, humor, and happine............................... of good a book. *Never the Bride* is more than that—it's terrific!"

—LOUISE DUART, comedic impressionist, TV host,
and author of *Couples Who Pray*

"*Never the Bride* is a love story with a kick! Not just funny, this book is rollicking, with a heroine who can change her own tires, guide her own free-spirited sister, and keep an outlook on life that caused more than one fit of giggles. This is the kind of book I want to read again, simply because it is so rich with meaning and so intelligently written; I want to make sure I've caught every nuance."

—HANNAH ALEXANDER, author of *A Killing Frost*
and the Hideaway series

"*Never the Bride* is a powerful and thought-provoking story with just the right touch of humor. At times I laughed out loud, and at other times I wiped away my tears. *Never the Bride* is a treasure of a novel and a must-read!"

—CARRIE TURANSKY, author of *Along Came Love*
and *Kiss the Bride*

"Engrossing as they are entertaining, the authors hit it out of the park with this delightful romantic romp, striking at the heart of a woman's deepest desire: to be known and loved for herself. Side-splittingly funny and devastatingly raw in turns. Having devoured McKay's inspired screenplay first, followed by this fabulously faithful novel, I can hardly wait for the movie!"

—SUSAN ROHRER, producer, writer, and director

"*Never the Bride* teaches us all powerful lessons about God's plan, control, and the peace that comes with surrender."

—JIM STOVALL, author of *The Ultimate Gift*

"Delightful, delightful, delightful is *Never the Bride*. Rene Gutteridge knows how to take a plot and give it an unexpected, soul-searching, humorous wow of a twist."
—LYN COTE, author of *The Desires of Her Heart*

"*Never the Bride* is a delightful book. Jessie is a wise-cracking, sarcastic gal I'd love to take to lunch. This book had me in stitches as I laughed with Jessie, in tears as I felt her pain and desperation. If you're looking for a book that's more than a romance, this is the book. This novel will speak to the heart of every woman who's ever sought the perfect man, by pointing her to the perfect romance."
—CARA C. PUTMAN, author of *Canteen Dreams*
and *Sandhill Dreams*

"*Never the Bride* is a pure delight! It's fun, refreshing, and witty, yet also profoundly insightful about God and His amazing love for us. I'll be recommending this one to my family and friends!"
—MARLO SCHALESKY, author of *If Tomorrow Never Comes*
and *Beyond the Night*

"For all those wannabe brides out there, *Never the Bride* is a refreshing look at how quickly we can sell ourselves short, while reminding us, in a witty and yet profound way, that there is a wannabe Groom who has always been there. Every belly laugh and every tear inspired by this book will hopefully cause each wannabe bride to realize she already is one."
—DENISE HILDRETH, author of the Savannah series
and *Flies on the Butter*

"I devoured every single page. *Never the Bride* is the best romantic comedy written in years! A page turner from page one."
—VICTORYA ROGERS, love coach, host of ManToKeep.com,
and author of *Finding a Man Worth Keeping*

"*Never the Bride* is a ticklish tale of one slightly neurotic woman's quest to find Mr. Right that leads to an unexpected encounter. Delightfully memorable, wonderfully thought provoking!"
—TAMARA LEIGH, award-winning author of *Splitting Harriet*
and *Leaving Carolina*

never
the
bride

By Rene Gutteridge

Boo

Boo Who

Boo Hiss

Boo Humbug

Scoop

Snitch

Skid

My Life as a Doormat

By Cheryl McKay

Never the Bride (screenplay)

The Ultimate Gift film (screenplay)

Gigi: God's Little Princess DVD (screenplay)

Wild & Wacky, Totally True Bible Stories series (cowritten with Frank Peretti)

Books by Cheryl McKay and Rene Gutteridge

The Ultimate Gift film novelization

never
the
bride

a novel

cheryl mckay &
rene gutteridge

WaterBrook
PRESS

NEVER THE BRIDE
PUBLISHED BY WATERBROOK PRESS
12265 Oracle Boulevard, Suite 200
Colorado Springs, Colorado 80921

Grateful acknowledgment is made for the use of select lyrics to "Love Unseen" and "Don't
Want to Know You," copyright © 2009 by Louis Rodriguez. Used by permission.

ISBN 978-0-30744-498-1
ISBN 978-0-30745-790-5 (electronic)

Published in association with the literary agency of Janet Kobobel Grant, Books & Such,
52 Mission Circle, Suite 122, PMB 170, Santa Rosa, CA 95409-5370.

Published in the United States by WaterBrook Multnomah, an imprint of The Doubleday
Publishing Group, a division of Random House Inc., New York.

WATERBROOK and its deer colophon are registered trademarks of Random House Inc.

Library of Congress Cataloging-in-Publication Data
Gutteridge, Rene.
       Never the bride : a novel / Rene Gutteridge and Cheryl McKay. — 1st ed.
       p. cm.
       ISBN 978-0-307-44498-1 — ISBN 978-0-30745-790-5 (electronic)
   I. McKay, Cheryl. II. Title.
       PS3557.U887N48 2009
       813'.54—dc22

                                                          2009001790

Printed in the United States of America
2009

10 9 8 7 6 5 4 3

For those who fear the
surrender of their
purple pens

one

You don't know me yet, so there is no reason you should care that I'm stuck on a highway with a blowout. But maybe we can relate to each other. Maybe you can understand that when I say, "Everything goes my way," I'm being sarcastic. Not that I'm usually dependent on such a primitive form of communication. I'm actually not very cynical at all. I'm more of a glass-half-full-of-vitamin-infused-water person. Sometimes I even believe that if I dream something, or at least journal it, it will happen. But today, at eight forty-five in the morning, as the sun bakes me like a cod against the blacktop of the Pacific Coast Highway, I'm feeling a bit sarcastic.

It's February but hotter than normal, which means a long, hot California summer is ahead—the kind that seems to bring out the beauty in blondes and the sweat glands in brunettes. I am a brunette. Not at all troubled by it. I don't even have my hair highlighted. I own my brunetteness and always have, even when Sun-In was all the rage. And it can't be overstated that chlorine doesn't turn my medium chestnut hair green. Actually, it's the copper, not the chlorine, that turns hair green—but that's a useless trivia fact I try to save for speed dating.

I'm squatting next to my flat tire, examining the small rip. Holding my hair back and off my neck with one hand, I stand and look up and down the road, hoping to appear mildly distressed. Inside, I'll admit it, I'm feeling moderately hysterical. My boss flips out when I'm late. It wouldn't matter if my appendix burst, he doesn't want to hear excuses. I wish he were the kind of guy who would just turn red in the face and yell, like Clark Kent's newspaper boss. But no. He likes to lecture as if he's an intellectual, except he's weird and redundant and cliché, so it's painful and boring.

A few cars zoom by, and I suddenly realize this could be my moment. Part of me says not to be ridiculous, because this kind of thing happens only on shows with a ZIP code or county name in the title. But still, you can't help wondering, hoping, that maybe this is the moment when your life will change. When you meet your soul mate.

Like I said, I enjoy my glass/life half full.

Even as an optimist, I see no harm in being a little aggressive to achieve my goals. So with my free hand, I do a little wave, throw a little smile, and attempt to lock eyes with people going fifty miles an hour.

And then I see him. He's in a red convertible, the top down, the black sunglasses shiny and tight against his tan skin. He's wearing pink silk the way only a man with a good, measured amount of confidence can. At least that's the way I see it from where I'm standing.

As he gets closer, his head turns and he notices me. I do a little wave, flirtatious with a slight hint of unintentional taxi hailing. I decide to smile widely, because he is going fast and I might look blurry. He smiles back. My hand falls to my side. I step back, lean against my car, and try to make my conservative business suit seem flattering. There's nothing I can do about my upper lip sweating except hope my sweat-proof department-store makeup is holding up its end of the bargain better than my blowout-proof tire did.

He seems to be slowing down.

Live in the moment, I instruct myself. Don't think about what I should say or what I could say. Just let it roll, Jessie, let it roll. Don't overthink it.

This thought repeats itself when the convertible zooms by. I think he actually accelerated.

So.

My makeup is failing, along with whatever charm I thought I had. I just can't imagine what kind of guy wouldn't stop and help a woman. Maybe I'd have more hits if I were elderly.

I do what I have to do. What I know *how* to do. I change my own stupid tire. Yes, I can, and have been able to since I was eighteen. I can also change my own oil but don't because then I appear capable of taking care of myself. And I'm really not. Practically, yes, I can take care of myself. I make decent money. I drive myself home from root canals. I open cans without a can opener. I'm able to survive for three days in the forest without food or water, and I never lost sleep over Y2K.

But I'm talking about something different. I'm talking about being taken care of in an emotional way. Maybe it's a genetic problem. I don't know. Somehow I became a hopeless romantic. A friend tried the exorcism equivalent of purging me of this demon when she made me watch *The War of the Roses* two times in a row, all under the guise of a girls' night, complete with popcorn and fuzzy slippers.

That didn't cure me.

I want to be married. I hate being alone.

I lift the blown-out tire and throw it in my trunk, slamming it closed. My skin looks like condensation off a plastic cup. I can't believe nobody has stopped. Not even a creepy guy. I stand there trying to breathe, trying to get ahold of my anger. I'm going to be late, I'm going to be sweaty, and I'm on the side of a highway alone.

"You need some help?"

I whirl around because I realize that I've just been hoping that even a creepy guy would stop, and since my world works in a way that only my negative thoughts seem to come to pass, you can see why the glass-half-full is so important.

The morning sun blinds me, and all I see is a silhouette. The voice is deep, kind of mature.

"Well, I *did* need some help," I say, fully aware that acting cute is not going to undo the sweat rings that have actually burst through three layers of fabric, so I don't bother. I dramatically gesture to my car and try a smile. "But as you can see, I don't now."

"You're sure?"

"Yes. But thank you very much," I say, *for stopping after I'm completely finished.* I trudge back to my car and start the air conditioner. Glancing back in my rearview mirror, I study the silhouette. He sort of has the same shape as the guy in my dream last night. My nightmare. It was actually a dream after my nightmare, where you feel awake but you're not. It wasn't the nocturnal version of *Chainsaw Massacre*, but it did involve taffeta.

He doesn't wave. He doesn't move. He just stands there, exactly like the guy in my dream. It's very déjà vu–like and I lock my doors. I put my blinker on, pull onto the highway, and leave him behind, driving below the speed limit on my flimsy spare tire all the way to work.

I work at Coston Real Estate. We're squeezed between a wireless store and a Pizza Hut. We stand out a little because of our two huge dark wood doors, ten feet tall and adorned with silver handles.

I push open one of the doors and walk in. Mine is the front desk. It's tall, almost Berlin Wall–like. People have to peer over it to see me, and I look very small on the other side. When I'm sitting, I can barely see over the top of it.

I walk toward the break room, past nine square cubicles, all tan and otherwise colorless. Even the carpet is tan. On my left are the real offices with walls.

Nicole, inside her cubicle, sees me. "What happened to you?"

We've been good friends ever since I started working here, ten years ago. She's African American, two years younger than I am. She has that kind of expression I wish I could wear. Her eyebrows slant upward toward each other, like a bridge that's opening to let a boat through. It's part *You're weird* and part *I'm worried*. She has sass and I love it. She's working her way up to senior agent and is one of Mr. Coston's favorites, but I don't hold that against her.

I don't answer because I'm busy staring at her new eight-by-ten framed family picture. It's very Picture People: white background, casual body language, all four wearing identical polos and jeans. I love that kind of husband, who will wear matching clothes with his family. They're so adorable.

"Jessie, seriously girl, you okay? You've got black smeared across your forehead."

I tear my eyes away from the photo. "Blowout on the highway."

The eyebrow bridge is lowered, and she chuckles. "Honey, you look like you changed your own tire."

I put my forehead against the edge of her cube wall. "I did."

"Oh. Wow. I wish I knew how to change a tire."

"No, you don't. Trust me."

She reaches under her desk and pulls out a neatly wrapped gift. "For you."

I smile. I love gifts. I drop my things and tear it open even though I already know what it is. "Nicole, it's beautiful!" It's a leather-bound journal with gold embossed lettering and heavy lined paper inside. "What's the occasion?"

"It's February. I know how much this month… Well, it tends to be a long month for you, that's all." She points to the spine of it. "It sort of reminds me of the one I brought you back from Italy four years ago. Remember?"

"Yes, it does."

"So, my friend, happy February. May this month bring you—"

"Love." From my bag, I pull out a folder and slap it on her desk.

"What is this?" She says it like a mom who has just been handed a disappointing report card.

"Just look."

Carefully, like something might jump out and insult her, she opens the folder. She picks up three glossy photos of several potential loves of my life.

"They're hot, aren't they?" I ask.

"Too hot," she says.

"There's no such thing as too hot."

"Suspiciously too hot, like an airbrush might be involved."

I grab the photos from her and turn them around for her to see. With my finger, I underline each of their names: CuteBootsieBoo, SuaveOneYouWant, OneOfAKindMan.

"Jessie CuteBootsieBoo. Mmm. Doesn't have a good ring to it."

"It's their *instant message* names, Nicole."

"Yes. And that makes it better?"

I sigh. "You have got to get into the twenty-first century, you know. This is the best way to meet a guy."

"You can tell a lot about a man by what he names himself." She looks up at me and shakes her head. "Seriously. You set up a date with one of these and they'll show up with a beer gut, a walker, or a rap sheet."

"None of them rap."

Nicole stands, grabs my arm with one hand and my stuff with the other, and whisks me to my desk. She nearly pushes me into my chair and drops everything in front of me.

"Chill out," I say as she walks away. "This service guarantees background checks. But if you happen to end up needing a restraining order, they'll pay for it."

Nicole gasps and whirls around.

"I'm kidding." But I have her attention now. I lean back in my chair, looking at the ceiling as my hands feel the leather on my new journal. "This'll be the year, Nicole."

"You say that every year. Especially in February, which is why I got you the—"

I snap forward. "But I've never taken control like this before. Three online match sites, one dating service. They find what you want or your money back."

Nicole walks back toward me and leans over the counter. "I didn't realize QVC sold dates. If you order in the next ten minutes, do you get two for the price of one, plus an eight-piece Tupperware set?" She reaches for my chocolate bowl.

I scowl at her but lift the bowl up so she can reach it. "What do you know about it? You got married right out of college."

"Don't remind me." She carefully unwraps her candy and takes a mini-bite.

"You never even had to try." I grab a piece of dark chocolate out of my candy bowl and get the whole thing in my mouth before she takes another bite of hers.

Nicole shrugs and leans against the counter. "Sometimes you just gotta leave these things up to fate." She goes back to nibbling on her chocolate.

I swirl my hands in the air. "Fate, God, the universe. They've all been asleep on the job of setting up a love story for me." I stand up. "No. I am going to make this happen myself."

Nicole doesn't look up from her candy. "Do you even know what it means to be married? To be chained to another person for the rest of your life? To pick up socks and wash underwear and care for a grown man like he's just popped out of infancy? Huh?"

I glare at her even though she's got eyes only for her candy. "It's got to be better than being alone. Or being a bridesmaid eleven times."

She bites her lip and finally glances at me. "But you know how…you kind of need everything to be a certain way."

I nudge my stapler so it isn't perfectly perpendicular to my sticky notes, just to show her I'm able to handle disorder. I try not to stare at it because now it's really bugging me. "Are you saying I'm a control freak?"

"With OCD tendencies. You can't expect everything to be exactly how you want it if you want to live through a marriage."

I stand and start walking slowly toward the bathroom. "I know what 'compromise' means."

Nicole follows. "Then why do you get mad when I have to check with my husband before we go out? That's what marriage is. You can't even poop without someone else knowing."

I glance at her to see if she's serious. She is. Part of me wants to tell her about my dream last night. I always tell her about my dreams. But she's really pooping on my parade today. We get to her desk and she sits down. I walk on.

I have these dreams. I'm talking nocturnal, not journal. Yeah, I dream in my journal. I admit it. I've written in one since I was fourteen, when I found a strange delight every time I drew a heart with a boy's name attached in squiggly letters.

But back to my nightmare. It started with me in a wedding dress.

That's not the nightmare. That part was actually cool because I was in a dress I designed in my journal when I was twenty-two.

The march was playing. I love the "Bridal March." Nothing can replace it. I cringe every time I hear a country song or bagpipes or something. My wedding, it's got to be traditional.

I was making my way down the aisle, rhythmically elegant, one foot in front of the other. My shoulders were thrown back, my chin lifted, and my bouquet held right at my waist. I once saw a bride carry her bouquet all the way down the aisle holding it at her chest. I shudder just talking about it.

The train fluttered behind me, like it's weightless or maybe there's an ocean breeze not too far away. It was long, bright white, and caused people to nod their approval.

I smiled.

Then the "Bridal March" stopped, halting like a scratched record. I looked up to find another bride in my place, wearing *my* dress, standing next to *my* guy. I couldn't see what he looked like; he was facing the pastor. But the bride, she looked back at me with menacing eyes, overdone with teal eye shadow and fake lashes.

I screamed. I couldn't help it. I closed my eyes and screamed again. When I opened them, I could hardly believe what I was looking at. A church full of people, looking at *her*. And what was I doing? Standing next to her in a bridesmaid dress.

Gasping, I looked down. Hot pink! With dyed-to-match shoes! I glanced next to me and covered my mouth. It was me again, standing next to me, in green. Dyed footwear.

And there I was again, standing next to my lime self, this time in canary yellow. On and on it goes. I counted ten of me before I woke up, gasping for air, clutching myself to make sure I was wearing cotton pajamas.

"Thank God," I said, but as I looked up, I saw a man in my room. He was backlit against my window, like the moon was shining in on him, but I don't think the moon was out. A scream started forming in my throat, but I recognized that he was not in a stance that indicated he was going to stab me to death. There was no knife. Nothing but an easy, casual lean against my windowsill. Truly, no less scary.

The scream arrived as I clamored for my lamp. I yanked the string three or four times before it turned on, but when it did, the man was gone.

I realize I am standing in the middle of the hallway near Nicole's desk. She is gabbing on the phone but looking at me funny. I go to the coat closet next to the bathroom. I always, always keep a spare change of clothes at work, just in case I have to do something like change my tire. Or someone else's. It's happened. I take out my least favorite suit, which is why I keep it here. It's lilac with a boxy neckline that makes me feel like I should be a nanny. I head toward the bathroom.

"Stone, get me the ad copy for the new Hope Ranch listings."

This is my boss, Mr. Coston, dragging me back to reality. He pops his head out the door as I pass by but yells at me like I'm down the hall. I don't think he even remembers my first name.

"Already on your desk, sir," I say.

He's in his sixties, with a loud but raspy voice and shiny silver hair that tops a permanent look of disappointment. "What happened to you?"

"Blown tire." I hold up my suit. "I was just going to change."

"Fine. Then get me a latte. Lighten up on the sugar, will you?"

"Right," I mumble as he disappears. "Lighten up on life, will you?"

I'm the office equivalent of a bat boy. I'm the coffee girl. It's this one thing that sort of drives me crazy about my job. I do a lot of important things, but when I have to run get coffee, I feel like I'm falling down the rungs of the occupational ladder. It makes me wonder. If I had a job I could get passionate about, would I be so desperate for a husband? I could drown myself in work rather than my dreams.

Well, either way, I'm drowning, and that's never good.

After I change and decide I really, really dislike the color lilac, I grab my purse and head for the neighborhood Starbucks. It's five blocks away and I like that. It gives me time to walk and think on such things as to why Mr. Coston has been married for thirty-four years, the exact number of years I haven't been married. He doesn't mention his wife much and doesn't even have a picture of her in his office. He doesn't wear a wedding band, and when he does take a vacation, it's with his buddies to golf resorts.

It just seems like the world could better balance itself out, that's all.

I'm nearly to Starbucks. People are leaving with their white and green cups of bliss. The putrid smell of coffee will soon replace the putrid smell of old rainwater evaporating underneath the sun. I'm not a coffee fan. I'm high strung. The feeling everyone wants by drinking coffee I have naturally, just like my chestnut hair.

I'm about to open the door, and then I see him, in all his glory.

two

He's sitting at one of the outside tables in front of Starbucks, busily texting. I pull out my phone and pause. I know exactly whom he's texting. My phone vibrates almost instantly.

PLAY HOOKY.

Before I go on, I have to explain Blake to you. It's complicated, but stick with me.

Blake is my best friend. We've known each other since we were kids. I grew up to be smart, sensible, and brunette. He grew up to be smart, sensible, and hot. We've been through a lot together, but I never could shake the attraction to him that I've felt since we were sixteen.

I remember the exact day he went from irritating to irresistible. We were at a birthday party. Our birthdays are nine days apart, and his mother was always kind to include me since my mom had a hard time organizing events, or even dinner, for that matter. Blake never minded. We shared many friends.

Anyway, it was the smallest thing. One second he was Blake. And the next, when he offered to pour my drink for me, he became more. My heart skipped a beat and for a second I thought maybe something was wrong. I stared at the fizz swelling over the top of the plastic cup, dribbling down the side. His finger caught it, swiped it. He took a napkin and cleaned the rest. He looked at me and said, "Sorry about that."

It's no *Casablanca* moment, but that's when it happened, when everything changed.

I've never spoken a word to him or anyone else about it, because there is a certain feeling of safety knowing that he is my best friend and that we're close for no other reason except we like each other.

It's just that he's also hot.

But trust me, I'm not going to do anything crazy like declare my love for him. I've seen *My Best Friend's Wedding*, and it doesn't end well for the chick friend.

Anyway, this is a usual routine for us. He texts PLAY HOOKY, and I meet him down at the Starbucks under the guise of getting my boss coffee. Since my boss is a Starbucks junkie, this has worked out well.

I snap my phone closed and decide to play a little trick on him. He's busy watching women walk by, so I sneak up behind him and in a deep, sexy voice purr, "Hey, baby, wanna share a latte?"

Blake sits up and whips around, his eyes wide. He sees me and cracks up laughing. I slide into the other seat at the table. "That was fast!"

"I was on my way here. Coston needed a latte, pronto."

I observe Blake for a moment. He always seems out of place at Starbucks. He works construction, houses mostly, and his clothes often have a fine layer of sawdust on them. He's rugged and muscular, with caramel wavy hair that complements his tanned skin. I like the fact that he always has a sunglasses line and that he refuses to wear anything but Ray-Bans.

For my birthday one year he bought me a pair, since I'd given him a hard time for years, declaring Target's were just as good. Turns out I was wrong. Ray-Bans rock. I still have the pair that he gave me. They're locked in my safe-deposit box because I couldn't live with myself if I lost a pair of two-hundred-dollar sunglasses.

He props his sunglasses on top of his head and grins, and by "grins" I mean melts my heart. "I've got something to show you!" He takes my hand and guides me through a small crowd. We are walking the opposite direction of my work, toward a two-block stretch of quaint shops.

He drops my hand and starts talking with his hands, which I notice immediately because usually he has them stuffed deep into his painter jeans. "She called the company this morning, asked for our help designing the inside of her shop. It's right up here."

I eye him suspiciously. "You build homes…"

"I know, but I think she just called, maybe because it's my dad's company, but—"

"Who?"

He stops and gestures toward a storefront. It's obviously unoccupied, but inside a couple of people are milling around. One in particular is catching Blake's eye. And mine. The plain glass window is busy with reflections of the street, but through all that I can see her. She's practically glowing among the dust and clutter of an unfinished room. And bending over. Let's just say she's…taut. All of her. Head to toe. Even her neck looks in shape.

I fold my arms. "You're gonna stop building homes to make, what is it, shelves or something?"

Blake smiles. "For Veronica Steele, yes."

I take a deep breath. I had never actually seen her in person until now. I'd seen a picture of her…okay, pictures. Lots of them. This woman, whose name sounds like she stepped straight out of Harlequin, USA, was Blake Lightner's college obsession.

We stand there for a moment, Blake observing Veronica and me observing Blake. He's got this weird expression on his face. It's part thirteen-year-old with an *SI* swimsuit issue and part dumbfounded, *Why didn't she choose me?* That part I can relate to.

Still, it irritates me. "What? And you need my approval? What do you see in her?"

We both look. We both know. Legs like a giraffe. Hair like a wild pony. Curves like a coastal highway.

"What's not to like?"

"She's just very giraffey. I mean, sure, her neck is long, her legs are long, but don't you think she's a little out of proportion? She's got short arms, or maybe a long waist, but either way, she's very giraffey." I know. I sound stupid. I get this way when Blake gets this way.

"I was thinking more along the lines of gazelle." He's staring like we're five-year-olds at the zoo and the zebras are mating.

"Well, good luck finding a vet for the two of you." I sigh a little. I'm being hard on him and I know it. The truth is, he's always loved Veronica. I'm about to apologize for my snarkiness when his attention is diverted by another woman walking by. It's just for a second, but I see it. "I'm not sure they can cure you of the bad case of shallow-itis you're suffering from."

Blake's gaze slides sideways. "I am not one of those guys."

"I hate to shatter your perfectly solid opinion of yourself, but people who hold on to old flames and refuse to let go are pathetic."

My words are harsh. Not as harsh as I want them to be. But Blake's sensitive, which is why I like him and why I hold back. And yes, that's holding back. Especially when I offer a small smile. I stand there for a moment, drowning in my own subtext.

Veronica is bent over again. We're both staring.

"Well," he says, and I can't tell at all if he's being serious or not, "is it curable?"

"This girl's gotta get back to work. Enjoy the show." I walk toward Starbucks, checking my watch. The line is long, but that is a good thing today. I need some time to cool off. I feel foolish. And hopeless.

How can I, Jessica Stone, compare to *that*? Leggy. Blonde. Owns a business. Steele will win over Stone any day of the week.

I sigh loudly—too loudly—and the woman in front of me turns, offering a sympathetic smile. "This line is barely crawling."

I stand on my tiptoes to see what's going on. Short on baristas? Nope.

"It's that she's blonde," I tell the woman in front of me, who is a carrot top—curly and afro-like.

She peeks around the line to look. "Yep. The men always feel like they need to chat up a blonde."

I didn't know redheads felt the same way. Huh.

"What is it about blondes?" I ask her.

She fluffs her curls. "No idea. I hate her. Look."

I stare at the young barista, who really doesn't seem to be doing anything out of the ordinary. She's taking orders, smiling at customers, counting change. But somehow when she does it, it seems sexy.

I am fully aware that I am discriminating by hair color. And I'm also fully aware of how shallow that makes me.

The redhead finally gets to the front and begins ordering. I chew a nail, wondering if I should text Blake, just to make sure things are okay. But then I notice a man. He's standing in the corner, near the wall of coffee mugs, noticing me. The second thing I notice is that when I notice him, he doesn't stop noticing me. He doesn't look away. He locks eyes with me, and I look away first. He's cute! Slightly rugged but not above a button-down cotton shirt. A nice, gentle smile. Compelling eyes.

"Ma'am?" By the tone, I realize the barista has probably been trying to get my attention.

"Oh, uh, sorry." I shuffle forward. "Grande latte, skim, extra foam."

"For?"

"Jessie."

I hand over the money and glance back at the guy. He's still staring at me. He looks familiar, but I don't know where I've seen him. It's not his face. It's…the way he's standing.

"Ma'am?"

"Oh, sorry," I say as the blonde dumps the change into my hand. I scoot out of the way and stand near the bar where the coffee comes out. The red-haired woman is standing nearby. "Hey," I say to her, "is it just me or is the guy over by the mugs staring at me?"

She nonchalantly glances over. "The motorcycle dude?"

I see the motorcycle dude. Scary and not at all looking like a latte guy. "No, the other guy, standing by the mugs."

"Um…"

"He seems kind of intense. I mean, to just blatantly stare, you know?"

She doesn't say anything. Now *she's* staring at me. I've got two people staring at me.

Thankfully my drink comes up. I grab two sugars and tear them open. I pour. I stir.

I wonder if he's still watching me. And then I realize that I had been so distracted by his intensity, I forgot to be cute. I look back up, this time with a cool smile on my face, but he's gone. I peer out the window. Maybe he's waiting outside. But no. He's gone. Probably the lilac suit.

I rip open two more packets and pour furiously. Stir so hard coffee drips. I grab four napkins and scrub the counter. Two more packets and I don't bother stirring this time. I secure the lid and walk outside.

Yes, sometimes I ruin his coffee simply because I'm in a bad mood. But the man should count his blessings. I could add something much worse than sugar.

I make it back quickly because when I'm mad I walk fast. I deliver the latte to Mr. Coston, who is busy on the phone explaining to someone that just because a person died in a house doesn't mean it's haunted.

Back at my desk, I gaze at the shiny silver banner that hangs across the wall behind me. It's been there for two weeks. It looks tacky against the marble lettering of Coston Real Estate. It reads, HAPPY TENTH ANNIVERSARY! The exclamation point bothers me. I'm certain that the banner was meant for a married couple. If not, then the exclamation point is unnecessary because maybe someone isn't excited about being at the same dead-end job for ten years.

I can't complain too much. They did bring me literally pounds of my favorite candy. I open my desk drawer and plunge my hand into a bag of dark chocolate M&M's. You wouldn't know it by looking at the situation, but I'm a bit of a risk taker. I'm allergic to chocolate. Not in an airway-closed-off kind of way, but I do swell. Sometimes my lips get puffy, and I won't lie, it's a good look for me. Other times I'm not so lucky, and an eyelid will droop or something. Dark chocolate and chocolate in liquid form give me the least trouble. But when I do indulge, I have to make sure I'm not due for a date or a presentation or something, because I never know exactly what's going to swell.

Since I'm stuffing my face with chocolate, why not continue down what Nicole would call a self-destructive path? I log on to Matches.com. The opening page has one match being lit by the other's charm. It's kind of cute, except the song is corny, so I turn down the sound. I log in and punch in my password, Dark Cocoa. My screen name appears: WELCOME, LEGALLY_BROWN.

The front doors of the office open. I quickly minimize the page and smile as my co-worker Christa enters. She peeks over the counter. "Hey, Jessie."

"Hi, Christa. How are you?" *And your perky, beautiful self?*

"Good. I can't wait for after work. You'll be there, right?"

I pause. I had no intention of going to her bridal shower in the break room. I was going to cut out early to avoid it. But the bright smile that must've won the guy—now fiancé—over starts to fade and she seems a little hurt. "Of course," I say. "Wouldn't miss it."

She claps her hands. "Yay! All right, see you then!"

She bounces down the hall, and all she's missing is a team to cheer for. I pull up my Matches.com page again.

Ugh. NO MATCHES blinks like a hazard light. Why did they have to make it blink? Blinking is for excitement and road hazards.

Maybe it's a subtle message that I'm on the wrong road.

It's noon and I tell Nicole I'll have to skip our planned lunch because I have to go get something for Christa. Nicole says it's fine because she wants to decorate the room a little more. How a break room can look any better with streamers is beyond me, but I let it go. I don't want to become that bitter person who stands people up at their bridal showers because I'm insanely jealous.

I find an open meter in the Paseo Nuevo district, parallel park like a moron, and walk a few blocks to get to the gift shop that is my home away from home.

I notice an awful lot of men shopping today. These are the cool ones, who are shopping a few days before Valentine's to get the exact right gift. They're thinking ahead, not running out and grabbing something in a hurry. Their women, whoever they are, are lucky.

I open the door to Malia's Gifts & Flowers. A robot Cupid, playing *Love Is in the Air,* pretends to shoot an arrow. I never liked Cupid. Thought he was a little creepy with his diaper and fat rolls.

I notice Malia behind the counter, sacking up some grand gift for a guy. She hands him change and wishes him luck. Malia is beautiful for her age. She's sixty-two and looks like she's forty, except she's all gray.

She has a youthful playfulness about her. She spots me and waves enthusiastically. I wave back, then block the door so the guy with the balloons, stuffed pink bear, and card can't get out.

He gives me a curious look.

I can smell his cologne. "Hi." I smile.

"Hi. Excuse me."

"Not so fast." I look carefully over his purchases and notice he had picked out a card that had made me snort out loud when I read it last week. Funny, but not so romantic. "Love the balloons. The pink bear is cute. But trust me, you'll want to write something personal in the card."

He looks down at it, a slight panic crossing his face. "I went with humor. Maybe I shouldn't have. I'm…I better go back…this is…"

I place a steady hand on his shoulder. "Listen, the card is fine. It doesn't matter what's in there. Just write something personal. You don't have to write an essay, just two or three lines that make her feel like you have thought this through." I let go of his shoulder and step aside.

He nods, gazing up at the balloons. "Maybe the balloons were a mistake."

"How long have you been dating?"

"Not long. Three months."

"Then it's perfect. It's too soon for jewelry, but this still says, 'I'm crazy about you.'"

"Thank you," he says, relieved.

"You're welcome." Malia is coming toward me, so I step toward her and embrace her with a hug.

"How are you?" she asks. "I didn't see you this weekend."

"Fine. The shop looks great! Love the Valentine's decorations."

"Yeah? I kind of think I went overboard."

"No," I say, gazing at the hundreds of hearts hanging from the ceiling. "It's the season for going overboard. For most people, anyway."

She pinches my cheek and begins walking toward the counter. "What brings you by?" She looks me up and down as I walk with her. "You eating enough, girl?"

"More than my share of my favorite food group."

Malia arranges a pile of fake roses as she talks. "How many times do I have to tell you? Chocolate is not a food group."

I grin and adjust the heart-shaped notepads. "Hey, I've got to get my antioxidants somehow."

Malia looks up at me, worried. "Well, are you at least carrying Benadryl?"

I smile. She's such a mom. "Yes, I've got my emergency supply here."

"Let me go microwave some organic spinach for you." She starts moving toward the back room. "I'll season it; it'll give you energy."

"And stick in my teeth." I grab her arm, and she stops, though it's obvious she's disappointed. "It'll be awkward," I say, "because I won't know I have green slime on my teeth and nobody will tell me. I'll get home, see it, die of embarrassment—and then I'll have to eat more chocolate. So I better pass."

She shoots me a mild look.

I begin to browse. "I need a bridal shower gift."

A customer approaches the counter, and I let Malia take care of him.

I wander the displays, looking for anything that doesn't scream Valentine's Day. I pick up a cloth doll with a mop of blond hair. "The bride's young enough that she might actually enjoy this," I holler as I hold the doll high enough for her to see.

I hear her laugh. She finishes with the customer and joins me.

"Did you know," I say, fingering the yarn, "that your son has quite the thing for blondes?"

Malia nods. "No curing a man of that." She reaches for a display and hands me a shiny silver heart-shaped frame. "She'll love this. One can never have too many frames."

"Thanks."

"I'll wrap it up nicely for you."

"You're a sweetheart."

She takes my arm as we head for the register. "You know, speaking of, I could introduce you to the guy who owns Fine Computer Techs. They do my Web site. He's single."

"Unless *fine* means something other than 'talented computer geeks,' I think I'll pass. Have we not committed to memory the last disaster you set me up with?"

"I swear I had no idea he would ask you for one of your kidneys." Malia's eyes grow wide at the memory.

I pull out my credit card and hand it to Malia. "Maybe I have commitment issues, because although his great-uncle Ned sounded completely fascinating, I wasn't ready to part with an organ."

Malia laughs. "I'm serious, though. This computer guy, he's a cutie. He'd be just right for you."

"I need more depth, Malia. He speaks binary, and I need more than just zeros and ones in my life."

She hands me my card and receipt. "He's fully HTML." She winks and begins looking for wrapping.

I smile. I love that she gets my jokes. Blake gets his sense of humor from her. The thing is, Malia has this track record with me. She's tried to set me up twelve times. Twelve disasters. Maybe because she never tried to set me up with Blake. I don't blame her. I act awfully uninterested to protect my own interests. But still. Can't his own mother see what a great couple we'd make?

Malia sets my gift aside for a moment to help a pregnant woman who has approached. She's wearing a short-sleeved cotton blouse with tiny tulips all over, and some khaki capris. Her shiny, youthfully golden hair is pulled up high into a ponytail. Her stomach is beautifully round, and she's rubbing the bottom of it with one hand, like the baby is already in her arms. I start rubbing my belly just watching her. Except when I do it, I look like I'm expecting chocolate-chip cookies.

"You ready, hon?" Malia asks her.

"Yes."

Malia peers over the counter. "Do you know if you're having a boy or a girl?"

"A boy."

"Oh, do tell us! Have you picked a name?" I see something in Malia's eyes…a longing for a grandchild of her own.

"Jonathan. It took three years for me to get pregnant, so my husband and I consider this little guy to be a gift of God. That's what Jonathan means."

I have to wonder: what name means "in desperate need of a man"?

Mr. Coston is in a particularly bad mood today. He sends me out twice more for coffee. I take my time and this time don't add so much sugar.

The atmosphere is somber for the afternoon. We've all been lectured three or four times. I try to focus, for once, on my work. By five I am exhausted and still have to attend the break room bridal shower. I turn off my computer, straighten my desk, dust, Lysol, squirt my hands, and then head for the break room.

A few people have gathered, and Nicole is trying to secure a streamer that has fallen. I climb on a chair to help her.

"Hey." She smiles. "Can you hand me some tape?"

"Sure." I reach for it and rip off a piece. "Nicole?"

"Yes?"

"Promise me when I get married you'll do something bigger—maybe outside the office or something?"

Nicole glances at me. "Honey, when you get married, we're going to give the Fourth of July a run for its money."

I hand her the end of the streamer. "Christa's nice. Maybe we should've done something more."

"She's a co-worker. We don't hang out on weekends. There's a difference."

"What'd you get her?"

Nicole stands on her toes and manages to re-secure the streamer. "A gift certificate to Pottery Barn. You?"

"A frame and a month's supply of antibacterial gel."

Nicole laughs. "Wow."

"It's practical. She's going to appreciate that after she shakes everyone's hand at the reception."

Nicole glances at me. "You're serious?"

"What? I tied a cute satin bow around it."

We are climbing down just in time to see Christa entering, surrounded by a half-dozen people.

"...and my fiancé tied my ring to the mistletoe and waited for me to notice. It was so adorable."

"A little unoriginal, don't you think?" I whisper to Nicole.

"I don't know. Jerry dropped to one knee, popped open the box, asked, and we ordered chicken wings, so it sounds kind of nice to me."

"I'm just saying, mistletoe is overdone. Now dropping it down the chimney, that's creative."

"Santa's got the corner on that market."

I sigh and sit on one of the folding chairs that we've put into a circle. Christa is popping her shoulders up and down, just as happy as any human being can be. It's genuine. And she doesn't seem to care we're in a break room.

"I'm just saying," I whisper again to Nicole as soon as she sits down beside me, "she deserves a more creative proposal than that."

"Jessie, some people are not creative. They're okay with things not having to be done over the top."

"I'm not over the top."

Nicole puts on her sales smile as she looks up at the arriving guests, but she turns sideways toward me and says quietly, "You dream big."

I can't respond for the moment because Nicole welcomes everyone, tells some nice anecdotes about Christa, and then begins the procession of presents. But as soon as I get Nicole's ear again, I whisper, "I like the personal touch. I like things not to be cookie cutter." I gesture to Christa as she pulls out a slinky negligee. People are giggling. "I'm simply saying that she's the type of person who would make her bridesmaids wear peach dresses with dyed-to-match shoes. When I get married, you're going to thank me for being a little more original."

"Like what? Scratch-and-sniff dresses?"

"Funny. *No.* Like maybe letting everyone wear what they want."

Nicole laughs. Hard. Nobody notices because they're all laughing about the fluffy bunny slippers Christa just unwrapped. "You've got to be kidding me," Nicole whispers. "You're not capable."

"Of what?"

"Letting us choose what we wear."

I smile at Christa "That's not true."

"So you're fine with your sister in a dress cut so low we can see her bellybutton ring and me wearing that off-white skirt I've had since—"

I wave my hands. "Sensibly. That's what I mean. Wear what you want as long as it's sensible."

"Uh-huh. But here's the thing. Your definition of sensible has a lot of parameters."

Just then Christa pulls out the antibacterial gel. "Ohhhh…um…the bow is lovely."

"There's more," I say, pointing to the bag.

She reaches in and pulls out the frame. Now she's gushing again. Good. I'd hate to have stopped all that gushing.

I turn back to Nicole. "You're still coming over Wednesday, right? Jerry's cool with it?"

"Yes, I'm still coming. And I think it's big of you to ask for help."

Christa is now pulling out his and her robes from Mr. Coston. "Oh! Beautiful!"

I sink into my seat.

three

i "I think the red looks good," Nicole says, leaning toward the mirror like I am. We're both staring at my jugular red lips, shiny like I've eaten a bucket of fried chicken. I glance at Nicole. She seems more sure than I feel.

"I don't know," I say, standing upright. "I mean, it's very, very red. It's the first thing you see coming. Is there a woman attached to those lips?"

"It fits you."

"Fits me?" I stare at myself, trying to see what Nicole sees. "I wear Burt's Bees lip balm with a hint of color."

"For tonight, though, isn't the whole idea to stand out?"

"Yes…" I turn away from the mirror and then look back quickly, trying to catch myself off guard. Still, the first thing I see are my red lips. "But I'm afraid my lips are going to upstage me."

"The guys will know what's coming."

I glance over at her. "What's that mean?"

Nicole smiles knowingly. At least I hope it's knowingly. She better not be winging this. "It's like foreshadowing in a book," she says. "The lips say a lot. And yours will get a chance to talk before you do."

"You're not winning me over."

Nicole turns me to her, puts her hands on my shoulders. "It's not a bad thing. You are a strong personality. There is nothing wrong with that. But it's misleading to wear powder pink and then light them up."

I turn back to the mirror, forcing her hands off my shoulders. "I don't light them up. I engage in conversation. We have eight minutes. There is no time for small talk."

"But it's still about first impressions."

"So my first impression is going to be about my mouth."

"Like I said, foreshadowing. Plus, you have great lips for a white woman." I slump but Nicole straightens my back. "You have to stand tall in this dress. And don't lean over or the lips will be a moot point, if you know what I mean."

"Zip me up," I say, grabbing my chest and now eying the dress, wondering if this little black number with the scoop neckline is such a good idea.

She zips.

I grab a towel and swipe the sink. Droplets of water drive me crazy. If people would just wipe up their messes, nobody would have to worry about leaning against the bathroom counter and leaving with dark wet smudges on their shirts. It's the small things in life, you know?

I check my watch. "Okay. 'Bout time to go. So you're sure? The ensemble works? I look inviting but not cheap? Happy but not peppy?"

She brushes some hair off my cheek. "You look beautiful, Jessie. You *are* beautiful. Remember that when you walk in. Hold your head high. You are a fine catch."

I hold my head high and feel like a fine catch. "I have a good feeling about tonight."

An uneasy expression passes over her face. "Just go have fun."

"I know, I know, my expectations always get me in trouble. But something's different. I feel different."

"There's power in red lipstick."

I laugh. "As long as it doesn't land on my teeth."

Her face turns a little serious. "Now. We need a game plan."

"Why?"

"Well, you know, last time it was…according to you—I'm using your own words—it was, um, grossly disappointing."

I grab my little black purse and shove my light-it-up lipstick inside. "I had an off night, that's all." I bustle around gathering my things so I can make a quick exit.

Nicole, however, perches on the edge of the bathtub and pats the spot. I wipe it with a towel and then grudgingly sit next to her. "As your friend," Nicole says, "—and again, you called me—I think you could try a different approach this time."

I push my cell phone into the tiny purse and zip the bag shut. "What do you mean?"

"Just minor changes, that's all I'm saying. I'm thinking that you completely take out their hair-color preference. You can't hold it against a person because they like a certain hair color, and then you've automatically put them on the defensive. I'm saying don't even broach that subject. Just be casual, let them do most of the talking."

"It's *speed* dating, Nicole. And it's a scientific fact that men who prefer blondes rarely mate with a brunette." I resist the urge to stand up.

"This is not a *Wild Kingdom* documentary."

"I've got to know something about them," I say, pressing my lips together. They feel very heavy.

"Yes. But you can tell a lot about a guy by what he asks *you.*"

I stop. I raise an eyebrow. She has a point. I'd never thought about that before.

"I know, I'm brilliant." She winks, stands up, and whisks me out of my bathroom. "And you, my darling, are going to make every man in that place speechless." She steps back from me and takes me in. "Audrey Hepburn, eat your heart out."

I slump again. "Please. I don't have the eyebrows."

Nicole laughs and reminds me to keep my shoulders back. "You call me tonight, okay? I want to know the details. You know I live vicariously through you."

We walk out the front door together and I lock up. "I would give anything for a family like yours," I say.

"Baby, you wait until it's the right time."

"Easy for you to say." I throw my shoulders back. "You're not speed dating on Valentine's Day."

★ ★ ★

It's a nice evening. The sun is low and glowing above the ocean water.
The salty smell entices me and I wonder if I might better serve myself
by just going on a long walk on the beach. I circle several downtown
Santa Barbara streets, trying to find a decent place to park. It's prime real
estate, though, on a Friday evening. I watch a man pull over and drop
his wife off before he goes to find a parking space. She gives him a quick,
appreciative wave. And, as if the heavens opened up with harp music,
a white Cadillac pulls off a meter and the man slides in, a half a block
from where he dropped off his wife. I slap my hand against the steering wheel. Maybe I should lobby for handicap parking *and* single-
woman parking.

I'm about to run late, especially if I have to park a few blocks away.
I give it one more circle. There! Up ahead! A meter, and it looks plenty
big for me to cram into. I accelerate. I'm only a quarter block away, but
up ahead…a Miata. Top down. The guy inside is alone, has black hair,
and sports a five o'clock shadow. No shades. Our eyes meet. Wow,
gorgeous, this one.

I grin and nod toward the spot, hoping he'll let me in. Technically he got there first—just by a second or two—but he's on the
wrong side of the street. His blinker is flashing aggressively. He lifts
his eyebrows and acknowledges me, pointing to the spot. I smile and
am about to mouth *thank you* when he waves, U-turns, and whips
right in.

My hands squeeze my steering wheel as I watch him check his
hair in the rearview mirror. A car lightly taps its horn behind me, but
I can't move. I just watch him.

He lifts his sleeve, glances at his watch, hops out of his car—and for the first time notices me still there. The car behind me swerves around and goes on.

"Thanks so much!" he calls. "I'm running late!" He jogs across the street.

I let my foot off the brake, and my Beemer crawls forward like it's suddenly aware it weighs a ton. I don't know why, but I can't even get angry about it. It was a genuine misunderstanding, apparently. I think I'd rather that this guy flip me the bird, screech his tires, and beat me to it.

My sister constantly reminds me that I'm a baffling embarrassment to our sex, as if one Jessie Stone could completely undo all of women's lib by wishing for a little chivalry. Of course, I know it and so does everyone else—I want more than chivalry. According to *Cosmo,* I should be strong and independent; the man is sort of like an afterthought. I'm just not wired that way. I wish I were. Believe me, if I could be anywhere else than a speed-dating session on Valentine's Day, I would be. But I'm no spring chicken, and all my life's dreams are seeping down the drain of time. I honestly thought I'd marry at the age of twenty-three, so it's been more than a decade of gulping down a lot of disappointment.

The sun has set, the streetlights are starting to pop on, and I find myself on a side street that doesn't even have a name or a working streetlight. The parking meters look ancient. It's not quite an alley, but with all the shadows of the nearby buildings, it might as well be.

Tears sting my eyes as I reach for my purse and my jewel-studded Mace can. Sniffling, I check my rearview mirror to see if anyone is around. Nobody. The street is completely empty, except for a cat next to a Dumpster, eying me like she might fight me for it.

I swipe at the tears. "No, Jessie. Don't." I get out of the car, trembling. Not that I haven't made long walks in the dark before. But with the ocean breeze and the sun down, it's cold. And yeah, I'm scared—even though I know how to grab a pinkie and force a guy to the ground, thanks to two years of self-defense classes where I swore I'd meet someone but didn't.

Blowing away my discouragement, I lock my doors and walk swiftly toward the main street. Suddenly, the streetlight right above me flickers on. Light spills across the pavement as if the sky found its flashlight. I laugh. I can't help it.

I glance behind me one more time and see someone, far away, leaning against something, I can't tell what. It's a guy, but it doesn't worry me. He's too far away.

I finally reach the main street and turn north. I check my watch right as I push open the door to Anita's. Inside a small table sits off to the right. Laurel notices me and checks me off her list.

"There you are."

"Sorry. Running a little late."

"No problem." She hands me my name tag with my registration number under it. "You're table ten."

"Thanks."

"Red."

"Pardon?"

"The lips."

I cover my mouth like a cold sore has popped up. "My friend's idea," I mumble.

"It's a bold look."

I hurry to my spot, eying my competition. Two natural blondes.

Four bottles. Two brunettes. A redhead. And a bald woman. I breathe in and settle into my chair, trying to look calm despite the fact that my lips feel like they're sizzling. I really think I should just go ahead and blot, but it's too late. The bell rings and the men, standing on the other side of the room, swarm toward the tables.

I brush my hair back and sit tall, clasping my hands on top of the table, then decide to go under for a more casual look. I smile pleasantly. Maybe eagerly. Like I said, I have a good feeling about tonight.

I center myself, remembering Nicole's advice—to focus on what they're asking me. That's a good plan. Sometimes these things can have a job-interview feel to them, though as I glance around, I do admire Laurel's sense of ambiance. Candles. Cloth table covers. Roses here and there.

I notice a man approach. He seems distracted by something a few tables away. He's walking toward me but not really looking at me. I shift and widen my smile. He glances at me, notices the smile, I guess, and smiles back.

"Hi." He shakes my hand. "Bob."

"Jessie."

Bob. Last year I moved into this new age bracket. It's thirty-four to forty-two. It was a little hard to get used to. I went from Skylers and Danes to Bobs and Larrys. Immediately I note Bob dyes his gray-ish brown hair, and that's okay. I have no problem with men dyeing their hair. Bob's has a Just-for-Men feel to it, but it's nothing I can't live with. He's about six feet tall, nice cheekbones, deep-set eyes, and bald-ing. I actually like the bald look, especially when they keep the rest of their hair short, which he does.

He glances down the row of tables again. I clear my throat. "Have I seat," I offer, since he's the last one standing.

He slides in and shakes his head. "I am so sorry. I'm being completely rude."

Self-awareness. I'm liking him already.

"It's just that four tables down…that's my ex-girlfriend."

"Oh."

"Heather."

"The blonde?"

"Yes."

We both look. She tosses her head backward and roars with laughter, deep from the throat. Across from her, the man's eyes light up as he watches. Bob's dim.

"I'm sorry," I say. It's obvious he still has feelings for her.

He shrugs and sips his drink. "But I'm here with you. Jessie."

"Yes."

"So, Jessie, what do you like to do for fun?"

Fun. Okay, first thing on this guy's mind. Not sure he's a catch, but we'll work with it.

"I like to read."

"Books?"

"Anything. Newspapers. Magazines."

"That's fun?"

"I love amusement parks." Love is over the top, but I had to go somewhere. I was losing this guy with books.

"Yeah? Me too! I once took a chick on this ride, and she threw up all over me. Oh man, you should've seen the look on her face!" He laughs hysterically and then glances over at Heather again. "It's just that it's going to be awkward, you know? I mean, she's very self-absorbed and probably thinks I'm here because I heard she was coming. I broke up with her, so it's probably going to be more awkward for her, and that's better. But the truth is that I'm kind of regretting it now and I'm wondering if maybe I should give it a second try."

Heather doesn't look like she needs anybody to give her a second try. She's radiant and, by the goofy look on the other guy's face, apparently witty. This is a downer. Bob doesn't see me even as a rebound type.

But I save face and lean across the table. "Why not? Maybe this was meant to be. You and her here on the same night. Coincidence?" I say this because I've been looking for my meant-to-be moment for years. I've personally witnessed several other people's, including now possibly one for Bald Bob.

His eyes absorb my comment. "You think so?"

"She's very nice looking."

"I know. She really is. And funny." He suddenly snatches my hand off the table. In the next second he drops it with a thud. "Sorry. I thought she looked over here."

"She was just scratching her ear."

"She does that when she's nervous."

"Ah."

Ding.

And that, possibly, was the longest eight minutes of my life. The guy now sliding in across from me is short, skinny, and bearing humongous white teeth. They're so big that you could make a case *against* whitener for this guy. A Caesar cut makes his ears look small, but a cute button nose and nice hazel eyes round him out well.

"Hey!" He slaps his hands together. "Roger!"

"Jessie."

"Jessie! Wow! You are beautiful! That hair! Look at that hair!" It feels like this guy has his Caps Lock on.

My fingers comb through the ends as I smile. But the smile drops when he reaches across the table to actually *touch* it. I'm about to suggest he stay on his side of the table when he produces a pop-up flower that he claims was growing out of my ear. He hands it to me and takes a little bow.

"Thank you," I say, twirling the plastic between my fingers. "You're a magician?"

"Baby, I can make magic happen anywhere, anytime. And I don't even need a dime." It comes rolling out of his sleeve and onto the table, shining in the candlelight. He picks it up and hands it to me as if it were a diamond.

I try to smile. "I bet you do this for all the girls."

His grin fades. I don't think he gets my joke, that I'm fully aware that's his plan. He's about to reach into his breast pocket. Fearing a string of rainbow handkerchiefs I say, "So, Roger, what are you looking for in a woman?"

"Magic!"

"What kind of magic? The kind that doesn't come with a top hat and a bunny rabbit?"

Oddly, Roger looks defeated again. "Actually, I was hoping to find a woman who would like to be my beautiful assistant."

I crack up. Roger is not joking, though. "Really."

"Oh, I'm sorry. I thought you were—well, never mind."

He points at me, shaking his finger. "You, actually, would be perfect. You're tall, beautiful, and obviously not afraid of wearing stage makeup."

I press my lips together. "I do like magic. I saw David Copperfield once."

"That guy's an amateur."

Sure. Everyone can make the Statue of Liberty disappear.

"What about Criss Angel?" I ask.

"Very theatrical and dark. That's so overdone. Why not go happy and bright?"

"Why not?"

And for the next three minutes he explains if we ever got married, I still wouldn't be privy to how he does *all* of his tricks.

The eight minutes are over, and my neck is hurting. I'm off to a rough start. Number three slides in. He's dressed in a suit and tie. He smiles politely, genuinely.

"Pat."

"Jessie."

"I like that name."

"Thank you."

"Okay, so I have a question for you. If you could do one thing in life right now, what would it be?"

I lean back, sort of blown away by the depth of the question after having a flower pulled out of my ear. I study Pat's eyes. It seems like he's getting me, getting that I'm really above all this. He seems to be too. Two lost souls, only eight minutes to find each other.

"Find my true love." His eyes tell me he can handle this statement. He doesn't even blink. "Do you think he's here? Tonight?"

This guy is intense. I sort of like it. He's making me nervous but in a good way. One hundred percent of his attention is focused on me. I pause, taking him in. Dark brown hair, wavy and sticking out a little behind the ears. I think his eyes are green, but it's hard to tell because they are reflecting a lot of light, especially considering the dim room. I am remembering Nicole's advice again—and liking this better. The guy's asking *me* questions. This is a guy who knows what he wants.

I tuck my hair behind my ears, fully aware of the silence. But I like silence sometimes. And I like that he doesn't feel as if he needs to fill it in.

"Eight minutes," I carefully answer, "is enough time to make me think I could be on the right track."

He likes my answer. I can tell. He's grinning and there are dimples! Real dimples! On both cheeks! And then…then…he leans forward. I studied this in a body-language book. This, ladies and gentlemen, means he's interested!

"I love brown hair," he says. "My mom had brown hair. A lot like yours. You plan on keeping it that way?"

"I wouldn't dream of another color."

"You have beautiful lips."

"Oh…wow…thank you." With all these compliments the lips might burst into flames.

"I'm sorry. Am I being too forward?"

"Eight minutes sort of requires it, doesn't it?"

"Well said. So," he said, balling up his hand and perching his chin there, "what do you do for a living?"

"Worry that I'm not living enough of life."

"I like you, Jessie. I can tell you're very smart. And funny. And deep."

One, he remembered my name without looking at my nametag. Two, he's totally getting me. Three, dimples. Four, he's leaning forward.

And now, even more. "You're really beautiful. I sense it comes from the inside. I feel like you know what you want. In fact, I feel like I already know you…like we've known each other for years. You've got a special quality about you that—"

Ding.

I grin but not fast enough. Pat is out of his chair. Midsentence. And gone to the next table. I blink rapidly. What just happened? I'm so special he can't finish his sentence?

I try to recover because I was drawn in. Pat had a way with words. Rolling up next is Newton. I'm about to introduce myself, but I don't get a chance.

"Okay, first things first. Do you like chicken?"

I pause. Is there going to be a punch line? Doesn't look like it. "Yes."

It's like a little red check mark has gone off in his head. "Great. What about allergies? To cats?"

"No. Just chocolate."

"Awesome. Willing to go organic?"

"Sure."

"Opposed to midwives?"

"Um…"

"If you get pregnant."

"I like the idea of a doctor around."

"Oh." Seems to throw him. I wait. "All right. Okay. Um, what about sushi?"

"Love it."

Wrong answer.

"But can live without it," I add.

"You're flexible?"

"Sure. I like a variety of foods."

"No, I mean, are you flexible physically? As in yoga."

Oh boy. Nicole was right. The questions can shed a lot of light. I'm bored already. Four minutes to go. I decide to have some fun.

"I can't even touch my toes."

Newton looks horrified, like I'd mentioned toe fungus or something. I keep a serious look on my face.

"Okay…um, would you be opposed to painting an entire room pink?"

"I'm color blind."

"Wow. Sorry to hear that. I'm really into the study of color and mood."

"Maybe that's why I have a mood disorder." I can hardly say this without laughing. Newton's face twitches as he tries to hold his expression.

"I'm sorry to hear that," he says, almost convincingly.

"Are you pitying me?"

Now his eyes are wide, like he's afraid he might've just crossed a mood-disorder line. I'm having way too much fun here.

"No…no, not at all. I think it's, um, courageous that you can even mention it—talk about it, I mean, to a total stranger."

"Total stranger? You mean you don't remember me?"

Newton is saved by the bell. He practically dives out of his chair. I am cracking myself up. That is, until I see the next guy. Ugh. Ugh. Ugh. Mr. Miata.

"Hi. Greg." He holds out his hand and smiles. It's obvious he doesn't recognize me from the parking incident.

"Jessie." Firm handshake. Nice ears. I'm trying to find something that will keep me from— "I'm the one you stole the parking space from." Too late. Must be the lipstick.

He carefully takes his seat. "Sorry? What?"

"This evening. I was going to take that spot you whipped into."

He frowns. "You waved me in."

"Actually, you pointed to the spot, and I thought you were being a gentleman and offering it to me. I was waving to say thank you."

Now, this can go either way. He can get defensive and make an excuse, or—

"I'm sorry." He smiles gently. "I really am. Why wouldn't I let a woman have that spot, right?"

I let a little of the tension go. "It's all right. I'm not really that mad. I mean, I was peeved at the time, but it's really just because I hate walking long distances by myself."

He truly looks mortified. "I wasn't thinking. I just knew I was running late, and I thought I'd had a stroke of good luck." He pauses. "And here I am with you…another stroke of good luck."

I giggle all breathy-like. I'm shameless as I decide his ears aren't his only good quality.

"So, I suppose you're looking for the kind of man that would think to give a woman the parking spot."

I nod a little. "I guess I am."

"What about a guy that usually thinks that way but had a weak moment?"

I smile. "I'm a big believer in forgiveness."

"Maybe it's the car," he says. "I just got that little Miata, and to tell you the truth, I feel a little silly in it."

I'm starting to think that this guy can steal my parking space anytime.

"It was one of those moments, you know, when you do something foolish because you think life is passing you by and you just want something great to happen. So you think a car is going to solve your problems. Do you know what I mean?"

I nod. "Yeah."

"So besides a parking space, what are you looking for in a guy, Jessie?"

It is striking me completely ironic that the guy that made me cry on a dark street seems to be connecting with my soul. I choose my words carefully.

"I'm looking for the kind of guy that can apologize for taking a parking space."

He leans back into his chair, not like he's leaning away from the conversation, but like he's getting comfortable.

Like he wants to stay awhile. A long while.

four

After Greg's eight minutes are up, I slip into some bad habits with the other fellows. I ask a few questions about their feelings on psychological compatibility testing and ask two men—and only two—to rate on a scale from one to twelve their fear of commitment. And yes, I'm perfectly aware I'm two shades of pink away from being Newton when I ask these guys how they might propose.

But hey, I let them ask a few questions too.

The evening ends with Ed, who sells used cars and keeps using my name like we're on the lot and I'm eying the sportier one I can't afford, but he's nice enough.

I watch Bob and Heather walk out, hand in hand. I slip into the bathroom to finally get this lipstick off my mouth and take a breather. But really what I'm doing is lingering.

As I leave the bathroom, the crowd has cleared out and Laurel is busy picking up her table and organizing the cards.

"Hey." She smiles. "How'd it go?"

I hand her my card. She eyes it, then me. "Last time you only checked two."

I shrug. "I'm giving these men the benefit of all my doubts. And there are many. Doubts." I bite my lip. "Look, Laurel, I know you're not supposed to, but can you check now? Please? I'm just very optimistic tonight, you know? I have a feeling."

"Let's see what we got."

She grabs the cards from my age group and flips through the men's. Then she flips through them again.

"What? Five?"

"Not exactly."

"Three?"

"No. Not three. I'm afraid no one picked you."

"Oh." I'm bleeding the color of my lipstick but I smile. "Oh, okay." I start to walk away, then turn back. "Can you check Greg's card again?"

She flips through and shakes her head. "No, sorry, hon. He's got five, but you're not one of them."

Tears sting my eyes. I'm hoping it's giving me the glassy look of aloofness. I bet not, though, judging by the way Laurel is tilting her head to the side. "If I didn't know better," she says with a sad smile, "I'd say it's gonna take a miracle of God to help you, honey. I mean, you're beautiful. And likable. I don't get it."

"Yeah? Well, when has God ever shown up to help me?" I turn on my chunky heel, push the door open, and storm out. I'm stomping and I don't care. I stomp harder.

"Hello, there."

Gasping, I turn. A man is standing near the wall outside of the bar, leaning, his arms crossed. He's staring, piercing me with—what is that, scrutiny? No, not scrutiny. Something else. I don't know. I don't care. I keep walking.

"Jessie."

I whip around, my hands on my hips. "How did you—" I glance down. I've still got my nametag on. I rip it off and throw it to the ground. But because I'm very much against littering, I stoop and pick it back up. The man is still watching me. I take a deep breath. I mean, this guy is cute. Looks a little familiar. Was he just inside? I don't know. But the air is out of my proverbial tire, as it goes, and I'm not feeling very chatty. Or charming. Or pretty.

I offer a small smile, then turn and walk toward my dark street, daring somebody to mess with me.

He takes the dare and scurries after me. "I want to talk to you." I keep walking. Who is this guy? Someone who hangs outside the bar, waiting for the pour souls who don't get picked? Championing for the strays? Good grief. "Trust me. Just for a minute." I can still hear his footsteps behind me. I turn and march right up to his…his…handsome self.

"Look," I say, trying so darn hard to seem polite, "I'm not in a good place right now. The last thing I want to do is…" I might as well be frank. "Is trust one of you."

"One of me?"

"Man. Males. Men." I step away from him. He does not look like a serial killer. In fact, he looks completely harmless, and had he been at my table tonight, I probably would've found him quite adorable.

But not now. Now he represents everything I despise. I don't say another word. Instead, I pull out my jewel-studded Mace and wave it in the air. It's the universal "you may be crazy but I'm crazier" sign.

He doesn't seem intimidated, even though I lurch forward a little. Instead, he simply stands there looking amused. Great. Glad I could entertain someone tonight. I walk backward a few steps and then turn down the street where I parked. I glance behind me, relieved he is not following.

As I head home, I dial Blake. Predictably it goes to voice mail, because he actually has a life and probably has a Valentine's date with Ms. Steele. "Blake, I hate you guy types. I never want to talk to you again! Just wanted to you to know." I feel better already. "Hey, when you get home from whatever you're doing, call me or hop online. By the way, I'm officially being stalked."

I cry as I drive. I don't heave-cry, where it's best to pull over, but tears are trickling down my face. I regret asking Laurel to sneak a peak. I would've rather just found out by e-mail like everyone else. Now I see why that rule is in place. And this is what happens when I break the rules. Other people break rules and live to brag about it. I break rules and live to be humiliated. I park on the curb outside the condo and dry my tears. The drive was good. It let me get some things out. I step out of the car to breathe in the coolness of the night. It feels safe out here. I suck in more air and try to remember there is a good reason that I am alive.

Then I spot him. I can't believe what I am seeing, and it nearly backs me into my car. My stalker is sitting on the small wall of the porch at the top of the stairs of my condo. Something deflates inside me. I have no energy for stalker or Prince Charming. Perhaps it's the irony that I can't get a date but strange men are following me home. Normally I would cower back into my car, but I decide not to. I decide, truly against my better judgment, to take this freak on.

He stands as I approach the steps of my condo. "Do you really believe I've never done anything to help you, Jessie?"

I don't know what he's talking about.

He continues speaking in a pleasant voice that doesn't fit my stereotype of freaky stalkers. "You can't accuse me of something like that and expect me to not show up and defend myself. Come on."

I stare straight into his eyes. "I'm not a big fan of men I don't know following me home. Would you get out of my way?"

To my surprise, he actually does. Then he takes a gallant bow and gestures toward the door. "As you wish." Terrific. Chivalry from a stalker. See? This is how my life goes.

I hold out my key, eying him. One startling move and I'm going to scream bloody murder. "How did you know where I live?"

"I've always known where you live. In San Diego, it was Carter Street until you were eight. Moved here when your dad was transferred. You inherited this place on behalf of yourself and your little sister."

My hand plunges into my purse and emerges with the cell phone. "Okay, freak. Time for the police." I accidentally dial 411 and have to start over, but he doesn't seem to be going anywhere fast, which is part of the problem. "What? Did you look me up on the Internet? That's really original."

With my other hand, I finally jiggle the lock enough and the door opens. I step inside, the phone still to my ear, and lock the screen door.

Stalker Dude sits back down on the wall. "They'll send Officer Garrety," he says. "He's got a great sense of humor. I love that about him."

"911. What is your emergency?"

"There is a stalker outside my door."

"A stalker, ma'am?"

"Yes. He followed me home from a bar. I mean, yes, okay, it was a bar. I wasn't there drinking or picking up men, though. Okay, I was picking up men—trying to—but it wasn't…um, well, it was speed dating."

"Speed dating?"

"Eight minutes, bell dings, change tables. That whole scene. Anyway, he's followed me home."

"Is this a guy you met there?"

"No. He was outside, like he was waiting for me."

"Sounds like a successful night."

"No, no. No. I left him at the bar. And now he's at my house. He, like, followed me home or something. And he knows where I lived when I was eight. Can you please just send someone?"

"Are you safe right now?"

"Yes. I'm in my house, watching him. He's not going anywhere, even when I threatened to call the cops."

"Okay, sweetie. Just stay put. I'll get someone over there."

"Thank you."

"It won't be long. Garrety is just around the corner," Stalker says.

"What are you, psychic?"

"Omniscient, actually."

Just then I see the patrol car. The lights aren't even on until he pulls to the curb, and then they flash. Two heavyset men emerge, lumbering toward my condo. The stalker, to my surprise, has somehow moved down the steps and is sitting on the hood of my car. When did that happen? During a blink? I open the screen door and step outside as the two officers pass right by him.

"Ma'am? I'm Officer Garrety. This is Officer Lakeland. How can we assist you?"

I point to my car. "He followed me home from speed dating. Please don't judge me. It's humiliating enough. But now he won't leave."

"Ma'am, who won't leave?" Officer Garrety asks.

I point again. "Him! And he should not be sitting on the hood of my car. He'll scratch the paint."

"How much ya been on the juice tonight?"

"Huh? None. Why?"

The chubbier of the two officers, Lakeland, pitches his thumb over his right shoulder. "There's no one sitting on that car of yours."

"What are you talking about?" I gesture toward the stalker, who hops off my hood. "He's right there!" He is now sauntering, literally sauntering toward me. "There! Look! He's coming…up…the…" Steps. Slowly. One step at a time. Then he hops up and sits on the small wall again, swinging his legs like he's nine. "See?" I point to him. The officers don't even look.

Garrety says, "I didn't know women your age still had imaginary friends."

"I haven't had one of those since I was six."

"Try nine," Stalker whispers. How does he know *that*?

Lakeland laughs. "Look, lady, whatever it is you're drinking tonight, you might want to try something a little less strong next time, okay?"

"I'm not drinking! What is this, some sort of horrible joke?"

Officer Garrety stops chuckling. "Okay, look, miss, normally for false alarms we can bring you in. But I have a sense of humor, and I'm willing to bet you're not having a good Valentine's Day, now are ya?"

I grind my teeth. "Oh no. It's terrific. It's getting better by the second."

Stalker steps right next to Lakeland and leans in toward me. "They can't see me. Only you can. Bet you wish I'd told you that earlier, huh?"

It's an odd thought, I know, but I seriously wonder if I'm being Punk'd, and am about to mention it to the officers/actors when Stalker turns and walks through my screen door. And by through, I mean like Casper. I feel lightheaded. I actually think my eyes roll back in my head. I'm not sure, but everything seems fuzzy.

"It's vodka," Lakeland whispers to Garrety. "Women don't do vodka well."

"Well," Garrety says in a loud voice, as if I've suddenly turned deaf, "we'll just call this a *dry run* and forget it ever happened."

"Think she's going to be okay?" I hear Lakeland ask as they walk down my steps.

"Look, she probably just got her heart broken or something, you know?"

I turn and stare through my screen door. There he is, sitting on my couch like it's his own home. I watch the officers get in their car and drive off.

Again, against my better judgment, I walk in. I am normally panic prone. Spiders. Mice. Snakes. Strangely, though, ghosts don't seem to trigger anything. I don't want to touch him, for fear that my arm will go straight through his, so I give a few exaggerated gestures. "Come on. Come now. Let's go. There's no need to make a scene. Let's go."

He settles back in the couch.

I feel remarkably calm, if not the slightest bit delusional. "Okay, this isn't happening. You are not happening. My parents sent me to a psycho head…head…shrinker when I was nine to get rid of someone like you. *You* aren't coming *back*!"

He grins. "I said no one else can see me. I didn't say I was imaginary."

I back away, clutching my stomach and feeling my forehead for a fever. I turn away from him, breathing hard and feeling like I probably should've had a drink. "Okay. Okay. I'm losing it. Okay. Officially losing it. Breathe. Breathe. Okay. Okay."

"You know," he says.

I cringe. I was hoping he might have disappeared.

"Dr. Montrose wasn't totally psycho. He just didn't get *you*."

Whether he's real or not, this guy's right. Montrose wasn't psycho. I was. Am. In the middle of being. I turn, jamming my finger into the air. "No. No. No. You don't get to just spout things, about me that I already know to…to trick me. I know these things, and therefore I could be making all this up. Yes, me. Making it up in my head. Maybe Montrose was right…"

I hadn't thought about that quack doctor in years. I hated that man. He was very tall and thin, with darker skin, thinning hair, and a tiny mustache that twitched like mouse whiskers. He wore perfectly round glasses that always made him look surprised and therefore made me feel like I was in some odd way always surprising.

I remember in one session, he said I should try bossing my imaginary friend around. My mother always told me not to be bossy, so this was very confusing to me, but I realize this might come in handy right now. So I look him in the eye, point my finger to his face and say— nothing, because he interrupts me.

"Your phone is about to ring. It's Blake. Your blonde-obsessed friend, as you so affectionately coin him. Don't answer it."

It rings. I look at the caller ID: BLAKE LIGHTNER. For a second, I almost snatch up the phone and scream for help, but I have no idea how I'm going to explain this, and Blake's probably calling about some fabulous date he had. So I withdraw my hand.

"Okay, *that* I wouldn't have known." So my theory that I'm going insane is unwinding. I look at him. "Who are you?"

"The one you accused of never doing anything to help you. Some people call me God. Occasionally in vain."

It's very odd, because I'm literally about to take God's name in vain. I'm not usually the cussing type. It's just that certain situations— this would be a good example—cause questionable language to invade my vocabulary.

"God. Right. God has shown up in my living room. That's funny." I let out a halfhearted laugh, because secretly I feel like I'm going to burst into tears. Of course, laughing makes me look just as hormonal and insane, and I fear that I may land in a psych hospital either way.

"Is that so hard to believe?" he asks.

I study his quizzical expression, beautiful eyes, square chin, and sculptured cheekbones. This is a guy that I'd notice, you know? If he'd been at speed dating, I'd have marked him down. So my insides wiggle at the weirdness of it all. Not that I ever imagined God coming down to meet me, but if he did, I'd, well, I just think he'd lean more toward the Morgan Freeman look with a voice like James Earl Jones, or he'd have long wavy hair like Colin Farrell tried. I don't know. This guy, he just doesn't fit the mold.

I cross my arms. "*God* has never been in the business of coming to my rescue. Or doing anything for me, for that matter."

"You gotta lay off those inflammatory generalizations."

I hold up a finger to retort, but my lips and finger freeze as I watch him hop off the arm of the couch and head out of the room.

"Where are you going?"

He doesn't answer as he goes upstairs.

I follow the stalker, a.k.a. God, taking two stairs at a time because he's vanished like he might've just floated all the way to the top. I'm out of breath as I fly into my bedroom. I stand in the doorway, my fists planted on my hips, breathing hard and trying to rationalize why I would follow a stranger into my own bedroom. This is how people turn up on *48 Hours*.

I decide I will stop referring to him as Stalker because that just makes me look like an idiot. Referring to him as God makes me look crazy, but I'll take crazy over idiot.

He is sitting on the left side of my bed, Indian style. I'm about to protest, because I never, ever, ever sit on my bed with my shoes on. It completely grosses me out when I see someone else do it to my bed or anyone else's. I start to demand he take off his shoes when I notice his boots on the floor. He's actually in his socks.

And surrounded by my journals. My journals! I gasp, because I notice he is also holding my feathered purple pen. Nobody holds my feathered purple pen! It's my own personal holy grail. My heart is pounding even as I stare at it.

I hold up my hands. "Back away from the pen. Please. Just put the pen down."

He does. Into the pocket on his shirt. And picks up one of my journals.

"Hey! Ever heard of the word *private*?"

"I already know your thoughts."

"That's right. You're psychic."

"Omniscient."

"And can I just add *intrusive*? I mean that in the nicest way."

He waves the journal in his hand. "Did you know that out of your one hundred nine journals, you have penned twelve hundred fifty-six ways a man could propose to you?"

Yes, I'm huffy, but I don't care. I mean, the gall of this guy. I would say he just pulled that proposal number out of the air, except I have a bad habit of counting things. Numbers like me and I like numbers. He is correct.

"Well," I say, gesturing toward the journals, "we see the way my pen translates into real life."

"Jessie, if you could ask me for one gift, what would it be?"

"If you are God, which I am not saying I believe you are, don't you already know?"

"I do."

"Then you tell me."

He plucks the purple pen out of his pocket, swings his legs over the side of the bed, and stands up. Normally this would cause me to instinctively reach for my Mace—or possibly toss my hair. Instead, I stand there, a little rigid, as he comes right up to me.

He's staring at me, directly into my eyes, like he might actually be able to read my mind. I should note that it's not a serial-killer kind of stare, where red flags are going off and every hair on your body is standing up like a Chia Pet. I actually feel kind of calm. His face is eight inches from mine, and I have to tell you, I'm a personal-space kind of gal. Normally I'd go all air traffic controller on him and fly him right out of my safe zone. But I don't. I just stand there like a geek, worried about my purple pen but not worried why this man is staring at me.

In a quiet, controlled voice he says, "You want your love story. So much so that you fight tears every night, wishing there were someone beside you." He points behind him. "Someone to sleep right there on that side of the bed. He has to be a left-side-of-the-bed sleeper because you've been sleeping on the right side far too long to change now."

I scratch my hairline, trying to hold back tears. "It's just personal preference. I'm not a bed zealot or anything."

He smiles. "You leave space for him. You want the one who matches the man you've written about year after year."

Drip. One tear down my cheek.

He walks into my bathroom. I follow him. "You're not asking too much," he says. "A guy who wipes up at the sink, who wears cologne to enhance and not cover up, and, these are your words not mine, 'someone who understands the importance of Lysol.'"

I feel weak. "What are you doing here?"

"I want to help you."

"Why? I don't even like you. I haven't stepped foot in a church since—"

"August 15, fourteen years ago." He exits the bathroom. I glance at the sink. Water droplets! I quickly wipe them up and hurry to follow him. He's standing near the window...like in my dream the other night. "I know it's hard," he says. "There are some things I just can't answer for you yet."

"Yeah. I can see that." I can also see him twirling my purple pen between his fingers like it's some kind of good luck charm. I let go of that theory—that it's a good luck charm—four years ago, but I still don't like anybody touching it. Blake grabbed it once to jot down a phone number. He never made that mistake again.

He smiles and stops twirling the pen. "I can write this story for you, if you're willing to give me the pen."

I stare at the pen. "Everything I've accomplished in my life, I've done myself. Me. Alone. Why should I trust you now?"

"You haven't asked me for help." He looks at the purple pen, and I study his expression. He seems to know its importance. "Of course, you can keep doing things your way. If that's working for you."

I look him in the eyes, study every minuscule movement on his face. He sits down on the edge of the bed and slips his boots on.

"So you take the pen. Then what? You want me to sit down, shut up, and stay out of your way?"

"Oh no. You'll be busy."

"Doing what?"

He finishes lacing up his boots and stands. He holds out the purple pen. I snatch it from him, my fingers quickly running back and forth over the feather. I take a deep breath of relief.

"You have twenty-four hours to decide if you want to give me that pen." He brushes by me and toward my bedroom door. I clutch my pen, thankful to have it back, then turn to follow him.

Except he's gone.

I hurry to the door to look down the stairs, but there's nothing. No movement, no footsteps. All is quiet.

I turn and go back into my bedroom. Not all one hundred nine journals are on my bed. Just a few, scattered around the bedspread like there's no particular order to them. There *is* an order to them, and I promptly return them to my closet and refile. My heart's not into it, but I straighten the bedspread anyway. Wrinkles bother me. But not as much as what just happened. I'm still having a hard time figuring out if I need to exorcize a figment of my imagination.

It's a weird thing, but I feel peaceful, like I've just had a spa day.

I decide to go brush my teeth, because cleaning anything always makes me feel better. I brush a full five minutes as I stare into my mirror, trying to find that nine-year-old girl who was so confused and so lonely. Is she back?

I finish up and decide to change into my pajamas and say good-bye to this Valentine's disaster once and for all. I go downstairs, check the locks, turn out the lights, and head for the bathroom to do a final wipedown.

But as I wipe up the water droplets and step outside my bathroom, I hear a loud thud downstairs.

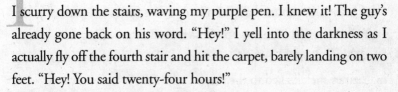

five

I scurry down the stairs, waving my purple pen. I knew it! The guy's already gone back on his word. "Hey!" I yell into the darkness as I actually fly off the fourth stair and hit the carpet, barely landing on two feet. "Hey! You said twenty-four hours!"

"Do you have a guy in your room?!"

The front door shuts, and there stands my sister, Brooklyn. Even in the dark, her bright blond hair shines like the moon is hovering above her. I flip on the light, only to notice two suitcases in her hands. She blinks at me, her heavy eyelashes batting in spite of themselves. Her gaze slowly climbs the stairs.

"Good grief, no. Not that I know of." I add this because the guy has proved he can appear without warning. I glance upstairs. Everything seems quiet.

"Then who are you talking to?" Brooklyn flops onto the couch, tossing a pillow to the floor. I walk over, dust it off, and put it back in place.

"No one. What are you doing here?"

She sighs and sulks. Vintage Brooklyn. "My play closed tonight. Gary kicked me out."

Not sure what one has to do with the other, but somehow everything in Brooklyn's life is connected. She goes through men like cats go through mice, and I am having a hard time feeling any bit of sympathy for her.

"I won't mention he fell for the leading woman."

Oh. Ouch. Okay, that helps. "Wow. You okay?"

"I don't know. I mean, I'm more concerned about why I didn't see this coming." She kicks her feet onto the coffee table. "I can read men, Jessie. You know that. I can look across the room and tell you if a guy is interested in me or not. So where did I go wrong with Gary?"

Where should I start? I keep my mouth shut and straighten the magazines she's kicked to the side.

"I think I need to reevaluate my life, Jess. Just try to understand why I seem to end up with dysfunctional men over and over."

I know this seems harsh, but it's the truth: these guys don't strike me as dysfunctional until Brooklyn gets ahold of them. Just a candid observation.

One of her suitcases has tipped over, and I lift it back upright. She is glaring at me. "I'm taking my room back. I don't care what you say!"

"I know. Your suitcases did the talking for you."

That steams her. She hates when I talk to her in a matter-of-fact voice. She's kind of a drama queen and tone is everything to her, so when I don't have a tone it freaks her out. I smile as she clomps upstairs. It's not the first time she's barged back in. My place is like her own personal halfway house.

My gloating fades as I find myself alone in my living room. It's been a Valentine's Day repeat, except for the weird God thing, but I'm halfway certain I'm going to wake up tomorrow to find myself remembering this dream.

Usually on a disastrous Valentine's Day, I would fill up at least five pages of my journal, but I don't feel like journaling at all. I fall into the cushions of my couch, adjust the pillows, and stare at my purple pen. Maybe, with the night I've had, it will start writing all on its own.

"What are you doing?"

I whirl around in my desk chair like I'm not expecting anyone to show up. The truth of the matter is that I keep expecting *him* to step right out of the wallpaper. But it's not him. It's Brooklyn, rubbing her tired eyes.

"It's three-thirty in the morning."

"I know," I say. "Sorry. Did I wake you?"

"No." She leans over me and snatches up the pill bottle that is on the desk. "What's this?"

"Give me that!" I claw at her arms, but she backs away and holds it up, squinting to read it.

"St. John's wort?" She raises a curious eyebrow and tosses it back to me.

"It's not what you think."

"You have a wart?"

Obviously it's not what she thinks. "It's an herb." I swivel back around and continue typing.

"What are you doing?" she asks.

"Why are you awake?"

"I can't sleep. I'm having life crisises, you know."

"Crises."

"Whatever. So what are you doing?"

"I'm just looking up drug interactions."

"For the wart stuff?"

I swivel to face her again. I look into her tired-yet-remarkably-taut-and-bright eyes. I don't think she has the ability to look disheveled. Her pajamas include a tight-fitting cami with matching figure-flattering pants. I look down at myself. I'm wearing running shorts and a T-shirt that would fit a gorilla.

"I had a bad night," I say. "A bad Valentine's."

She grabs a cushion off the sofa and sits on the floor. I try not to be bothered by it, but why not grab a chair or nearby stool? Why remove a cushion? "Me too." She smiles a little and explains the whole night to me. I hurt for her. As immature as she is, I don't like to see her hurting.

I lean in to hug her. "Maybe we should've spent Valentine's together, watching romance movies."

"Or," she says, holding up a finger, "action flicks. Kind of sticking it to the idea of romance." She tilts her head to the side. "Except you can't let go of romance."

"I'm getting close."

"No, Jess. You're the very definition of hopeless when it comes to romantic."

"It's funny." I sigh. "You're independent and always have a guy. I'm codependent and can't find an eligible man to save my life." I lean into my chair and stare at my cuticles. "Brooklyn, do you remember when I was nine? I don't know, maybe you were too young to remember what happened."

"I was one, but I figured it out later," Brooklyn said.

"You did?"

"I knew something was wrong when I was playing tea with my dolls and Mom totally freaked out on me. I was just doing voices for all the girls, and she's asking me if I'm seeing people."

I laugh. "I had no idea that happened."

Brooklyn stands and moves to the kitchen. She puts the kettle on. "Well, Mom was very diplomatic about the whole thing, I guess. She told me you had a 'sunny' imagination but that sometimes it went a little too far and that if I started having more than dolls show up at my tea parties, I should talk to her about it."

"Wow." I join her in the kitchen, pulling up a bar stool to the breakfast bar. I open the St. John's wort bottle. "Well, it wasn't a good experience. It was the first time in my life that I started feeling like I was different."

"Different is good, Jess."

"Except in speed dating." I dump a couple of pills in my hand.

"You didn't." She hands me a glass of water.

"I did. It was awful." I throw my head back and down the pills. "And now look at me. I've become a pill popper."

"Jess, you're not a pill popper."

"I am! You can pill pop herbs too."

"Pill poppers don't stop to determine if there will be drug inter-actions."

"I just thought…" I set down the pills. How do I explain that I'm hoping an herb will keep God away from my purple pen?

"So you okay?" Brooklyn asks as she retrieves two tea mugs. "I hear women mostly have nervous breakdowns in their thirties." All right, that was as deep as she is capable of going. Sometimes you just have to accept people for who they are.

"I'm fine." I smile and nod.

"Good. Can you fix the tea? I have to get back to bed and medi-tate." She's about to leave the room, and then she turns back and smiles. "The good news is that I should sleep good. Gary used to suf-focate me in bed, you know? Arms around me, feet next to mine. Now I have the entire bed to myself!"

And off she goes, bounding up the stairs to freedom. I wait for the kettle to whistle, make two cups of Sleepytime tea, and head upstairs. I deliver the tea to Brooklyn, but she's fallen asleep in her yoga posi-tion, except she's now face forward into her comforter, where she's snoring. I take my bottle of pills to the bathroom. At this point, I decide, an herb is not going to help my delusions. I'm beyond help, I think.

I sit on the edge of my bed, my tea in hand. The sheets are cold. The room feels empty, and not in a clean, organizational sort of way. Just a few hours ago a man was here, and as weird as it was, it was at least another warm body. But now I'm alone again. I force myself to finish my tea. Then I fold back the comforter, turn off the light, kick off my slippers, and slide under the sheets.

The darkness is suffocating.

Nicole has come with me to get coffee, desperate for caffeine. One of her kids had croup overnight, and she's talking about how she had to hold him in front of the freezer for twenty minutes. Frankly, compared to my evening, it's just a little boring, but I listen anyway. Or try to. I'm very distracted because as we approach Starbucks, I realize the man I saw earlier this week, staring at me by the wall of mugs, was the man in my bedroom last night. It jolts me to a stop. Nicole turns around.

"You okay?

"Yes, sorry." I start walking again, keeping a wide eye open for him.

I order for Mr. Coston and then glance up at the menu. "I'll have whatever drink you have that has espresso but doesn't taste at all like coffee."

Nicole leans in. "What are you doing?"

"Ordering."

"For yourself?"

"Yes. I'm tired."

"You hate coffee."

"I'm desperate." Oh, how I wish I could explain how desperate. Really, I am hoping that this legal form of drug will somehow get the blood flowing back to my brain. Caffeine is supposed to help migraines, so why not hallucinations?

Nicole looks very worried. "The last time you tried espresso you were shaking so badly you couldn't type."

"I've got the presentation this morning, and I feel like I've been run over by a truck."

The barista clears her throat. "So, you want to try a mocha, extra chocolate?"

"Sure. Tall, please."

As Nicole orders, I wait for mine and stare at the wall of mugs, waiting for him to vaporize into the room—but nothing happens. I glance around at the customers, searching for his face.

Nicole slides up beside me. "You know, I think it's a big deal that Mr. Coston is asking you to do this. It means he believes in you."

"Ten years later."

"He's not an easy man to work for, but he's a good businessman."

Our coffee is ready. I dump sugar into Mr. Coston's, and we head back to the office. I sip pure putridness. The extra chocolate is barely helping.

"You haven't mentioned how your Valentine's event went," Nicole says. "You were supposed to call me."

I cough. "How do people spend this much on coffee every day? Three bucks? You could buy a sandwich!"

"You're avoiding the topic, so I have to assume it went poorly."

I glance behind me. I feel like I'm being followed but see no one. "It was fine. Four or five guys picked me. None of them my type."

"Sorry, babe. Better luck next time. But you know what, I'm proud of you. I mean, you go to extremes, but at least you're not waiting around for Prince Charming to show up on your doorstep, you know? I think a lot of women have this false expectation that the one that is meant for them is just going to *poof!* appear out of nowhere."

"Oh…uh, yeah. That's, um, ridiculous."

We arrive back at the office. I'm about to head to Mr. Coston's to deliver his coffee when Nicole grabs my arm. She is staring at the banner. "Why is the exclamation scribbled out?"

I shrug. "It just didn't fit."

"Why?"

"It's too much excitement for me in the morning."

"Honey, maybe you need to start drinking coffee if that's how your mornings are going."

I'm sipping as fast as one can sip a hot nasty beverage, but I still can't shake the feeling that I'm being watched. I check the time and hurry to deliver Mr. Coston's coffee. I place it on his desk. Normally he doesn't even look up, but this morning he says, "I bet you had some trouble sleeping last night, didn't you?"

"Pardon me?" I about drop my coffee.

"Nerves?"

"Huh?"

His eyebrows flatten out. "About today. The presentation."

By "presentation," Mr. Coston is referring to the thirty seconds I'll stand and give a short report on listings to the senior agents. "Oh. Yes. Up all night."

"Don't be nervous." He smiles. "You've been with me a long time, Jessie. I wouldn't have asked you to do this if I didn't think you were ready."

I try to play the role. "It's an honor, sir." Yes, occasionally, I have been known to suck up to the boss.

Twenty minutes later we are filing into the conference room. Three senior agents from the other offices, all in white shirts and gray ties, sit on one side of the table, looking as if they'd rather be somewhere else. I never can remember their names because they only come in once or twice a year. Usually I'm there taking meeting notes, and I just call them Larry, Moe, and Curly in shorthand. But that small detail of their names might be helpful today.

I lean in to Nicole, who is sitting up straight with arms on the table and hands connected at the fingertips. She is smiling and nodding to everyone. If she starts to wave, this may become her Miss America moment.

"What are their names?" I whisper.

"Who?"

"The suits."

"From left to right, Mr. Wallace, Mr. Keegan, Mr. Brown. You should shake hands and introduce yourself."

"Why? They've seen me at other meetings."

"Yes, but usually in a corner and looking very bored. They need to know you're part of the bigger picture."

I try to sit up straight like Nicole and smile. "You know I hate this kind of thing."

Nicole smiles. "I think Mr. Keegan is single."

I glance over. No ring. And no way. He's a decade older and looks like an expression might kill him. But I decide to take Nicole's advice. She is savvy in these things. I stand and lean over the table. "Hi, I'm Jessie Stone."

They look at me. Blink. Blink. I hold out my hand. They each shake it. I sit down. Awkward. Nicole shoots me a look. I whisper out the side of my mouth, "It's them, not me. I smiled."

Mr. Coston flies in, carrying folders, juggling his coffee, trying to button his jacket. "Good morning, gentlemen. Coffee, anyone? Soda?"

Thankfully everyone says no, because that's my job. Mr. Coston stands at the end of the table near the whiteboard, and I get comfortable, sipping my coffee carefully and trying to swallow without tasting much. I want to close my eyes, think hard about what happened last night. I can only wonder if insane people know they're insane. I don't think I'm insane because I'm rationally thinking that I *am* insane, and insane people think they're sane. Of course it can be argued that sane people don't see God or have visits from God. Insane people may claim to have visits from God, but I'm willing to bet these visitors don't look like the God who showed up on my doorstep. All Prince Charming–ish. So I'm not sane or insane. What does that make me?

Jessie Stone, ladies and gentlemen: the first woman to discover there's actually a third option.

"Jessie?"

I glance up. "I'm sorry…yes? Um…?"

"You have the report to pass out?"

"Yes, of course." I quickly stand and start passing out stapled stacks of paper.

Mr. Coston continues. "Despite the typical slump for this time of year, not to mention the current housing market, we've had a better-than-average showing count. Nicole, outshining us all. Congratulations."

Nicole smiles and nods. I give her a congratulatory wink.

"And I'd like to introduce Jessie Stone to you. She's been with us for ten years. She is reliable and passionate for what we do here."

Grin. Sell it. *Sell it.*

"Jessie, can you update us on listings?"

"Sure." I move back to my chair and pick up my notes. I decide to remain standing because that seems more professional. And I am, after all, passionate about real estate. "We have ten new properties—"

And then *he* appears, walking straight through the door like it's made of air. He is dressed in slacks and a polo, and has his hands in his pockets. He smiles at me. I don't smile back.

"—um, that came in from the God Development Project."

"God?" Mr. Coston's voice shoots through the room.

"Gabe. Sorry! Yes, Gabe. Not God. How ridiculous of me to—"

He speaks. "Jessie, I have to tell you something. Before you give me that pen, you should know a bit of what you're in for."

Suddenly someone kicks my shaking leg. It's Nicole, staring so wide eyed at me that for a moment I think maybe my pants have dropped. But no, I'm simply making a fool of myself. I try to refocus, though I can't help watching him move to the other side of the room.

"Um. And the condo renovations in Montecito—"

"I said you'd be busy. And I am compulsively true to my word."

"Be quiet! *Quite,* I mean. Be quite…lovely. The Montecito condos, that is. They'll be ready for showings."

"Did you hear me?" my imaginary friend named God asks.

"You said twenty-four hours!" I whisper, foolishly thinking that somehow a whisper would go unnoticed. I try a smile. "In twenty-four hours. They'll be ready. Just finishing up some minor touch-ups. You know how that goes. We want everything to be perfect. Mr. Coston expects no less." I glance at Mr. Coston, who looks ready to intervene for me at any second.

He seems to relax a little as I sit down. I keep my focus on Mr. Coston, staring so hard at him that Nicole keeps glancing at me.

"Send a photographer today," Mr. Coston says. "Let's get these on the premier listings."

"You have to find a way," says God from across the room, "to share your proposal ideas with other people."

"What?" I whisper, turning my head to look at the man no one else can see.

"A photographer," Mr. Coston says loudly, looking where I am looking and obviously seeing nothing. He looks back at me, and I force myself to look at him, smiling. "The one who takes pictures? Pictures that you can upload to our Web site?"

"Yes, of course." My hands are shaking, and it's not from the espresso, I can tell you that. I ignore God for the few more minutes we are in the meeting—even though I am all too aware that he is pacing on the other side of the room. Mr. Coston finally finishes up, and I bolt out the door and straight to the ladies room. I check under the stalls. I'm all alone.

Except. *Poof!* There he is, sitting on the sink counter.

"Is this funny to you?" I ask.

"Is what funny?"

"Making me look like an idiot. Why didn't you show up at Starbucks? We could've talked there. You have to come into a meeting?"

He turns on the faucet for no particular reason, it seems, except to let his hand play under the water. "I'm kind of on my own schedule. I'm not in the habit of checking if it's convenient."

I put my hands on my hips but I don't say anything. That does sound very God of the universe. And it feels foolish arguing that he's not working with my schedule.

"So," he says, "to recount what we're doing here. You are going to be participating in, well, let's just call it show and tell. You're going to help others, Jessie. I'm really into that, you know."

I take two paper towels, move to the sink, and start wiping off the water droplets he's making. "You're trying to tell me that while waiting for my own proposal, you want me to help other women get the ones I have been dreaming about my whole life."

"That about sums it up." He smiles and holds his hands up to dry in the air.

I snatch two more paper towels and dry up water droplets from the other sink. "And how do you, oh wise one, propose I do this?"

"That's up to you. You know how you're always bemoaning that all these people around you are getting engaged?"

"I do not moan. I merely point out."

He looks down at me, and for a moment I catch a glimpse of who he really is inside that young man's body. I squirm. The moment passes, and he says, "Share those creative serenade ideas from your journals with the guys who need your brilliance. I particularly like the one that involves the daisies—oh, and the ball of fire."

I grab another towel. Water spots seem to be appearing out of nowhere. God hops off the counter. I start wiping. "How many proposals do I have to share? Three? Four? Nine hundred?" I need a number. Numbers comfort me.

But he is gone. Naturally. And right on cue, Nicole comes barging in. "There you are!"

I toss the paper towel in the trash. "You know when I get nervous I need to wipe things."

Nicole stands there with her hands on her hips, not smiling. "Okay, first of all, no more coffee for you."

"It wasn't the coffee."

"Secondly, what just happened? I've always known you to be quite confident in front of people, Jessie."

"It was nothing. I'm sorry I embarrassed you."

Nicole took her hands off her hips and took a few steps toward me. "You didn't embarrass me, but I am worried about you. You just seemed very unfocused."

"I've got a lot on my mind."

"Sweetie," she says and comes in for a hug, "I'm just so worried about you. You don't seem like yourself."

"I know." I lightly tap her on the back and then head out of the bathroom. She scurries after me.

"Do you want to talk about it?" she asks, hurrying up beside me.

"Yes, but I can't. You wouldn't understand."

"You always say that, Jessie. But I think you'd be surprised if you just shared it with me."

I reach my desk and sit down. Nicole leans over the counter, looking at me. Should I tell her? I can't. I don't know how to explain it. "This place, Nicole, is good for you. You love what you do and you're good at it. But it's just a job for me, you know?" Much better reason than explaining how God was pacing the boardroom.

She nods. "I think Mr. Coston senses that and wants to give you more responsibility. That was what this morning was all about."

"And I blew it." I reach for chocolate but think twice. I'd hate to swell today and have to deal with *that* on top of everything else. I tend to swell more when I'm stressed.

Nicole smiles at me. "It wasn't as bad as you think."

I lean back in my chair and put a hand over my face. "No. I'm sure I came across as endearingly abnormal."

Nicole laughs. "You're always endearing, my friend. No matter what. Listen," she says, reaching all the way over the counter and straightening the stapler for me, which I thought was very nice, "I'll talk to Mr. Coston, okay? Tell him to give you another chance."

"You are the best!" I lean forward and squeeze her arm. "But that's okay. I don't want you to have to wipe up my messes for me."

The strange thing about it, though, was that messing up the presentation didn't seem like that big of a mess—which got me to thinking.

And that can be dangerous.

six

Malia's store looks a little empty. All the candy is half off, and I've got an arm full of assorted dark chocolates as I make my way to the checkout. The day after Valentine's is truly, along with Easter and Halloween, the best time to buy candy.

I'm relieved to have made it past Valentine's Day again, though perhaps not with my sanity intact.

I heave my candy onto Malia's counter. She chuckles.

"I can always count on you to help relieve my inventory." She holds up a discounted Valentine's card I've picked out and raises an eyebrow. "Something you want to share with me?"

"No, not at all. You know how I like to buy cards for my future husband."

"How many cards do you have for him?"

"Oh, you know, I don't keep count." Fifty-two. I lean on the counter. "So, I've got a crazy idea."

She looks up at me with a big smile. "Yeah?"

"What if I rented space from you and opened a little business?"

She looks intrigued but not sold. "What kind of business?"

"A sort of consulting firm. For men. On how to make the perfect proposal. A mind-blowing proposal. I'd help them plan the whole thing, and that would hopefully bring more gift-giving, lovesick, paying customers into the store." I eagerly rub my hands together. "So, what do you think? Can I move in?"

Malia squeals. Don't be alarmed. She's a squealer at all things exciting. She squeals at babies and small animals and good hair days. She reaches over the counter and pulls me into a hug.

"I love it! Oh, sweetie, I've been wanting you out of that dead-end nine-to-five for so long! If it means I get to keep you all day—" Malia stops. "You're turning pale."

It doesn't surprise me. I feel the blood draining out of my head. *Quit* my other job? I hadn't thought of that. I was thinking more like a supplement *to* my job. I look at Malia, who is frozen between elation and hesitation. She's watching me to determine what she should do next.

"Can I really do this?" I whisper.

Malia looks directly at me. "Jessie, the way you've stepped up all your life, how you've done what you had to do, like taking care of your sister—it amazes me. But she's old enough to take care of herself now. You can take a risk. You can do this. You *can* do this."

I take a deep, liberating breath, then bite my lip. Is this even sensible? I mean, quit the reliable job that has paid the bills for so long? Quit the familiar job that I've just spent ten years at?

That wretched exclamation mark morphs into a question mark.

"I can do this. I can, can't I?"

Malia pounds the counter. "You can, baby. You can."

"I can! Okay. Okay. Yeah. This feels right."

Malia rings up the last of my candy and the card. "Why don't you write some ideas down on paper, your vision, your practical needs, all that. We'll talk about it tomorrow." She puts my stuff in a bag but holds up the card. "May I take a peek?"

"Sure." I smile.

She opens the card and reads. "'You're absolutely divine.'"

I shrug. "Just seemed to fit at the moment."

I don't know why it surprises me anymore, but it always does when I find Brooklyn sound asleep in the middle of the day. I have a strange internal clock that won't allow me to sleep past eight, and that's on the weekend. Plus, I have no idea how someone can wear a mask while sleeping. I get annoyed when my hair brushes against my face.

I walk into her room, already a pigsty, kicking clothes and high-heeled shoes to the side. I throw open the curtains. Bright beaming light warms my skin and makes me blink. Brooklyn doesn't even stir. I clap my hands. She manages to groan.

"Hey! Get up! It's the afternoon, for crying out loud."

She rolls over. "I've got my alarm set for five. Leave me alone."

"Five? That's when you should be getting off work. *Work*." I throw back her comforter, and she curls her knees to her chest. Bouncing on the end of the bed, I say, "If you are moving back in, you need a job."

"I have a job."

"Volunteering at the community theater doesn't count."

"Jessie, later. Please." She tries to pull the covers back over her, but I won't let her. "My lower eyelids get puffy when I don't sleep. Plus I get moody. I'm liable to start crying at any moment, so just let me sleep."

I wish she could see my unmoved expression. "You have always been my favorite drama queen. Now get up." I pull her arm and manage to get her into a sitting position. I tear off her sleeping mask. "You no longer have a boyfriend to pay your bills."

"Yes, Jessie, I realize that, which is why I'm drowning my sorrows in a day's worth of sleep. Or trying to." She almost tips over again, but I catch her and get her to her feet. Then I let out a gasp. "Hey, you better make it to the bathroom and get some cream on that thing."

That pops her eyes open. She has no idea what "that thing" is, but by the look on her face, if it requires cream it's enough to get her out of bed. I smile. I am so stinkin' clever it kills me.

I go downstairs and start some battery acid / coffee for her. I keep it around for Brooklyn, who can't manage to tackle a day, or the end of a day, without it. I hate the smell of it brewing, though. It's so bitter and skunk-like. Like a good beverage gone bad.

Ten minutes later she plunks down the stairs and spills onto the kitchen table, managing her behind into a chair. "I feel like I'm dying."

I bring her a cup, doctored with sugar-free sugar and cream-free cream.

"Straw."

I hand her one, but only her white sparkling teeth manage to thank me.

I sit down, put my elbows on the table, and get ready to watch her expression. "Here's the deal. I'm starting my own business."

She barely looks up from the coffee she's hovering over. "Is this a Mary Kay sort of deal?" she asks between sips. "Because if so, you're going to have to start wearing the stuff, and you know how you hate makeup."

I get up. "I can do makeup. Red lipstick, no less." I pull out the bread and peanut butter.

"Red is not your color."

I grab the jelly from the fridge. "Shut up and listen. It's a service for men who want to make a splash proposing to their future wives. It'll be in Malia's store."

She nods her head slowly, as if tasting a new food. "Sounds interesting enough."

"I know." I put the sandwich on a plate and put it in front of her, then sit down at the table with her. "There's nothing else like it out there. I believe in this, Brooklyn. So much so that I'm quitting my job."

She shoves the sandwich in her mouth and says with her mouth full, "Huh? You—Jessica Esther Stone, a woman for whom risk is a four-letter word—are going to leave your very reliable and well-paying job to start a business? That's funny." She crouches over her coffee again. "Do you have any mochaccino?"

I notice a few drops of coffee near her mug and grab my rag. "We'll be adding a service to the shop Malia already runs. We'll stage proposals for guys who want to ask a girl to marry them."

Up her head comes. "We?" She pulls the straw out of her coffee. It drips. I return with the rag and realize she may be dripping on purpose because she knows it drives me nuts.

"I can't do this myself, Brooklyn. But I have to share my creative proposals somehow."

"Have to? Why?"

"I just do."

She bites into her sandwich again. "Well, I have to say, over the years you've come up with some really amazing ideas."

I clap my hands—"I know!"—and then realize I sound like a cheerleader.

Fortunately Brooklyn doesn't seem to notice. "And men need help in this area. They seriously don't have a clue."

"I know!"

Brooklyn seems to be contemplating, which is a good sign because she rarely thinks about much.

"So?" I ask. "Interested?"

"I guess. If we must." She slurps her coffee.

It's not gung-ho, but we are talking about Brooklyn here. Maybe more excitement will come later. I watch her watch her coffee. She's always loved straws. Now she uses them primarily for cosmetic purposes, but as a kid, she was obsessed with them. She'd drink the milk out of the bottom of the bowl or use it for canned chicken noodle soup. I bought straws in bulk and still do. She even has a way of squeezing them and running the tip between her teeth like floss. And anytime she's nervous or upset, she likes to chew on them.

We went through a lot of straws back in the day. I had a pocketful at the funeral. She chewed through all of them in two hours.

I study her face. She doesn't look much different than when she was a kid. She's got a perfectly round face, ruddy and bright cheeks, and eyes that dazzle like a disco ball. She really is very adorable.

"Brooklyn, do you…"

"What?"

"How to say this." I try to make eye contact with her, but she's playing with her straw. "Um…does God ever, you know, talk to you?" All casual-like.

"Huh?"

"Talk to you."

Brooklyn laughs. "No. But I occasionally give him a piece of my mind. In fact, just last night I questioned why in the world he would create a dork like Gary Griffin. I mean, what's the point? The guy's a moron."

"Right. Yeah. So when you're talking to God about Gary the moron, does he…" My hands start talking, and I have to put them in my lap. "He doesn't show up, does he?"

"Yeah, right." She chuckles, but then stops. With the straw dangling out of her mouth she stares over the table at me. "Are you okay? Or do I need to call Dr. What's His Name?"

"I'm joking," I say, standing to grab my rag again.

"Yeah, well, that kind of sense of humor can put you in a straitjacket." She tosses her straw onto the table and stands. "I'm going to go shower. Can I borrow your stuff?"

"Yeah," I sigh. Borrow away. Why not? I watch her climb the stairs and disappear. I let out a tense breath. Why in the world would I broach this subject with Brooklyn? With anybody, for that matter. I sound like a quack. "I sound like a quack!" I whisper to the ceiling. But I am alone, and if this or the conversation moments before is any indication, I'm starting to understand why.

seven

As Brooklyn leaves for her night out, I am preparing for my night in. I get in my comfy clothes, fix some canned soup, curl up on the couch, and work on my proposal for Malia. I can't write fast enough. All kinds of ideas are flowing, and after two hours, I've managed to put together a terrific game plan, along with a budget and long-term goals.

Yet, even as I am focused on the task I have been ordered to take on, I feel him...okay, *Him,* nagging at me. I keep looking around, but He is not here. I listen carefully for noises downstairs, but all is quiet.

However, in the midst of the silence, there is a whisper. I don't hear it with my ears. Deep in my heart, where I hardly ever go, something is being said.

I walk to the kitchen and make myself some tea, contemplating what it is that lingers in my heart. Not words. Not thoughts. Something else, yet complete and clear.

I take my tea and go to the computer, which is already on and logged in to one of my online dating pages. I sit there for a moment. I don't understand why this is hard. These dating sites have never worked for me. And somewhere inside of me I always felt I was worth more than a profile on a page.

Still, my fingertips hover over the keys, barely touching their tops.

I sense Him, like He's poised over my shoulder. "Give me a second, will ya?" I say. "I'm not fast like You. I didn't create my little online world here in six days, you know."

I don't feel much sympathy back, so I sigh and hit Delete.

ARE YOU SURE YOU WANT TO DELETE YOUR PROFILE?

I stare at the question. I feel like I'm deleting myself. Or a version of myself—a hotter, sexier, more interesting version of myself, with pics of me, only in good lighting.

After this is gone, what is left? I chew my lower lip and try not to burst into tears. This is way harder than I thought it would be. Yet I have a sense that things can't move forward until I give this up. But it's like a smoker quitting cold turkey. I'm afraid of the withdrawal symptoms.

I punch the Enter key.

YOU HAVE BEEN DELETED.

Gee. That sounds promising.

I look up. Don't really know why. He has yet to hang from the ceiling like a bat or something. "Okay. All canceled. Satisfied?"

No reply.

I take my purple pen out of my pocket and run my fingers through the feather on the end. My twenty-four hours is almost up.

It takes four attempts, but I finally lay it on the desk and swivel around. "Here it is," I say, pitching my thumb over my shoulder. "I'm ready. Come on. There's a purple pen here." I twiddle my thumbs and swivel in long, slow circles in my chair. "Just awaitin'…"

Nothing.

I'm growing frustrated. He shows up when I don't want Him to and doesn't show up when I do. Who does He think He is?

Oh yeah.

Okay, so maybe I need to go to Him. Yes, that would be the proper, perhaps reverent thing to do.

And where would one find God at ten o'clock in the evening?

I stuff the pen in my pocket and grab my keys.

I didn't really take into account how creepy churches are late at night. No glowing windows. Just haunting light shot straight into the sky, highlighting a steeple that from my angle looks more like a dagger.

We've already established I have an active imagination.

I don't know why, but I actually go to the front door to see if it's unlocked. Somewhere inside of me it seems like a church more than a grocery store should have twenty-four-hour access. But no, locked up like a bank vault. As it should be, with the thousands of dollars' worth of sound equipment they've got in there.

I slink along the front wall, hiding in the shadows while acknowledging to myself that I really should go back to church. Maybe if I'd made myself go and dragged Brooklyn with me, she would've turned out a little more, I don't know, like me. Of course, the question is, how would I have turned out?

I realize I should pay more attention to what I'm doing. If you're going to break into a church at night, that should be your focus. I slide around the corner and am facing west now. The regular sounds of the night—distant traffic, dogs barking—bring a strange comfort. I look up into the sky. It is surprisingly bright. The stars pulse like they're dancing to the rapid beat of my heart. Honestly, I have never done anything like this before. I have never shoplifted or cheated on a test or exaggerated on my dating profile. I believe in honesty and that people should not break into buildings, especially churches.

However, I am breaking in only to deliver something important, not to take anything. And I happen to know how to break into buildings with little damage because of the numerous times my sister has gotten us locked out of the condo.

I realize how I must look, with my purple pen hanging out of my pants pocket, my tire iron tucked under my shirt, and my eyes wide with what can only be described as guilt.

I'm on the secluded side of the church, where they keep the garbage cans and don't keep the landscaping. It's very alley-like except there's not another building very close. A window, right above the air-conditioning unit, catches my attention. I should've brought a flashlight—but there is only so much one can stuff into a size A bra.

I give a quick glance around and decide it's now or never. I hop onto the air-conditioning unit. The window is old and not super easy to pry open. It's creaking like it's doing a haunted-house impression, but finally I manage to shove it open enough to crawl in. I stuff the tire iron back in place.

Dusting off, I find myself standing in an office and being distracted by the coffee stains on the desk.

Move along, move along.

The door is locked, but from the inside. I unlock it and am now in a pitch-black hallway, which does not have the benefit of outside light. I let my eyes adjust as I follow the hallway around in a semicircle. Finally I come to the foyer and the sound of somebody tinkling. I pray it's not me. Turns out it's actually a little cherub fountain.

And beyond the fountain is the sanctuary. The doors are open, and the room seems to glow like a firefly. Not sure where the light's coming from, but it's definitely not as black as the rest of the church.

I like the stained glass and take a moment to observe it, then decide I better get my business done. Ahead is a lavishly decorated altar, with beautiful white floral arrangements and tall, thick, stately candles.

I start down the center aisle. Then can't stop myself from humming the "Bridal March," which then causes me to saunter like I've got a train flowing behind me and a hundred pairs of eyes watching me. I clutch my purple pen like a bouquet and take my time. Heel, toe. Heel, toe. This is a once-in-a-lifetime moment and you don't want to hurry it. I've seen girls rush down to the altar like they're afraid the guy's not going to wait any longer. I say make 'em wait!

I grin and nod, pretending to see people I love as they express their adoration while I pass by. Up ahead are Brooklyn and Nicole, side by side in bridesmaid dresses any woman would kill to wear. Nothing taffeta, nothing dyed to match. Simple. Graceful. Eggshell white with a scalloped collar and arm-flattering sleeves.

I reach the altar, pretend to hand my bouquet off, and turn. To nothing. I try to imagine what my groom will look like, but the only thing popping into my head is *Him.* Maybe that's because I need a good dose of reality—that I am here not for my own wedding, but to turn over my favorite purple pen to God, the pen that has written down a thousand hopes and dreams.

The wedding music is still playing in my head.

It's like a compulsion. Before I know it, I've actually stepped onto the green-carpeted stage and grabbed a microphone.

"To my husband…"

I shake my head. I'm being ridiculous. But I've always wondered what my vows might sound like spoken. I've written them a hundred times, a hundred different ways. But I've actually never said them out loud.

"To my husband. I have waited so long for you. You have filled up the pages of my life before you ever touched my heart. But when you did touch my heart, you filled it more than words could ever express…"

I smile. This is sounding pretty goo— *Ahhhh!*

"Freeze!"

I throw my hands up. The microphone drops to the carpet with a thud, but the purple pen is still in my clutches. A bright blinding light bounces toward me. I can't see a thing; I only hear footsteps on the carpet.

"Don't move!" More instructions. Okay, freeze. Don't move. And come up with something clever. Quickly.

"Surrender your weapon! Now!"

Weapon? I look up at my hands. Oh, the purple pen. I've got lights and presumably guns pointing at me, and still, it's a little hard to hand it over. *Surrender* the pen?

"NOW!"

I swallow and gently bend my knees. It takes three tries, but I finally set it on the carpet and stand back up.

The light lowers and behind it are my two best friends: Garrety and Lakeland.

"Oh, it's our favorite speed dater," Garrety says.

"Looking for your imaginary friend?" adds Lakeland.

I walk, as calmly as possible, off the stage.

Garrety peers at me. "Is that a tire iron sticking out of your—"

"Look," I say, "I know how this appears."

"It appears as though you jimmied the window open above the air-conditioning unit, which incidentally is tied to a silent alarm, and you're now trying to steal valuable sound equipment."

"I wasn't stealing anything. In fact, I was giving God my..."

"Yes?" Lakeland leans in.

"My, um..." I look longingly back at my pen.

"What's your name?" Garrety asks.

"Jessie Stone."

"Lakeland, let me have a moment with Miss Stone."

"Sure." Lakeland steps to the back of the church and begins examining the sound board. Garrety sits on the highest step on the stage and pats it, indicating I should sit next to him. I do, because really I don't see that I have any other options. I eye my pen, sitting on the carpet. The tire iron is awkwardly sticking out of my shirt, but I decide to pretend it's not there, because he hasn't mentioned it again and so I probably shouldn't either.

"Now, young lady, why don't you tell me what's going on."

I feel my eyes moisten. "It's very complicated, Officer."

"It always is. Just start from the beginning."

I shake my head. "I don't even know how to explain this."

"When we came in, it sounded like you were rehearsing for a wedding."

I nod solemnly. "Yes. I was."

"So speed dating paid off?"

"No. I'm not even dating anyone. How pathetic is that? I've just always wanted to be married. I know it sounds stupid, but there's something in me that needs that. I want it. I've dreamed my whole life of finding the right guy. But I'm thirty-four. Time is running out for me."

Garrety shifts awkwardly. "You know, I was once like you."

"You?"

"Me." He smiles and rubs his bulging waistline. "I know, hard to believe. But I'm actually quite the romantic."

"I can see that, I really can."

"I've been married and divorced twice, and I can speak to the fact that as terrific as romance is, it's not enough to carry you through the hard times. My first wife I married straight out of high school. She went to the prom with me, so I figured that was enough to get her to go through life with me." He chuckles. "No such luck."

"I'm sorry," I say, patting his arm.

"After that, my self-esteem was pretty low. So I married a woman I thought was too good for me, just because she showed some interest. I thought I was pretty lucky that any woman of that caliber would even look in my direction, let alone date me." He sighs a little. It's obvious to me he's still in a lot of pain over it. "Anyway, the entire relationship was tumultuous. She never 'got' me, you know? She didn't understand anything about me. She didn't even think I was funny, and that was the real dagger. I was never the best-looking guy around, but everyone had always told me I was funny. Then here was this woman saying I wasn't."

I lean in to him. "God thinks you're hilarious. He says you have a great sense of humor."

Garrety eyes me. "Huh. So…that's why you're here? Because you hear God talking to you?"

I lean back against the step and cross my arms over the tire iron. "Let's just say He likes to get into my business."

"What I would've given for Him to have gotten into mine."

"You believe in God?"

"After two divorces and a midlife crisis, you start thinking that maybe the way you're doing it isn't working." He lowers his voice. "And, ma'am, I'm not trying to be offensive here, but you're displaying some behaviors that might benefit from seeing a doctor."

I roll my eyes. If he only knew.

"All right, let's get you on your feet." He stands, pulls me up by the arm, and gestures for the tire iron, which I pull out and hand to him. "You have the right to remain silent. Anything you say can—"

"You're arresting me?"

Garrety raises up his hands the way I raise up my hands when Brooklyn says something unbelievable. "You did just break into a church. And the evidence was just sticking out of your shirt there. So my hands are tied. Sorry." Except as he cuffs me, it's my hands that are tied.

Lakeland returns. "Nothing appears to be missing. We're trying to get ahold of the pastor."

"I didn't take anything!"

"All right, ma'am, just remain calm," Lakeland says. I take one last look at the pen I'm leaving behind before they walk me out the front door of the church and put me in the squad car.

"I hope he's worth it!" I yell at God, but the only one who hears me is Garrety, who shoots me a look indicating I should seriously consider getting a doctor.

eight

I've actually never been to jail. At least for something I've done. I've bailed Brooklyn out four times. Once I let her spend the night in there, just to give her a reality check. But now—as I lie on the cold metal bench, staring at a molded, rotting ceiling—I suddenly feel very bad about doing that.

The place reeks of urine, pot, and other unmentionables. I breathe shallowly, through my mouth, and stare hard at the ceiling like it's the face of God. How could He let this happen? I was there obeying *Him*. Doing what *He* asked. I contemplate this for hours while hoping Blake checks his voice mail. I contemplated calling Brooklyn but decided I'd rather get harassed by Blake. My thoughts return to God, me, and the purple pen.

"And I get thrown in jail for it?"

Oops. Said that out loud, which causes the only other person in the holding cell with me to look over. Ugh. She's wasted, with greasy hair and an expression that indicates she'd like to converse.

"That's what I said." The woman shrugs. "I mean, where does it say I can't pass out on a sidewalk, you knoowww?" A sloppy grin emerges.

I sit up and turn my back to her, bringing my knees close to my chest. All this over a stupid purple pen, which is now *not* in my possession. Perhaps I'm the only person to get thrown in jail for possession of nothing.

Well, I did break into the church—but seriously, should a church *really* have locks? I mean, isn't that counterproductive?

I hear keys rattle and turn to see Garrety unlocking the cell. I jump to my feet, and he waves me over. I glance at my cellmate, but she's passed out again and about to fall off the bench.

"Thank you!" I say, stepping out of the cell. "That was so disgusting!"

"Keep that in mind next time you decide to do something crazy, okay, Speedy?" Garrety says.

"I only went speed dating once." This month.

"Uh-huh." Garrety locks the cell and leads me down the hall. "By crazy, I meant breaking into the church."

"Oh, right." I wanted to add that's only touching on crazy, but I'm more concerned about getting out of here. Garrety gives me my tire iron and keys back, and I sign a few papers. He nods to something behind me. I look around and it's Blake, laughing it up with the female officer at the desk.

"Now there's a nice fellow," Garrety says quietly. "Good looking. Comes to get you out of jail. Why not some guy like that?"

"Yes. Why not?" I glance at the ceiling hoping God is eavesdropping on this conversation. Blake must have noticed us, because when I look back at him, he is watching me, grinning like he's just been given the right to harass me for the rest of my life.

Garrety reaches out to shake my hand. "Stay out of trouble, you hear?"

I shake his hand. "Yes. Thank you, Officer." I turn and walk toward Blake, who is chuckling. "Shut up," I say as I walk through the front doors of the station. The morning light screams at me, and I block it with my hand. I really want to sleep.

Blake scrambles behind me, laughing out loud now.

I walk quickly toward the car, which is parked at the curb. "I said shut up! Thanks for coming to get me. But shut up."

He opens the car door for me and notices the tire iron. This causes even more laughter.

I get in as quickly as I can. "'Shut up' includes insidious laughter over my most inconvenient predicament."

"Hey. I'm the one that came and bailed you out. And sorry, I just got your message. I was asleep." He shuts my door, then goes around and gets in, the laughter cranking up again. Finally, his laughter settles. "Jessie, seriously, what were you doing?"

I hold my hand up. "Talk to my Fifth Amendment."

"What were you doing?"

I drop my hand into my lap. "Nothing. Now, can you take me back to my condo so I can change and come up with some clever excuse for being late to work?"

He starts the car. "Nothing, huh? Excuse me for stating the obvious, but you don't break into a church in the middle of the night for nothing."

"I'm a woman. In case you didn't notice. I don't have to make sense."

He grins. It's so unfair when he does that. I can't be mad at him when his dimples show. I cross my arms, though, and hunker down in my seat.

Blake whistles for a few minutes and then says, "Wasn't that your parents' church?"

"Yes." I look out the window. I don't want to talk about this.

"So...what were you doing there?"

I don't answer.

"The officer said you were rehearsing for a wedding or something." A chuckle escapes. "I'm sorry, I'm sorry..."

"No, you're not."

"Da, dum, da, dum."

I try not to smile. "Do you have any idea how much I hate you right now?"

"You love me. Admit it." Dimples.

I laugh—I can't help it—and then notice we're heading north. "Where are we going?"

"Just settle down. I paid two hundred dollars to get you out of jail, and that means I choose where we go."

"I need to get my car back, get changed, and get to work."

"You're going to be playing hooky for a while."

"I can't play hooky! I have responsibilities, Blake. People are depending on my dependability."

"Yeah, well, you can explain to them how those wonderful character traits landed you in jail. Later. Right now, I've got something to show you."

"Another blondie?"

He shoots me a look. "Careful. My shallow-itis is contagious."

Stung.

"Besides, what are you cracking on me for?" he asks. "Clay Matthews was a blond."

"You know," I say, rubbing my temples, "I've had a bad enough night without you bringing that jerk up."

"I'm just saying, Clay Matthews was a blond."

"Clay Matthews was the punk who *left* me for a blonde."

"Oh. Right. Well, I never did understand what you saw in that guy."

I close my eyes, my head resting against the seat. "His name was Clay. I thought he'd be more moldable."

Blake laughs. I love when he gets my jokes. "So, the perfect husband search—how's that going for you?"

"As a matter of fact, it's going fab—" My ear is tickled, and I swipe at it. "Stop touching my ear!"

"I'm not touching your ear."

I glance behind me. There *He* is, with my feather pen, about to tickle my ear again. He winks. "I am *so* not talking to You!" I say, giving Him a hard look.

"What?" Blake says, glancing at me. "What did I say?"

I turn and face forward, trying to calm myself. "I'm sorry. I wasn't actually, um, talking to you. I mean…I was just letting off some steam."

My ear is tickled from the backseat again, and He says, "Don't be mad. I'm gifted at turning bad into good."

"Whatever! What are you, um, going to show me, Blake?"

Blake glances at me and shakes his head. "You'll see." Then he smiles. "So, back to the perfect husband hunt. You're one and a half months into the new year. What are you waiting for?" Blake asks.

"That, my friend, is a great question. What *am* I waiting for?" I nod toward Blake, hoping *He'll* get a clue.

Blake starts in on some diatribe about how women put too much pressure on men to be perfect, which gives me a chance to turn around in my seat.

God smiles at me. "You left this at My house." The purple pen is tucked in His pocket, barely showing out the top.

My eyes narrow. He knows I can't say anything with Blake in the car.

"So," He continues, "no filling up journals with your grand ideas about this story anymore. But, I do need you to start blogging online."

Blogging? I turn back around in my seat, facing forward—or, more accurately, away from Him. I detest bloggers. Blogging is like going to a party where everyone is that one guy who has an opinion about everything. Ugh. If I blog, I'm going to have to take back all those nasty things I've said about bloggers.

Sigh. Well, at least I probably won't get arrested for it.

We've wound our way up the side of a mountain that overlooks Santa Barbara. This used to be where we'd hang out sometimes as teenagers. I try to admire the view, because it's breathtaking, but I'm fighting the imaginary conversation I have going on in my head with Mr. Coston— while also fighting off the attention of the possibly nonimaginary friend in the backseat, who is now dangling my purple pen.

"It's just up there," Blake says, pointing. We turn into a neighborhood filled with magnificent, never-in-my-lifetime homes.

"This is the development our company has been working on for a year. They should be ready in about four months. Most of them are sold."

"What? Building shelves for Veronica lost its luster?"

Blake's smile fades. He actually looks a little wounded, and I regret my sharp tongue. "Yeah. That didn't quite go over. She and her new *husband* are opening that shop. The one whose last name she hadn't taken on yet. Oh, but she will. In case you were worried."

"I wasn't. Sorry."

He shrugs. "Come on, I'll show you around." Blake hops out of the car.

I quickly turn to the backseat. "The story that You're writing for me—it could be a very short assignment for You, You know." I nod toward Blake as he rounds the back of the car.

God raises an eyebrow.

I smile innocently as I open the door to the car. "Here's what You need to write: *Blake wakes up to Jessie's irresistible charms.* Does that sound easy? No rewrites necessary."

God smirks. "Charm. Yeah, you were really charming back there. As charming as an ulcer."

"Hey! I thought You were loving and all that." I glance at Blake, who is already at the front door of the house.

"I am. Now go." God shoos me out the door. "He's here to show you something special. Maybe you should pay attention to that rather than hair color, which is really beginning to become an obsession with you."

"Jess, come on!" Blake yells.

"Okay. I'm going. You stay in the car. You are very distracting!"

I follow the stone driveway up to the house, which is nothing short of stunning. The scene takes my breath away. The house over-looks the water. The sun is shining straight through the unfinished walls.

"What do you think?" Blake asks as he gestures toward the front.

"Amazing. This is really great, Blake."

He grins. "I know! Come inside!"

I shove my hands in my pockets, only to discover…my purple pen. Huh? "Um, yeah, I'll be there in just a sec. I left something in the car." I race back to the car, open the door, and slide in. I turn to the backseat, but it's empty. "Are You here?"

No answer. I look back to the house and gasp. There He is! Inside the unfinished house! I hurry back up the driveway only to run into Blake inside. "What do you think? This is where the living room is, with a double-sided fireplace. The other side is the kitchen. Want to see?"

"Definitely. For sure. Just give me a sec to, um, you know, look around. I want to get the big picture."

Blake smiles proudly and nods. I hurry off. Man, this house must be, like, three thousand square feet or something. "Wow!" I yell. "Man, this is enormous! Love the layout!" I hurry through the rooms, glanc-ing into closets and bathrooms. I turn and nearly run into Him.

"Hi," He smiles. "Looking for someone?"

"Funny. I thought I told You to stay in the car."

"Yes, well, I'm working on your bossy side. You probably won't believe this, but not once in the history of the world have I actually taken orders from a human."

I bite my lip. "Sorry. I see your point. I just forget because You look…well, You know."

"Cute?"

"Um. Yes. That's the word I wasn't looking for."

He gestures to Himself. "It's just something I borrowed for the occasion."

I laugh. "You're funny." I take the pen out of my pocket. "I got arrested trying to give this to You. You can't give it right back."

He doesn't reach for the pen but instead gestures around Him. "So, what do you think of this house? Needs a few more walls, some paint. You like chartreuse?"

"Okay, let's stay on point here. I am being abundantly cooperative. Time to do Your part. Write, write, write."

"Wouldn't take much to make it a home. It's missing your veranda, though."

I relent and glance around a little, taking in the fresh sawdust smell, which I actually love. "And double front doors, chandelier in the foyer, an office overlooking the water, and a porch swing." I wave my hands. "You're getting me off track here."

He's looking at me in a way that makes me think I should, perhaps, do some internal searching.

I sigh. "Okay. So I made a *light* suggestion to You. Sorry. But don't You agree? Wouldn't Blake be the perfect match? Just picture our photo albums."

"I am not accepting nominations."

I can hear Blake walking around the front of the house. I lower my voice. "I've cared about him forever. If I'm hoping for something that won't happen, would You just tell me so I can get over it?"

"Jessie, you need to learn to trust Me. If you do, the next man you kiss could be the one."

I get *slightly* caught up in the moment but snap out of it. "No offense here, but You're not exactly what I'd called an expert in romance."

He looks amused. "Really?"

"Parting the Red Sea: majestic and very powerful—but not, You know, romantic."

"Have you read Song of Solomon?"

"Is that in the Old Testament?"

"Yes."

"Then no."

"You might start there. And you'd be surprised how into brides and grooms I am. One Bride in particular." He plucks the purple pen out of my hand and drops it in His shirt pocket. "I created romance, and I don't want to see you in any relationships off script. My script. The one I'm writing."

"Okay, so I'm off script duty. But what am I blogging about?"

"You'll figure it out."

"See? That's what I mean. Sometimes You're very nonspecific, and for an organized person, I just need a little more—"

"Jessie?"

I whirl around. "Need a little more, um, crown molding."

Blake grins. "Oh, that's coming. Believe me. What do you think?" He gestures around him. Pride beams from his face.

"It's great, Blake. Really. Very, very nice."

"This one's still available. You in the market?"

This makes me smile. "Soon. Very soon. Okay, not very. And maybe not soon." I sigh. I really wish God could at least give me a hint or a timeline or *something*. Maybe I should buy Him a BlackBerry.

nine

I was born with a guilty conscience that to this day can't be explained. It's one of many odd parts of my personality. I think it's a mutated gene or something, probably from my mother's side. Brooklyn does not have this gene and doesn't feel the slightest bit of guilt over things she really should feel guilty about.

That is why I think it is terribly odd that I am feeling not one ounce of guilt at this moment.

My slacks are wrinkled, my hair is in desperate need of product. Normally I'd be standing in the bathroom with hot water steaming out of the faucet, trying to force the wrinkles out. Or furiously combing/cursing my hair to get it just right.

Instead I'm skipping up the front steps to the office building. The day is glorious at sixty-five degrees, sunshine spilling out of the sky in abundance. I look up and grin, opening my arms like I'm Mary Poppins or something.

I fling open the front door of Coston Real Estate. I wave at my desk as I pass by. I start to wave at Nicole, but as she sees me she gasps so loudly I clutch my heart and wonder if I'm about to die in some freak office accident. Racing out of her cubicle with wide eyes, she hurries up to me and clasps my shoulders. "Are you okay? Are you okay?"

I step back. "Nicole, I'm fine. Why?"

"*Why?* Do you know what time it is?"

"Afternoon-ish."

She gasps again. "Something is very wrong. You always know what time it is."

"Nicole, I'm fine." Whisking her back into her cubicle, I say, "Really."

"What's wrong?"

I sit in her seat. "Didn't you just hear me?"

She walks around her cube like a squawking chicken. "Jessie, you're the type of person who would miss work without calling in only because you were murdered. Do you know what I mean?"

I grin. "I know. I know! I feel so liberated."

"You're late on purpose?" Her gaze stops on my clothes. "Isn't that what you were wearing yesterday?"

I put my elbows on her desk and lower my voice. "I was in jail."

"What?"

"I know. Crazy, isn't it? But yeah, in jail. Me!"

Nicole stands absolutely still. "For what?"

"Nothing. It was really a misunderstanding. I broke into a church. But not to *steal* anything. I was leaving something there for God and—"

Nicole grabs her purse and digs through it. Her hand emerges with a pill bottle. "Look, I want you to take these. Take two now and one tonight. They're my hormone pills, and it's the next best thing to an antidepressant—"

"Nicole, look at me." I stand up and throw open my arms. "Do I look like I'm depressed?"

"Isn't the first sign of depression that you stop taking care of yourself—like showering and changing clothes?"

I laugh her off as I take a seat in the small chair next to her desk and gesture her toward her own. She looks like she needs it. "Look, Blake bailed me out of jail, then I went with him to look at some houses he's building. That's all."

Nicole sits. "That's all? But what about work? I mean, Mr. Coston was about to have a heart attack this morning."

"Because he had to go get his own coffee?"

Nicole's eyes narrow. "No. I had to, actually, but that's not the point. Jess, you're a normal, dependable employee. You don't just not show up."

"I'm quitting."

Nicole stares at me for a moment, then opens her pills and pops two, swallowing without water. She looks at me again. "What is happening to you?"

I smile. "I'm starting my own business."

"I'm sorry?"

"Don't be sorry." I laugh at my own joke. "It's going to be wonderful."

Nicole reaches for her phone and then pulls her hand back again. She looks at me carefully, as if trying to decide which of us needs to be hospitalized. "Why would you start your own business? Don't you know how risky that is?"

I stand up. This is too exciting to stay in one place. "Yeah, I know. And I'm the least likely person to take a risk, aren't I?" I pace two or three steps inside the cubicle.

"You can't even open the bathroom door without a using a paper towel."

I step closer to her. "I know this is hard to understand, Nic. It's hard for me too. I mean, this isn't like me at all." I stop and turn to her. "But I've had a kind of…spiritual awakening."

Nicole looks desperate. "That's how cults start."

I laugh and reach to grab her hand. "Look at me. Don't I look happy?"

She nods, tears forming in her eyes. "Yeah, you really do."

"It's time for me to move on, you know? Brooklyn is old enough to support herself now. And you know, I don't even like real estate. If I hadn't inherited the condo, I'd probably be renting."

Nicole shakes her head, but then she smiles. "I still can't believe it." She laughs, stands, and hugs me. "I'm actually really proud of you. I don't know how I'll make it through the day without you, but I'm happy for you."

I hug her back. "Hey, our friendship goes well beyond the walls of this place. You know that."

She sniffles and releases me, giving me one more looking-over. "It's just…your hair. I've never seen the bed-head look on you before. When will you tell Mr. Coston?"

"I guess right now."

Nicole bites her finger. "I wish I could be a fly on the wall for that conversation."

"Please. It's not going to be a big deal. I'm replaceable."

"He depends on you way more than you know."

"Who knows? Now maybe he'll have a chance at getting his coffee fixed right."

I knock on his door, and he waves his hand, not bothering to look up. Then he holds out a finger indicating that he does not want to be interrupted, so I just stand there until he finishes writing. Finally, he stops and looks up. "Jessie!"

"Hello, Mr. Coston."

He looks me up and down. "Don't tell me your tire blew again."

"Why would I tell you that?"

"You look like you've been under a car."

"Oh. No, I haven't."

"Well, where *have* you been? You didn't bother calling, and that is not like you." He sips his coffee, eying me and waiting for an answer.

I take a step into his office. "Yes, I realize that, Mr. Coston. And I'm really sorry. I know this is highly unusual."

"I'll say. And to tell you the truth, not very well timed. I allow you to do some presenting at our weekly meeting and you're very distracted. Now you're showing up a half a day late for work. Normally when I give an employee more responsibility, they sort of rise to the challenge." He glances at his BlackBerry, then back at me, like he's expecting a response.

"Yes sir. I completely understand. It's just that, well, Mr. Coston, I hate real estate."

"Huh?"

I realize it's hard for Mr. Coston to comprehend life outside of real estate, but I give it a shot. "I think I've got other things inside me, you know? Things I'm more passionate about."

"It took you ten years to figure that out?"

"I had some responsibilities that required me to have a stable job."

He sets his BlackBerry down and leans on his desk, giving me his full attention. "That's what I thought you were, Jessie. Stable. But I don't know the person that I've seen over the past few days."

I take another step forward. "I know I've been acting strangely, sir. I've just got a lot on my mind, and some, um, unusual circumstances to deal with."

"So what are you saying?"

"I'm quitting."

I'm truly shocked by his expression. It seems he is taking this awfully personally for a guy who until recently regarded me only for my coffee-retrieving skills.

I quickly add, "Of course, this is my two weeks' notice. I'd never just leave you hanging." Yes, I realize it would be way more dramatic to walk out, free as a bird, but I'm not wired to be that irresponsible.

Now he's staring at his Starbucks cup, like it's the one quitting. "I think you're making a big mistake."

"I'm starting my own business."

He looks up, petrified. "Really? You?"

"Why?"

"You just don't seem like the, well, the business-minded type." He gives a sad little smile like that's the hardest thing he's ever had to say.

"I've learned a lot from you." Gag.

But it works. He looks thoughtful now. "Well, okay. Whatever you say. But I'll need you to stick around for about four more weeks."

Under normal circumstances, I would nod and be agreeable, but instead I say, "I can't."

"You can't?"

"I don't want to." What is *wrong* with me? It's like I'm a hardened criminal already. His office phone rings and I start to answer it, because that's my job, but I accidentally knock over his coffee, which spills in a spectacularly messy way. I gasp and hurriedly start blotting with Kleenexes.

He shoos me away from him as he stands and backs away from his desk. He looks angry as he stares at me, but I don't know which part of all this is making him angry.

After some more blotting, he regards me, looking partly resigned. "Well, Jessie, I realize I can't stop you if your mind is made up, but if I had a job like yours with a future in a company like this, it would take an act of God to get me to quit."

It is the end of the workday of my last day of work. Mr. Coston decided not to take my two weeks' notice. Nicole has helped me box all my stuff. I leave written instructions for the next employee, things he, or more likely she, will need to know, such as line five doesn't actually light up so you have to guess if someone is holding. Little things like that. I drop my jumbo roll of paper towels into the box. Nicole is taking down my shiny ten-year banner. She rolls it up and stuffs it in.

"Something to remember us by," she says.

"Isn't this incredible?" I whisper. "Me? Quitting? With nothing totally lined up. I mean, I feel like…like…"

"Brooklyn."

"Yeah, kinda."

"Well, don't get too carried away. You *are* starting your own business, and that's going to take a lot of faith."

I smile. "I happen to have a lot more faith these days, so it's perfect."

A horn blares outside.

"Speaking of Brooklyn," I say.

"I thought Blake was coming to get you."

"Yeah. He, uh, was. Then he had an appointment. That's what he called it. Probably a date." I shrug like I don't care. She helps me with one of my boxes as we head toward the front door. "I can't believe you quit your job."

"And broke into a church," I say.

"Yes. And went to jail." She shakes her head. "I don't know why you won't give me details."

"I will. Someday. I promise. It's just that right now, I think I've given you all you can take."

She laughs. "Yeah. I might need to digest this a little first." We step outside to cooler temperatures, more like the middle of February should be. She hands me my box and wraps her cardigan around herself. "Good luck. Call me, you hear? I want to know how everything is going."

"I will, I promise. And come by the shop next week, okay?"

We hug awkwardly around the box. I juggle my things down the stairs and have to knock on the window for Brooklyn to notice she needs to pop the trunk. I put my stuff back there, then get in the passenger seat, shifting trash around on the floorboard to make room for my feet. I wave at Nicole as she goes back in. Brooklyn starts to drive off but I say, "Wait."

"What?"

"Hold on."

"Did you forget something?"

No, I did not forget something. But I want to remember this moment...the moment that I walked away from everything that was secure and reliable in my life. Just walked away. Gone. Done with. Over.

"Can I go now?"

"Yes, fine. Go."

We drive for a little bit. "So, um, how does it feel to be jobless?"

My chest tightens. "Very free."

Brooklyn slaps the steering wheel. "I know! Isn't it great? See what I've been talking about all these years?"

"Now all we have to keep us afloat is our business."

A silence passes between us. I roll the window down and let the breeze tickle my face. But even with the cool breeze, I feel hot, so I crank on the air. I fan myself. I pull my hair up off my neck. The next thing I know I've grabbed a McDonald's sack off the floor of the car and am hyperventilating my way into a stroke.

"I can't breathe! I can't breathe!" It really feels like the bag is not giving me my air back. Brooklyn pulls over.

"Jess, calm down. Just breathe slowly."

"I am! I can't catch my breath! I think I'm having a heart attack. My chest hurts."

"Do you want me to call 911? Or should I take you to the ER? Do you even have medical insurance anymore?"

I look at her over the paper bag that is rapidly deflating and inflating. I'm pretty certain my insurance continues for a month or so, but right now nothing seems sure.

"I can take you to the free clinic. I go there all the time when I need my birth-control pills filled."

I roll my eyes and try to get a grip. The last place I want to end up is at a clinic. I close my eyes and…pray. *God, please help me.* Slowly, I feel myself calming down. Brooklyn looks tense.

"I'm fine," I say.

"You're not helping my confidence level here," she says. "I mean, you're actually making me feel like I might need to go out and get a real job." She pulls back onto the road, driving slowly.

"Look, Brooklyn, give me a break, okay? This is a big thing for me."

"I'm just not used to seeing you, like, freaked out." She glances at me a few times.

I grip the door handle. "I'm not freaked out. I'm having a normal response to the job equivalent of jumping off a cliff. I'm fine now. Did you get the sign ordered?"

"I think so."

"You think so?" I neatly fold the McDonald's sack in my lap.

"I placed the order. I mean, that's what you told me to do."

"Turn here," I say, pointing toward Waverly Street.

"Why?"

"Because we need to go to the grocery store. I hope you like ramen noodles."

ten

"Come on, it's time to hang the sign in the window!" Malia yells. "It just arrived!" Brooklyn is separating her eyelashes with a paper clip. I'm writing out a deposit slip. I drop everything and rush to Malia, who is at the front of the store.

"Thank goodness," I say. "That took forever." A whole week to be exact. In the meantime, we'd been arranging our little corner in Malia's.

We stand at the large plate-glass window that has been rearranged to include fewer floral arrangements and knickknacks to make room for our sign. Malia is pulling the sign out of the box, but it takes the three of us to get it out. Malia threads the hook with hearty rope, and we hoist it up.

Together the three of us steady and secure it.

"Come on!" Malia squeals. "Let's go outside and take a look!"

We file outside and stand in front of her store. It actually takes my breath away. Carved from wood, with fancy lettering, it's painted in vivid, romantic colors: Stone Serenades.

"I like it," Brooklyn says. "It really stands out here in the window."

"It does!" Malia says, squeezing both of us into sideways hugs. "I can remember when both of you were born! Now look! Your own business."

I smile, but inside I'm quivering. Maybe it's excitement. Or nerves. Or both. I don't know. It just seems strange for my name to be on something. For me to *own* it. A feeling of pride rushes over me. Momentarily.

"You okay, hon?" Malia asks me.

"Yes, fine. Exciting, right? Really, really—really!—exciting."

Malia checks her watch. "Time to open up shop! You girls ready?"

Brooklyn and I look at each other and grin. "Ready!"

Two hours later, I've rearranged our little area eight times. We have business cards, fliers, a cute floral arrangement to warm the counter up, and three different forms for our men to fill out. But no men. I decide to lay three feather pens out for them to use, just for the sake of irony. If a feather pen can't write for me, at least it can write for someone. I can only assume God sees and appreciates the selflessness of it all.

Brooklyn has spent the last hour redoing her makeup and separating her lashes, again, one by one with a paper clip. She's now studying herself in a tiny compact mirror, pushing at the skin under her eyes. "Seriously. Six pounds of groceries could fit in these bags. Do I look old?"

I look to Malia, who is sitting behind her counter reading a Harlequin novel. "Malia, does my sister need to be committed to the convalescent home?"

"I hear there are a lot of single men there." Malia smiles, then goes back to reading.

"Funny," Brooklyn huffs, snapping her compact closed. "Look, it's going to take me awhile to get on this new schedule. I mean, eight o'clock in the morning? It's the crack of freakin' dawn."

Malia and I exchange knowing glances.

"And where are the customers, exactly?" Brooklyn asks. "And why isn't there a coffee shop closer?"

"It's going to take some time," I say. "A lot of this is going to be word of mouth. Right, Malia?"

"That's how my business grew. A few loyal customers recommended me to their friends."

"We just need to make a good impression," I say, "so that's why you, flopped over the counter like you're dead, are worrying me."

Brooklyn groans. "As soon as that bell chimes, I promise I'll be chipper and lovely. Until then, let me rest."

I check my watch. "This is probably a good time to show you this. I special ordered it for you."

Brooklyn's head jolts up. "A gift?"

"Not exactly." I pull out a box from under the counter, open it, and remove a stuffed bunny suit. Holding it up, I wiggle it to try to get another expression to come to Brooklyn's face. But it's total deadpan.

"What is that?" she asks, her voice low.

"It's a bunny suit."

"I can see that. Halloween is months away, and usually I go as a witch."

"Look, we need some gimmicks, okay? Something to get people to come in. A cute girl in a bunny suit, standing on the corner of the—"

"I don't think so!" Brooklyn says, grabbing the suit and throwing it on the counter like it's a real rodent. "And why would you buy a bunny suit? Shouldn't we have a cupid or a heart or something?"

"Look, money is tight and the bunny was on clearance. Just hear me out," I say as Malia comes over to see what's going on. "You're an actress, right?"

"Yes, but—"

"And the one thing that Gary said drew you to him was that you were willing to tackle tough roles?"

Brooklyn puts her hands on her hips and narrows her eyes. "Uh-huh…"

"This is your moment to shine, Brook. I mean, our business depends on it. We have to bring in customers or we'll have no income. Do you get what I'm saying?"

She is standing there, arms crossed now, not saying a word.

"Let me put it to you this way. If we don't get some customers coming in, you're going to be forced to buy Cover Girl makeup and use hair products from Wal-Mart."

Growling, she snatches the bunny suit off the counter. "Fine!" she says. "But I'm not doing this all day!"

I nod my head energetically. "A couple of hours, tops. When the traffic is heavy out there. And listen, I heard this is how Jessica Simpson got discovered." Totally making that up, but I gotta feed her a bone. It seems to work.

"I can play it up, believe me. Before we know it, we'll have a ton of gorgeous guys coming in. Now, can I take my lunch break, please?"

I check my watch. It's barely after ten. "Yeah. Go on. I'll hold down the fort and try to keep all these gorgeous men at bay, okay?"

Brooklyn grabs her purse. "Not that I'm complaining, but opening this business is no way to remedy singleness. Every single gorgeous man who enters these doors is going to be in love with someone else."

I watch Brooklyn fly out the front door. I sit back down on my stool, pondering her words as I stroke the bunny suit. I actually hadn't thought of *that*.

Terrific. So I'm in a life-or-death-and-taxes job that I took on to be obedient to God, and there's absolutely no chance of meeting my Prince Charming.

I realize I'm choking the bunny. I need some dark chocolate. *Now.*

I know I am sleeping well when I open my eyes and I'm on my back. Any other position tends to signal some sort of nightmare or a battle with stress-induced insomnia. This morning I am on my back, but for some reason, my eyes fly open like I've just experienced something terrifying.

"Ah!" I scramble backward and grab my sheets. My head hits the wall.

"Morning, sunshine." God smiles.

I catch my breath—only to feel slightly embarrassed to be caught sleeping in. My guilty conscience is kicking in again. "It's Sunday. My day to sleep in." I'm not sure if I'm trying to convince myself or Him.

"Correction. Your day to go to My house. Legally this time." He sits on the edge of my bed. "The pastor dropped the charges and has been praying for you. The least you can do is say hello."

I groan and cover my head with the sheet. When I peek out, He's still there, tapping my purple pen against the nightstand He's perched on. Yes. He's actually sitting on my nightstand, His legs curled up to His chest, holding the clock, the only thing on the table.

"I had a dream about You last night."

"Oh?"

"Don't pretend You don't know everything."

He laughs. He actually gets my jokes. That's funny. "So you're talking about the one where you want to have Me incarcerated?"

I nod.

"And you're the judge, plaintiff, and lawyer?"

"Uh, yes." I throw the sheets off, and my feet hit the floor.

He hops off the nightstand and starts making my bed. "I kind of liked the part where I, acting as My own defense attorney, dump all those purple pens out on the table as evidence."

"Yeah. Hysterical." I wiggle my feet into my slippers and move to the other side of the bed to help Him. "I am upset. You've put me in a position of meeting only unavailable men."

"Nothing is impossible with Me. Now, come on. Time to get ready." He gestures toward the bathroom. I go in and grab my toothbrush.

"You know," I call through the open door, "it didn't go so well at the shop. We didn't have any customers. Not a single one. We could use some help, especially since all this was Your idea. Did I mention I won't have health insurance anymore?"

God pokes His head around the corner. "Listen, I have to go. Sunday school is starting." He smiles. "I'm just messing with you. I can be in more than one place at a time." I laugh. "But I should let you get ready. Make sure you say hello to Pastor Landry, got it?"

I pull the toothbrush out of my mouth. "Yeah, sure. Fine. Hi to Pastor Lan—wait a minute. He has a son, doesn't he? My age, right?" I smile at the mirror. "Did his son grow into a hottie? Still single?"

God calls out, "See you there. And don't forget Brooklyn."

"I just can't believe you're being this mean!" Brooklyn's wearing a dress, but it's got a length problem. It would barely pass at a bar.

I put on my blinker and turn toward the church. "I'm not trying to be mean, Sis. We need to go. Mom and Dad went and they took us. Don't you remember that?"

Brooklyn presses her cheek up against the glass. "All I remember is that I worked my butt off this week and I just want to sleep *in*."

"You can take a nap this afternoon. Until then, I need you to take this seriously. We need a lot of help from upstairs." I smile. "Plus, I hear it's a great place to meet guys."

"Ugh. That doesn't sound fun. Really, it doesn't."

I shrug. "I don't know. I mean, guys that get up on Sunday morning and go to church are at the very least responsible."

"Whatever. We've never liked the same kind of guy anyway." She slouches in the passenger seat.

I pull into the church parking lot. It is packed with cars, but I see a sign: Visitor Parking. Perfect. I pull in and open the car door.

"Come on, let's go."

We both get out of the car. Brooklyn, irritated as she stuffs her compact into her sequined silver bag that moonlights as a disco ball, trails behind me. "You're shocking my system. This is a lot of change. I mean, I'm happy you quit your job and everything, but you're kind of dragging me into your nightmare."

"Trust me. You don't know the half of it." I gaze up at the church, bright white and beautiful. Amazing what a little sunshine can do. I glance at Brooklyn. "Now shut up and try to look a little less immature."

"You can't say 'shut up' in church."

I'm about to smack her with my denim purse when a deacon opens the door for us. "Welcome."

"Thank you," I say, smiling pleasantly as I take a bulletin with a dove on it. I stop in the foyer, and Brooklyn comes up beside me.

"Wonder if you're famous."

I smile and nod at strangers as I whisper, "Shut up!" to my sister.

"You're going to make God mad with that foul mouth of yours."

"Nobody's going to recognize—"

"Jessie Stone!"

We both whip around. There is Pastor Landry, arms open wide. He is wearing his black pastor's robe and a look of delight. "Pastor Landry," I say quietly. "Hello."

He reaches in for a hug. I pat him lightly on the back. "I haven't seen you since the funeral." He steps back and looks me up and down.

"I know. I'm sorry. And sorry about the other night too."

"No need to explain," he smiles.

Thank God. Literally.

"And who is this?" he asks, holding out a hand to Brooklyn.

"My sister, Brooklyn."

"Brooklyn! My goodness, sweetheart, you're a grown woman now! It's hard to believe so much time has passed."

Suddenly, a man appears next to the pastor. He attempts a smile three times before it finally pops through. His cheeks flush right there in front of us like he's just done vodka shots. He keeps trying to make eye contact but doesn't manage to. Now he's staring at Brooklyn's rhinestone stilettos.

"Do you remember my son, Gavin?"

"Hi, Gavin. How are you?" I say.

"Yes," he answers.

"Oh, uh, good." I look back at Pastor Landry, who is grinning enough for both of them. "Gavin here is in charge of marketing at the church."

"Marketing? For a church?"

Gavin nods. "Yes. We put up billboards, send out postcards, and actually walk neighborhoods to invite people to come."

"Seems to be working. Looks like you've got a full house."

Pastor Landry takes my hand. "Jessie, anytime you want in, no problem."

Gavin finally makes eye contact with me. "I'll unlock your door…I mean, our door…for you anytime."

"Thanks. I appreciate it." Between the heat off Gavin's and my cheeks, we might be creating nuclear energy. "Obviously, I should've called first. I just didn't want to disturb anyone."

"You're not disturbed…I mean, you wouldn't be. Disturbing, I mean. Us." Gavin is back to staring at Brooklyn's shoes.

I rub my hands together. "Right. Okay. Well, I guess I should let you go. Sounds like church is about to begin."

"Would you two like to be my special guests today?" Pastor Landry is wide eyed with anticipation. "I always reserve two extra seats, right on the front row, for special guests. You could sit with Gavin here and—"

Brooklyn steps forward. "Oh, that is so kind. But unfortunately Jessie has one of those overactive bladders, so we have to sit near the back, you know, just case she needs to bolt."

I *really* want to slap her, but then again, I *really* don't want to sit on the front row either.

"Of course," Pastor Landry says. "I understand. You won't believe what an enlarged prostate will do. Well, it was good to see you." And off he goes.

Gavin leans toward me before he walks off. "You know, they have a pill for that problem." He smiles like he's just given me insider trading information. And he's gone.

I punch Brooklyn in the arm. "What did you do that for?"

"You're telling me you want to sit on the *front row* with Mr. Awkward?"

"No, I do not." I cross my arms. "But why'd you make up the bladder thing about me?"

"Jess, there is no way they'd believe *I* was old enough to have an overactive bladder. Now come on, let's get in there before all the back rows are taken."

Aggravated, I follow her in, and we manage to find an outside spot at the back. I cross my arms and stare forward.

"What? You're mad at me?" Brooklyn asks. "I just saved you."

"I know." I sigh. "I appreciate it, though maybe next time we can leave my organs out of it."

"It just came to me. Sorry."

"I guess I thought maybe Gavin might be…you know…maybe he was going to be…"

"Hotter?"

"Yeah. He was a really cute twelve-year-old."

"He's not bad. I mean, his nerves could use some nicotine or something, but he's probably not allowed, you know?"

The music starts and we stand. I grab a hymnal for us. I don't sing, mostly because I sound like a dying animal, but it's good to hear the words. They bring me comfort, and I remember them from when Mom and Dad used to bring us here. The crowd is diverse. Many sing—some like they mean it, others because that's what you're supposed to do, I guess. I look for Him. Surely He's got to be around here, somewhere.

The music ends and Pastor Landry comes to the podium to speak. A chill runs down my spine as I flash back to the night when breaking into a church made sense. I look at my sister, who is studying her cuticles. Maybe a lot has made sense to her over these years. Maybe wading through one relationship after another made some strange sense to her.

I tune in to Pastor Landry as the congregation laughs at some funny story he's told that I missed. I command myself to pay attention.

"If you have been waiting for God to do something for you, maybe you feel He's made you a promise, I can almost guarantee the next thing that happens will seem like the exact opposite. It's a test of your faith. Will you trust Him while you wait?"

And then I spot Him, standing behind Pastor Landry, and I swear

He winks at me. I close my eyes. A test of my faith? *What* faith? The only thing I've had faith in my whole life was that true love exists and romance is still alive. I mean, test Moses. Test Billy Graham. But why test a nobody like Jessie Stone?

I sit through the rest of the sermon contemplating this. Soon enough it is over, and Brooklyn and I are filing out with the rest of the people. As we head down the steps outside the front of the church, Pastor Landry shakes my hand again. "Come back, please. It was so good to see you."

"Thank you, Pastor. Your sermon was very…inspired."

Gavin springs toward us. "Jessie, again, let me know if you need to break in…I mean, give me a call…about getting in."

I manage a smile. That poor boy flushes more than a toilet.

"Yeah. Thanks, Gavin. And good luck with marketing and getting people to come—" I stop. "Brooklyn! I just got an idea!"

eleven

Brooklyn and I stand in front of the jewelry store's large window. Precious stones gleam and glitter in the afternoon sun. Brooklyn is drawn to the four-carat dazzler surrounded by alarm-triggering lasers and a four-inch box of glass. "Look at this!" she gasps. "It's platinum! I love platinum. That diamond is extraordinary."

"Uh-huh." My expectations, I guess, are a little lower because I'm staring at the dainty gold ring with a tiny diamond on top, barely visible to the human eye. But I like it. Simple. Beautiful. I don't want a guy going into debt to buy me a ring. Doesn't anyone realize that once you marry the fool, you'll be paying for your own ring? I mean, maybe I'm a traditionalist, but there seems to be something wrong with that scenario.

We're at the jewelry store because although Gavin didn't end up being a candidate for my love story, he did give me a fabulous idea for boosting our business. Instead of waiting for clients to come to us, we go to them, even before they know they're in desperate need of our services.

I nudge Brooklyn out of her trance. "We've got work to do."

"All right, fine. What's the plan?"

"Well, I don't think we should stand out here. It may leave the impression we're staking out the joint."

Brooklyn shoots me an evil grin. "You are on the most-wanted list now."

"I say we go in there, act casual, just—"

At the same time we notice a young man walk past us and into the store.

"He's got the vibe," Brooklyn whispers. "Young, nervous, hoping he can afford what he wants to give her."

"I agree. He's not here to buy a watch. Come on, let's go in."

We enter and separate to opposite sides of the store. The guy looks midtwenties, with honey blond hair, a nice physique, and plenty of dressing style. An older, chic-looking woman in a black suit is helping him. I try to inch my way closer so I can at least hear the conversation when I am stopped by outstanding customer service.

"Hello! May I help you?"

I look up. *Hello, gorgeous.* Wow. Bright blue eyes sparkle against the mood lighting of the showcases. His engaging smile causes my heart a little hiccup. I can't decide how old he is. There's a maturity in his face, but not a wrinkle on his skin.

"Ma'am?"

"Yes. Sorry. I'm looking for…" I glance down and realize I'm in front of a huge case of engagement rings. "A ring."

"Maybe getting an idea of what you like?"

Okay, now, how to play this? "Yes" means I'm not available. "No" means I have to come up with something about earrings, which are on the other side of the store, far away from Soon to Be Groom.

"Well, it never hurts to look, right?"

"Never." He pulls out a tray. "I like this ring. It's extremely romantic." I'm not kidding, he actually takes my hand. "Hmm. A size-five ring, perhaps?" Yes. Right on the mark. He takes the ring and slides it right onto my hand. A warm sensation crawls up my neck, and I stare forward—because if I don't, I swear my eyelashes will start batting.

"It fits perfectly." I hold out my hand and admire it.

"You have lovely hands. Any ring would look spectacular."

Yes, folks, I know he's paid to do this sort of thing, but it doesn't mean it's not fun. I hold the ring up, pretending to be thoughtfully admiring it, but in reality I'm wondering if this is the chance encounter I've been waiting for. I glance around for God or my purple pen or some sign that gives my eyelashes the green light to go for it.

Nothing.

"Let me show you this one, that's set with—"

"What are you doing?" It's Brooklyn.

I yank my hand away. "Uh…"

"Brooklyn?" my new love says. I look up to see the handsome man's face registering something as he looks at my sister.

"Oh my gawwshh!" Brooklyn gasps. "Jimmy?"

"Yeah! Oh my gosh! How long has it been?"

"Oh my gosh, I have no idea. Three years?"

"Like five!"

"Shut up!"

"Seriously, oh my gosh!"

Oh brother. I quickly slide the ring off. How this guy went from suave salesman to Valley boy, I have no idea, but I step aside to let these two exclaim the English language to death while I try to focus on the real reason we're here.

I move over a couple of cases, within earshot of our target, and pretend to be studying cuff links as I eavesdrop.

"What about this one?" the saleswoman asks.

"Hmm. I don't know. How much is this?" He's chewing a fingernail.

"Three thousand."

"Oh. What about this one?"

"Lovely choice. Look at the diamonds that encircle the band. And see how the—"

"How much is it?"

"Four thousand, five hundred."

"Oh."

Poor guy.

"I bet she's worth every penny," says the saleswoman.

Now that's just *wrong*. Obviously the guy's on a budget. Now if he goes practical, maybe he's giving the impression she's not worth it. Terrible!

"We have financing, no interest for ninety days."

"Oh, um…"

"You're already preapproved."

"I am?"

"Yes sir." The saleswoman gestures to the ring sitting on the counter. "She'll never forget the moment you give this to her."

He sighs and runs his hands through his hair over and over and over.

The saleswoman smiles. "I'll just go get the paperwork?"

"Um, okay. Yeah. I think that would be…she'll really like this."

"Honey, when she shows her friends what you bought her, you'll be the only star in her everlasting sky."

I think I actually snort out loud here. The saleswoman eyes me, then locks up the case before disappearing to an office. I glance at the guy. He's grown pale and looks like he's checking his bank account via cell phone.

Brooklyn's still catching up with Jimmy, so I slide up next to the guy. He's kind of breathing hard.

"Hi." I hold out my hand. "I'm Jessie Stone."

He looks confused. "Oh, um. Do I know you?"

"No." I hand him a business card. "But you look like you might need some help."

He reads the card. "You help guys set up the perfect proposal?"

"Here's the deal. You could spend five grand on a ring, or spend far less on that ring and propose to her in a way that will make her completely forget about the ring altogether." I lean in and talk softly, as if I'm sharing a deep dark secret. "The truth is that women want to feel special, and money just can't get you all the way there. Big ring? So what? Lots of guys can do that. But a proposal that takes her breath away— that's what will make her know that what you feel for her is real."

He stares at me for a moment, then glances down to all the rings. "You know, I really was looking at this one." He points to a single solitaire, small but exquisite. "It just looks like her."

I nod approvingly. "What's your name?"

"Daniel."

"My number is on there. Call me, and we'll help you give her something to remember for the rest of her life."

A relieved smile is accompanied by a handshake. "Thank you. Thank you so much. I will."

The saleswoman returns with a mound of paperwork in her arms. "All right, Mr. Taylor, let's get started here with—"

"I've changed my mind," he says as I slide back to the cuff links.

"Excuse me?"

"I want this one."

"The…the…single solitaire?"

"Yes."

"But…um…I thought you said she'd love the one with the—"

"I think *you* said that."

I'm beaming with pride as I hear him explain he'll be writing a check. I find Brooklyn, who is still chatting it up with Jimmy.

"Oh, hey, Sis. This is an old friend of mine. Jimmy."

I smile. "Hi, Jimmy." Grabbing Brooklyn's arm I whisper, "Let's go. I snagged a customer."

"Can you guys get me into a basketball game?" Daniel pretends to dribble and then takes a jump shot with a flier he's taken off the counter and wadded up. "Score!"

"Why?" Brooklyn asks, flipping a bunny ear out of her face. She's just come in for a fifteen-minute break. She really does look adorable.

"You know, so I can jump on the court during halftime and pro-pose." He holds up a finger. "Oooh! Maybe I could even dunk one!" He flies straight up and dunks the air.

Brooklyn and I glance at each other.

"Daniel, about Lila. She likes sports?" I ask.

"Not so much. No."

"What does she like?" Brooklyn asks.

This causes a full thirty seconds of thinking. Then, "Manicures."

"What else?"

More thinking. "Cocker spaniels."

I have a funny picture of three dozen cocker spaniels racing toward her, all carrying a rose. But Daniel's on a budget.

"Anything else you can think of? Something that might lend itself to some romance?" I ask, cueing Brooklyn to go hit the music on the iPod that's set in portable speakers.

But even with Frank Sinatra playing, Daniel looks completely out of ideas. "I mean, I don't know. I know she likes breath mints and bur-ritos with no onions. Um…sunless tanning lotion. Tartar-control toothpaste. Let's see here, she likes the toilet seat down." He smiles sheepishly. "Still working on that one."

"What about places? Any places she likes? Perhaps a park?"

"She's not fond of the outdoors. Allergies."

Oh boy. This is harder than I thought it would be. I try a differ-ent angle. "If you had a free Saturday and you told Lila that she could pick whatever she wanted to do that day and you'd do it with her, what would she say?"

Daniel wads up another flier and moves his feet around like an opponent is nearby. But he's still clearly thinking about it. Then he stops. "Got it. She'd want to go to the mall. And she's very picky. Not any mall. She always wants to go to the La Cumbre Plaza."

"The mall." I smile. "The mall. Yeah, we can work with the mall."

"We can?" Brooklyn asks. "What's romantic about a mall?"

"I can see it in my head. Yeah. This will work. This will work!"

Brooklyn eyes me, and I can read it on her face. She's wondering if I really am seeing something or someone that the rest of them are not.

"Daniel, what's your couple's song?"

"Um…"

"Something that reminds you of her?"

"I know. 'Wild Thing.'"

I can't help but smile at this guy. He's totally confirming why our business is going to thrive. "Trust me, Daniel. That's not your song. Think love song…something that makes her always want to dance with you."

"Okay, gotcha. Um, I'd say 'Still in Love' by Brian McKnight."

"Excellent." I fly behind the counter and grab a pencil. "So Saturday's the day?"

"Yes."

"All right. We've got three days to pull off a proposal that she'll never forget!"

twelve

I sort of feel like the wedding coordinator, except I'm the proposal coordinator. It's Saturday, and Brooklyn and I have walkie-talkies hooked to our hips. Brooklyn is outside the mall, waiting to spot Lila coming in. I'm standing with Daniel in front of Monster Electronics, which is directly across from Sephora. He's dancing around like he's on a basketball court, but I read it as excitement. I've found the guy dribbles when he's happy.

I check my watch. "Okay, it's almost time. Lila should be here any minute. You definitely told her the north entrance, right?"

"Yeah. She likes that entrance because of the Brass Buckle."

"Super. Now, you'll meet her at the front, and you've got a plan to get her here without stopping in a dozen stores on the way?"

"Yeah. I'm going to tell her there's a sale on mascara. She'll head straight here."

"Perfect." I nod to our cameraman, Jake. "Everything set?"

He pitches a thumbs-up.

Brooklyn's voice crackles through the walkie-talkie. "Green Honda Civic spotted. I think it's her. She's looking for a place to park."

"Brooklyn, tell us when she gets out of her car." I turn to Daniel. "Okay? You ready?"

"I, uh...no."

"No?"

"No. I'm not quite ready."

"Daniel, it's time! She's here! You're not having cold feet, are you?"

"I'm just...well, I don't know what to say. I mean, we've got all this fancy stuff set up, and I think I might just, well, just...blow it."

I take his shoulders. "Daniel, trust me on this. I'm a professional. Nothing's going to go wrong. We've rehearsed this a dozen times. I've got everything ready to roll."

"Not you. Me. I don't think I'm going to live up to all this." He gestures toward all the big-screen televisions that are about to show Lila the time of her life.

I suddenly see the problem. I try a calm voice. "Daniel, she's going to love all of this. It's going to be a dream come true for her, but what she cares most about is you. If you weren't here, this wouldn't mean a thing."

"But what do I say? I'm not very good at talking unless it's about basketball."

I put a hand on his chest, over his heart. "This is your moment to tell her exactly how you feel about her. Just pour out your heart, and it will be perfect."

He nods. "Okay. I can do that. I don't have to rhyme, do I?"

"No poetry needed. Just be yourself."

"She's getting out of the car," Brooklyn says.

"Okay! Hurry to the front door of the mall!" I send Daniel off. "Brooklyn, she's headed for the front doors, right?"

"Yeah!"

"Okay, get back here."

I hurry to Roger, who is the salesman in the big-screen television department. He's holding a remote the size of a small boom box. "Okay, Rog, we're all set, right?"

"Yep. Just hit this button and the music starts. Just hit this button and the TVs turn on. Just hit this button and the picture show starts. Just hit this button and the—"

"All right, so you're good to go?"

"Good to go."

"On my signal."

"Yes ma'am. And afterward, we're still okay to hand out store coupons?"

I slap him on the back. "Absolutely. I can't thank you enough for helping us out."

"My pleasure, Miss Stone. I'm a romantic at heart. I took my wife out to a skyscraper, had a candlelight dinner, and proposed."

I clutch my heart. "Roger, that's beautiful."

"That was twenty years ago. And we're still going strong."

If I were a cartoon character, my pupils would've turned into little hearts. Brooklyn rushes toward me and grabs my arm. "They're headed this way."

"Say a prayer for Daniel," I whisper. "He's not sure what he's going to say to her."

Brooklyn's eyes roll. "Please. A ring says it all, doesn't it?"

Maybe to some women. But not to me.

"Here they come!" Brooklyn claps, alerting Jake and Roger. I hold my hand up. On my cue, the music will start rolling.

Lila is oblivious. She is holding Daniel's hand and in the middle of telling some story. Daniel is wide eyed and trying not to look obvious, but I can tell he's about to burst with anticipation.

I hide behind one of the fifty-eight-inch televisions. Brooklyn is behind a cardboard cutout of a zebra selling Dish TV. They're just about to the store when I cue the music.

It's louder than it would normally be for the store, and this immediately catches Lila's attention. She stops right at the entrance and looks at Daniel. "Babe, it's our song!" She's clutching her heart. She does a little twirl in his arms and laughs. I cue the picture montage, and as she swings back around, she spots herself on the television screen. "Hey!" She gasps. "Hey! That's…that's us!"

Daniel wraps his arms around her as they watch the pictures. Lila is covering her mouth, and before we know it, a small crowd has gathered, sensing something spectacular is about to go down.

I signal to Roger to slowly lower the volume of the music.

As the pictures come to an end, Daniel turns to Lila and takes her hand. "Lila Suzanne, I've loved you since the day I met you in Mrs. Collins's class in third grade." Crowd coos. Lila's eyes go moist. "You know, when you glued my sleeve to the desk. I knew then I'd want you to be my wife. Well, okay, not really. I mean, I liked you a lot, as much as a third-grade boy can like a girl."

I'm grimacing. *Come on, Daniel, don't get sidetracked.*

Daniel takes her other hand. "To tell you the truth, the day I knew

I wanted to spend the rest of my life with you was when you brought in that eighty-piece bucket of hot wings for me and the guys when we were watching the game on TV. I mean, that was incredible. You're incredible. You're the swish in my jump shot, baby."

Lila giggles, which seems to make Daniel choke up with emotion.

"Now," he says, "and for the rest of my life, I choose you. I hope you will choose me." He gets down on one knee and opens the small black box. "So?"

If you weren't watching the situation and you heard the scream, you'd probably call 911. After curdling the blood of five dozen mall shoppers, Lila pulls Daniel up, jumps into his arms, and kisses his forehead over and over. "Yes! Yes! Absolutely!"

Fifteen televisions show the moment as the cameraman zooms in on Lila's hand. Daniel slides the glittering (and quite elegant, if I do say so myself) ring onto her finger. She admires it for a moment, but just as I predicted, she's caught up in *him.*

The mall crowd explodes with cheers. They are loving every bit of this romance. I watch Brooklyn as she makes her way around, passing out business cards. That's my girl.

Daniel and Lila kiss, sealing the deal and causing tears to sting my eyes. The electronics department is suddenly closing in on me, and I swear I see an electrical cord move my direction; I slowly back away and find an exit door.

Busting through it, I march forward with my head down, breathing in and out until my head doesn't feel light. Nearby I hear a fountain. I walk to it and sit down, letting the water lightly spray my skin. I pretend I'm at the ocean.

I don't have to open my eyes to know He's there. I'm starting to sense Him nearby, even when I can't see Him. I keep my eyes shut, because I know if I open them, a whole lot of tears are going to come rolling out.

"I don't want to be that person," I say.

"What person?"

"The one that hurts every time I see someone else get what I want."

"Why is this so important to you?"

I open my eyes and let the tears dribble down my cheek. I don't bother wiping them. It's no use. I *am* that person, and a beautiful young woman named Lila got what I've always wanted. The irony, of course, is that I'm the one who made it all come true for her.

Well, okay, Daniel was involved a little too.

"You read minds," I say. "Don't You already know the answer to why this is so important to me?"

"I need you to know. Say it."

Say it. I don't know that I've ever said it, outside my journal anyway.

I finally look at Him, look Him in the eye like He's always looking into mine.

"I want to know that I'm going to be somebody's choice." I sniffle. "I'd like to know *when* I'm going to be somebody's choice."

A woman walks by and gives me a look. "What?! Never seen a girl talk to herself before?"

"Try your earpiece," God whispers.

"Why are You whispering?" I whisper back. "Nobody can hear You, remember?" But He does have a good idea. I throw my cell phone earpiece in.

"I know how you feel," God says. He sits down beside me on the edge of the fountain.

"Yes. You read minds. We've established that."

"Jessie." He touches my arm. It throws me a little. I don't recall Him ever touching me before. It's like warmth and coolness all at the same time, like when you're at the lake and the top of the water is warm and the bottom is cool. "I know how you feel."

The tears drip again. "You are trying to win over the entire world, so I hear. I'm asking for just one person to love me. One. Is it really that hard for You to write?"

"No."

I stand up. "I mean, out of the seven *billion* people in this world, You can't find one who can see me?"

"That's six billion, nine hundred eighty-six million, three hundred fifty-four thousand, and two. Wait. Three." He reaches down to touch the water.

"Funny."

"And over half of those are women. Fourteen percent of men fall within a ten-year age span of you." He scoops some water in His hand and lets it drip slowly back into the fountain. "But when I factor in at least one-third of what you think you need, that really narrows down the choices, especially when you consider how many men have no idea they're dripping liquids everywhere, and if they did know, they wouldn't clean it up."

I sit down again and lean toward Him. "Aren't You known for defying, not defining, the odds?"

He smiles. "I'm simply shooting straight with you."

"So. Basically, it's impossible." I yank the earpiece out. At this point I don't care who sees me talking. "I just want…I want to walk into a home, see it filled with crazy in-laws, cousins, uncles, aunts, grandparents. Even if they're all bickering with one another, talking over themselves, a few kids of my own thrown in and a—"

"Jessie!"

I don't move a muscle but glance sideways. There is no—NO—mistaking that voice. The way he always used to put a little extra *hiss* in my *s*'s.

"Jessie Stone?"

I brace myself and turn.

"Clay Matthews." Clay, Clay, Clay. Clay who broke my heart. Clay who seems to be in all my nightmares. Clay who is looking perfectly gorgeous at the moment. A smile pops onto my face like my brain had to slingshot it there.

He opens his arms. "In the flesh. I just saw your sister inside. She told me you guys have a business, something about helping people put together marriage proposals…"

"Yeah, we do."

"Well, how are you? It's been…how long?" He comes in for a hug, but we both lean to the same side, then to the other side. Finally we manage it. I start to pat him as if he has shingles. He's squeezing me like I'm citrus.

"Yeah, it's been a while." I know to the day how long it's been.

"How've you been?" he asks.

How have I been? Hmm. Well, after having my heart ripped to shreds, I've recovered quite nicely and am now having conversations with God. "Great. Great. Life couldn't be more—"

. I'd almost forgotten He was there, but I sense Him hovering behind me like a jealous boyfriend. Of course, I can't say anything because then I'd look like life wasn't going well and I was talking to imaginary things. That's not the impression you want to give an ex. Not too many times in life are you lucky enough to give an ex any kind of impression, but here I am, business owner, dressed nicely, obviously pulled together. I'm even wearing makeup. Clay seems to notice. He's stepping back and taking me in.

"You look terrific."

I don't know whether to twirl or gag. "Thanks."

He grabs my hand. "Hey, I am so glad I ran into you—"

"Yeah. Me too." I feel my face grow hot.

He gets an excited, nervous look on his face. "I want to hire you to help set up my proposal to Gwyne. Remember Gwyne?"

I tip backward a little. Thankfully, two unseen hands steady me.

"I'm sorry…Gwyne?" I'm a horrible liar, especially with God standing right behind me, but I give it my best shot.

"She's tall, blond—"

I hold up my hand to stop him. "Oh yes. Of course. Gwyne."

He nods. "Yes, well, I want to propose, and I want it to be spectacular, but I'm just not the kind of guy that can come up with stuff like that."

"I know—I mean, sure. Most men aren't. That's why we're in business." But it's true: Clay was the least creative man I'd ever dated. Still, no need to make him feel small and pathetic.

But I want to.

★★★

Clay meets us at the shop Monday at noon. He wanted to visit that same day—he's anxious and eager, which stings even more—but I put him off. Clay never seemed anxious or eager as far as we were concerned.

Brooklyn is busy flirting with another customer she is supposed to be helping plan a dream proposal. Malia's noticing too, and we keep an eye on it. But sitting across from me at a side table right now is Clay, who is leaning forward, tapping his foot, and looking like he's about to detonate.

I've got a pad of paper in front of me and am holding a pencil, jotting notes mostly for something to do, because so far we haven't even talked about the proposal. Clay's been catching me up on his life. Whoopee. "Okay, well, I know you're anxious to get back to your lovely bride-to-be, so tell me what Gwyne likes. What is she into?" Besides stealing boyfriends.

"Me." He grins.

An eye roll is begging me, but I resist.

"No, um, seriously," he says, "I'd say boats. Gwyne loves boats and the water."

"Okay, that's good. We can work with that. We have a special deal with the city to use piers on weeknights." Well, not yet. I'm working on it. But it sounds good.

Clay's face lights up. "Oh, wow, that sounds unbelievable. Yes, I can see it. That could be amazing!"

"But the fees are high." I have no idea, but I should probably ask for a lot of money in case I need to bribe somebody.

"Money doesn't matter. She's worth it. Every penny." His day-dreamy eyes are suddenly on me. "Jess, this is so…"

Jess? Now it's Jess? I lean forward. "What?"

"You, me. Here like this. And it's not weird. It's like these past couple of years haven't gone by."

"Three."

Clay puts an affectionate hand on mine, and now Malia's keeping an eye on me. I ignore her and attend to my customer.

"Well, what are friends for?" I smile.

"Yeah." He smiles back, and I remember why I fell for him. That smile undid me the first time I saw it. But I keep myself guarded. All this enthusiasm is for a woman I got dumped for, so really, I don't have much to smile about.

Except I'm getting ready to make some good money off him.

I'm smiling again.

Suddenly my cell phone beeps, indicating I have a text message, and to my ever-grateful ego, also a life, in case Clay was wondering.

DITCH THE SLIMY PUNK AND LET'S GO PLAY.

I laugh hysterically when I read it, because it's very funny—though if it had been a reminder to pay my bill, I would've laughed anyway just to seem like I had a fun life. I manage to glance out the window. There is Blake, making a face through the glass.

thirteen

I'm sitting on the beach, on a blanket that Blake has provided, watching the tide sweep the sand. I'm reminded as I sit here that there are perks to owning your own business. You can take off in the middle of the day and come to the beach. It's not as crowded as the weekend, and I am enjoying my little space on the sand.

A family nearby romps around, oblivious to whatever trouble there is in the world. They are catching Frisbees, tackling one another to the sand, sunbathing, and swimming. *That's what I want.* In case He's listening and taking notes.

Blake returns and hands me a chocolate shake. That's why I like Blake so much. He just knows. He knows that I've seen Clay, prepared his dream proposal, and now need chocolate in liquid form.

I take a long sip. "Ah. Thank you, my hero."

"Anytime." He smiles. It's a knowing smile from the kind of guy who would take the time to rescue a girl from her perfectly happy ex.

I recline, sipping my shake, watching the waves, and trying to remember my life with Clay. The memories are clustered together into two groups—happy times and horrific times. The happy times seem smaller, even though there were actually more of those. I wade through the pile, remembering roller coaster rides, long walks on the beach, movie nights, Chinese takeout.

Yet there it is—that one moment. That one moment when I learned Clay was seeing someone else.

And of all the people who had to tell me, it was Blake. It had crushed me from every side. Not only was my boyfriend cheating on me, but the guy that I most wanted to notice I was desirable had to break the news to me that I wasn't.

I remember the first time I saw Gwyne. I was across town at the Super Target, delighting in the clearance bins, when I saw Clay walk by. I nearly fell over the merchandise.

But he wasn't alone.

He walked up to *her* as she was surveying the large line of size-small spandex. And not the capri length either. I watched from the kitty litter aisle as he poked her in the ribs and then said she'd look good in the baby blue one.

I couldn't take it anymore and wandered to the light bulb section, which at the time, I won't lie, seemed very dark. I ended up on the candy aisle with a basketful of chocolate—and an hour later the left side of my face was blown up like a balloon animal.

I take a long gulp of the shake and then say to Blake, "Was there ever a generation that had to live without chocolate?"

"I don't know. I don't spend time pondering such atrocities."

"Yeah." I sip some more. "I wouldn't need chocolate at all if Somebody up there would just do what I ask." I stare at the sky. It's blue and bright and expressionless. Not even a cloud floats by.

I am about to take another sip when I notice Blake staring at me. "What?"

"Who are you talking to?"

I go back to looking at the sky. "What? You don't talk to God?"

"Not usually and not at the beach or in the middle of a conversation. Plus, I'm not totally sure about this, but if I remember the Bible stories correctly, God's usually the One handing out orders." He watches a long, lanky redhead in a pink bikini pass by.

"Oh, He's good at that, believe me." I watch the redhead also— to guess at what he sees in her. Over me. "But He's a good listener too. That's what I don't get. He's got the world at His fingertips, literally, and I have only the best ideas for how my life should go. So why doesn't He just, you know, do His thing, make it happen. Huh?"

Blake wiggles the cup I'm holding. "Drink more chocolate— though I think I'm about ready to introduce you to something a little stronger."

I give him the thumbs-up but don't follow his suggestion. "My ideas don't include planning the marriage proposal of my ex to the girl he cheated on me with." I gesture toward the sky and add loudly, "And if you ask me, it's a little more than cruel! I'm even blogging now."

Blake looks at me. "You are? I thought you hated blogs."

"I do." I prop myself up on my elbows. "It's a little therapeutic. It's totally anonymous. It's okay, I guess."

"Let me get this straight," Blake says. "You're mad at God, so you took up blogging?"

And then I see two feet. Standing right at my head. I look up and there He is, like an umbrella shading me from the sun; I feel the relief from the sun but can see no shadow. *Nice.* He's dressed in casual khakis and a Hawaiian shirt, which makes me laugh out loud—until I spot the purple pen in His pocket. He crouches down next to me.

"Hi," God says.

If I say anything to God, I'm going to look weird—which I am, but Blake doesn't need to know that. I sit up and face the water. "God needs to start writing me some new material. That's all I'm saying." I slurp my shake until it's dried up.

"And that's all you should be saying because you're kind of talking weird," Blake says.

"Am I?" I answer Blake with a question for God. "Because it sounds extremely reasonable to me."

"That's it. More chocolate for you." Blake hops up.

"Extra chocolate, please."

"Yeah, no kidding." Blake jogs on the sand toward the canteen.

I quickly turn to God. "Do You need something?"

"Just a little bit of attention."

"Any particular reason? Because I'm really enjoying a nice time at the beach with the perfect man whom I'm hoping You think is suited for me."

God sits down where Blake had been sitting. "I like spending time with you."

This causes me to pause. Takes my breath away, actually. I drop my straw. "You do?"

"Yeah? Who knew?" He laughs.

I don't laugh, because honestly, it just seems like His timing is always off—and on purpose, if you know what I mean. When I expect

Him to show up, when I need Him to, He's nowhere to be seen. But when I'm perfectly happy, sipping chocolate through a straw and playing hooky with Blake, He blows in like a sandstorm. I gather my knees to my chest and stare at the water. "Well. We gotta talk about Your sense of timing. Don't take this wrong, but You are not the One whose company I want right now."

"Oh. Okay." He stands, suddenly. I sense disappointment in His voice, and I watch Him walk away from me, down the beach.

"Are You ever going to write him into my story?" I call after Him. "Just throwing it out there!"

He doesn't even slow down, just keeps walking, His hands in His pockets and His shirt fluttering in the breeze.

I jump up and chase after Him, and before I can stop myself, I've jumped onto His back. We topple into the sand.

"Gimme the pen!" I grab at the pocket on His shirt, but He plucks the pen out and holds it above His head. I push Him to His side and make a grab for it, but before I know it, I'm on my back with palm-tree-printed fabric batting at my face.

"I just want to borrow it for a few minutes. Come on."

He smiles and dangles it just out of my reach.

"If You don't, I'll torture You by singing."

That gives Him a good laugh. "Yes, I've heard you in the shower. Not pretty. But in case you haven't heard, I do love when people sing. To Me."

"Yes, well, thanks for the degree of tone deafness You gave me." I chuckle. I try to snatch the pen from Him, and He bolts. I chase after Him. "Give me that pen!"

I dig into the sand, trying to get a better position, and then I start laughing, like there's a feather tickling my chin. Or maybe it's that I must look completely ridiculous running around in the sand all by myself. I drop my arms and catch my breath. He stops running and turns, walking back to me with a big grin on His face.

With my hands on my knees I say, "When You said, 'Let there be man,' did it not occur to You to add, 'Let there be man for Jessie'?"

God laughs. He likes my jokes. That's kind of mind blowing, considering hardly anyone thinks I'm funny except Malia and Blake.

God dangles the pen just out of reach again and says, "Face it. I'm more powerful than you."

That's the understatement of the year. Yet, oddly, it hits me right in the chest, like I'd never considered it before. In my world, in my way, I was the powerful one. I stare at the pen as the sunlight glints off it.

He smiles and holds the pen out to me, this time within reach. "But you don't really want it back, do you?"

I look at Him and concede with a small smile. I dust the sand off my pants. "Technically, this is all Your fault. And by 'this' I mean me." I gesture toward myself. "The way I am."

"Really? Please, do enlighten Me." He sits in the sand, and I look at my pants for just a second and then sit down next to him.

I stare into the sky again. "You gave me this great mom."

"Yeah."

"And then You took her away."

He puts my pen in His pocket. "I have watched you lie on your mother's grave and cry."

"For hours."

"Yes. For hours."

"Before she died, she started these savings accounts for Brooklyn and me. For our weddings."

God chuckles affectionately. "She is such a romantic, just like you."

"She's had me thinking about my wedding, my dress, my Prince Charming, since I was six. And maybe I thought something magical would happen, You know? Maybe along with that money, she also left a wish for me to find the perfect man. Once she was gone, I thought she was up there directing my path to him."

"Instead, it was Me."

"Yes, and that's where things get confusing. I always felt like that's what Mom wanted for me, to have an incredible wedding, just like she did. And I'm failing her every day that goes by."

"It's not about the day, Jessie. It's about a lifetime."

I turn to look at Him. "With whom? Just tell me that?"

"No."

A shadow moves beside me. "What are you doing?" It's Blake, standing over me with another shake.

I fly to my feet. "Um…just having some fun."

Blake normally would have a comeback, but instead he's just standing there holding the shake. "I could see you from the canteen. You were like rolling around in the sand. I thought you were having a seizure. I almost called 911."

I try to laugh this off. "You're being overly dramatic. Can't a woman roll around in the sand?"

Blake is still staring at me and it's getting awkward, so I pull him down and we land in the sand together. There. Now we're both sandy and he has to shut up about it. My shake has sloshed and there is ice cream sliding down the side of the cup. Blake attempts to wipe it up with his fingers.

"If I wanted to capture the attention of one of you frustrating men, what do I do, oh wise one?"

"That's My name." I glance behind me. God's still there, sitting a few feet away. I smile, but right now I have to ignore Him. Blake is already suspicious.

"So? How do I capture a man's attention?"

"Is that why you were rolling and running around in the sand by yourself? A whole beach full of people noticed."

"Funny. I'm being serious."

Blake sighs. "I don't know. I mean, get creative." He hands me the shake, all cleaned up now.

"I'm an examples kind of girl. What's the most creative way a woman has ever tried to get your attention?"

God puts His mouth right next to my ear and says, "And what do you need this information for?" I keep my back to Him.

Blake is thinking, then he shrugs. "I can't say that a woman has done anything creative to get my attention."

"We have failed you as a gender?"

"I don't know. I mean, the very idea that a woman is trying to get my attention makes me wonder. It's sort of like I should be getting hers, you know? If she's all into me already, there's nothing that fun for me to do."

"You have failed us as a gender."

Blake smiles. "I know. Sounds shallow. But you asked. Generating mystery is always a plus."

"What, like a secret admirer?"

"It's a start."

"Are we twelve?"

He thumps me across the shoulder and bolts. I jump up and chase after the turkey. Yes, he's twelve. I look back. God is sitting in the sand. He's watching the waves now. I want to go back, but...

"Come on, Turtle!" Blake is running backward, a puckish expression beckoning me. I chase after him and don't look back.

fourteen

I make it home way after dark and begin to scarf down Chinese take-out. Brooklyn somehow has the energy to go out after work, and I resist giving her a lecture. She's not little anymore, but I see her that way. I still remember when she couldn't button her pants or tie her shoes or reach the cereal bowls in the cabinet.

"Hey, um, God, maybe You could watch over her tonight. Make sure she doesn't do anything stupid, or hook up with Stupid, if you know what I mean."

Silence. He's not around. I don't feel Him near. I wonder if He's still at the beach, sitting in the sand.

The rest of the workday went well. Brooklyn and I did some pre-liminary planning for Clay's proposal. It didn't seem to sting as much after I spent some time with Blake and drank two chocolate shakes.

I slurp my lo mein and wonder what reason God could have for not hooking me up with Blake. I mean, I know I'm not God and can't see all things, but sometimes there are things that feel so natural and so right. As humans, how do we know that they aren't? What do we have other than our instincts?

Exhaustion keeps me from pondering deeper. I trudge up the stairs and throw on a T-shirt. I wash my face, brush my teeth, rinse with Act, take my vitamins, and floss. The bed calls me, but so does my laptop, glowing in the dark room. I decide to do a short blog about mystique. So far I've blogged about the Art of Wooing, Proposals Done Right, and What Men Need to Know About Women. I don't understand why God wants me to blog. Maybe it's to let off some steam, though if I blog about what's going on with me and God these days, I'm certain to lose readers. Oh yeah. I don't have any.

But wait. I lean toward the screen, peering through the darkness. There's a comment left! By…JessieFan? I have a fan? The subject line reads, THANKS FOR JESSIE'S CORNER.

> Jessie, I appreciate everything you've written to help us clueless guys know how to relate to women. I hope one day soon I'll get to involve you in a proposal to a special girl. Please keep posting. How does a man win a girl's heart? J.F.

I lean back in my chair, cross my arms, and smile. JessieFan. That's secret admirer–ish.

The sound of an out-of-tune piano indicates I have an IM. Probably Blake.

Nope. Turns out it's God. At least that's what His screen name reads. Very well could be a cute guy who knows it, flaunts it, and thinks he is…but under the circumstances, I'm betting it's the real deal.

GET TO THE GLORY WEDDING CHAPEL AT 1 P.M.

"Huh?" Like the screen can hear me. But God can, so I say it again. Louder. "Huh?"

No answer, but another IM pops up.

TAKE THE RED TILE DISTRICT TROLLEY.

"That's not what the 'huh' was for," I say loudly. Sometimes I think He has a hearing problem. "I'm a little more worried about this wedding chapel thing. I mean, don't You think I should meet the guy first? Sure, I know whoever You pick is going to be the perfect guy for me, but it's a little awkward to just show up and get married. Plus I don't have a dress, and I—" I stop blabbering and take a breath. Okay, I'm getting way ahead of myself. I should just show up, do what He says.

Obey.

Yeah. For once. I think He would appreciate that.

I shut down the computer and crawl into bed, first tucking in all the covers and smoothing out the wrinkles. I set my alarm, then swing my legs under the sheets, sinking into my feather pillow. It feels good to get off my feet.

"Hey." Brooklyn's in the doorway.

"Hey."

Through the darkness, she walks toward the bed. She kicks off her shoes, and the next thing I know she's crawled into bed with me, punching her feet to untuck the covers at the end. "I'm exhausted."

"Me too. Why are you back so early?"

"I dunno. Just wasn't that fun tonight. I mean the gang was there and everything. Thankfully Gary was nowhere to be seen. But it just got old after a while."

I smile into the darkness. "Probably best," I say. "We've got a long week. I've been working a little on Clay's deal. I think we'll have some—"

Snoring.

I take her hand in mine, like I used to when she was little, and I settle into a deep, dreamless sleep.

It's like I am tapped on the shoulder by dread. I sit straight up in bed, and the first clue that something is wrong comes with how the light enters my room…from up high. It is sort of blinding, and I shield my eyes as they water.

I barely see the alarm clock through the tears. But I notice something immediately. The dot is gone.

The a.m. dot.

"What time is it?" I shriek as I rub my eyes frantically, trying to clear them. But Brooklyn isn't in bed. My heart sinks. If *she's* already out of bed, *how late is it*?

Brooklyn comes around the corner, brushing her teeth and grinning through the foam. "Lazy head."

"What time is it?"

She spits and returns. "After noon. I beat you up. 'Course I went to bed before the moon came out, so that probably explains it. But I feel so— What's the matter?"

I grab the alarm clock. "Is it 1 p.m.? Is it? Is it one?"

"Don't have a cow. You don't turn into a pumpkin if the clock strikes twelve. Maybe sleeping in did you some good."

I jump out of bed and scramble to my closet. "What time is it, Brooklyn? Exactly. The exact time."

"You just looked at the clock."

"I set it fast. Often. It gets a little out of control sometimes."

"It's twelve-thirty."

"No. No! I have no time to get ready!"

"For what?"

"One of us needs to be at work right now! Why aren't we at work?" I throw on a yellow blouse and appear in front of her. "What about this? How does this look?"

"Canary-ish."

"Then help me! Help me pick out something!"

"Good grief, calm down, woman. What is the occasion?"

"It's…it's hard to explain. I'm going to a wedding chapel."

She sets down the toothbrush and moves past me into the closet. "Okay, midday wedding, you'll want a spaghetti strap—"

"No, it's not a wedding. At least I don't think so. I can't—I can't look like I'm showing up for a wedding, even if there is one, because then I look desperate. Do you know what I mean?"

"I have no idea what you're talking about."

We stare at each other for a moment, and then Brooklyn spots something in my closet. She grabs a pair of black slacks. "Here. Dull for me but wears well on you. Add that aqua, sleeveless number right there and you'll be fine."

"Really?" I quickly shove myself into them. "This is good?"

"Come on. To the bathroom. Let's do your hair and add some makeup."

"I don't have time!" I protest, but then I look in the mirror and realize I better make some time.

"Here, put this cream on."

"What's it for?"

"Your face."

"I know that. But I don't need—"

"Trust me, you do. Now let me fix your hair." I dab on the cream as I watch Brooklyn pull my hair back. She finishes, and I'm not kidding, I look worse than when I got up.

"Brooklyn, what did you do? My hair looks all tangled and pieces are falling out and—"

"It's called a messy ponytail. Trust me, it's a good look. It makes you look sexy."

"It looks like I didn't try to fix my hair at all."

"Exactly. Now, let's go with a light gloss." She swipes some across my lips, but I can't really get my eyes off my hair.

"I just don't know. I mean, it looks like I got up but my hair stayed in bed."

"Sis," she says, turning to me. "Do you trust me?"

"No."

"But am I a fashionista?"

"Yes."

"Maybe I'm wrong about this, but by the way you're acting, I'm thinking there's a guy involved, right?"

"I don't know. Maybe. It's...complicated."

"You look fabulous. You're screaming, 'I'm sexy without trying.'"

"I'm more comfortable with, 'I'm trying not to be sexy.'"

"Just go! It's twenty till."

"Oh!" I rush downstairs, grab my bag, and run to catch the trolley.

I like the trolley. Aside from the fumes that seep in, it's a nice ride. The seats are comfortable and face inward so you don't have to turn to look out a window. An elderly couple sits across from me. The woman is fussing over the man's collar, and he lets her. Afterward he pats her lightly on the cheek, and they go back to watching the scenery pass by.

"Red Tile District, next stop." The trolley slows and two other people get off with me.

As I step off the trolley I think at first I hear God clapping for me. But no. Turns out it's a clap of thunder, and before I'm on the sidewalk, it's pouring.

"Show-off," I mumble. Just like God to make sure I'm incapable of hiding behind hair, makeup, and somewhat stylish clothing. Though I think my hair might've actually improved.

Heavy with extra water weight, I drag myself toward the chapel. It's getting cold and I feel myself shiver, but maybe that's just anticipation.

The chapel is small, known mostly for impromptu weddings. A few celebrities have made their mistakes here. It's always open but mostly bare, probably so people won't steal things. I look around and I'm alone, so I sit in a pew near the back and listen to the rain let up.

Perfect timing for the rain. Of course. God has an ornery side.

My dad always used to tell me God had a sense of humor, but I never believed him. What kind of God would steal parents away?

I never did much asking *why me* when my parents died. I wasn't the only kid who'd lost her parents. Why *not* me? A stretch of bad luck was easier to swallow than a God who decided it was their time to go. A well-meaning old woman told me at the funeral that my parents were so special that God wanted them in heaven with Him. I remember thinking that was the most selfish thing I had ever heard.

I try to squeeze the moisture out of my hair and shirt. It's really no use. I'm drenched and there's no hiding it. The question is, what am I doing here? And why is He so late?

I hear the door creak open. Strange. Usually He doesn't use doors.

I turn and He's smiling at me and about to say something, but I cut Him off. "Don't even 'hi' me." I stand up. "First of all, not funny. I mean, if You had to bring rain, why not drop a hint and tell me to grab an umbrella?" I walk toward Him. "Second, You're late. I realize you have Your 'business' to run, but since You 'own' Your own 'business,' You can be wherever You want, whenever You want." I hold up my hand to stop Him from interrupting. "Third, You better make this quick because I have to get to work. As You might recall, I have a small business to run, and if it doesn't run, I might be sleeping on the streets. So…" I pause. I smile, because He's still smiling at me, with a look of amazement on His face. "I'm sorry. I shouldn't be, you know, me so much. I get a little wound up. So…what are we doing here?"

"Well, hello, you two." The voice comes from behind me. I whirl around to find a minister walking up the aisle, black robe and all. He's grinning expectantly. "What can I help you with today?"

I realize something. "Wait a minute. *"You two?"* You can see Him?" I pitch a thumb behind me.

God looks unnaturally surprised, but not as surprised as the minister, who is looking at God and nodding.

I throw up my arms and laugh. "Oh, right. Of course. You're a man of God. You two probably meet on a regular basis." I cross my arms and smile at God. "So? What's going on here? Is there a special reason we're here or is it just to chat?"

God smiles. A little. I've never seen Him smile a little. Usually He's either not smiling or He's giving it His all. God glances back and forth between me and the minister. "I just stepped in to get out of the rain." He is now looking at me. "It's still raining. Maybe we could sit and chat."

I feel myself growing a little angry. "You didn't bring anyone with You?"

"Bring anyone?"

"You know what? Forget it. You two have fun chatting. I have to go to work. And blog or something." I march out, pushing the door hard as I exit. Not surprisingly, it's sunny. The pavement is still wet, though, and it splashes on my ankles as I return to the trolley stop.

Is it just me, or is God playing head games?

fifteen

Enter.

Enter.

Enter.

But no amount of pounding on the Enter key will get the error message off my computer screen. It has, however, gotten Malia's attention. She's staring at me over her book.

"I'm fine!" I say loudly, before she has a chance to ask.

"You sure you're okay?"

I roll my eyes. What did I just say? But then again, this is Clay's proposal day, and Malia knows, deep down inside, I'm not fine. I simmer down as I hear the bell ring, indicating a customer has come in. Malia leaves her counter to go attend. A lump forms in my throat. Why can't anything go right?

Enter.

Enter.

Enter.

"I hear if you spit on it, that works." Malia now stands above me, smiling.

I can't smile back. "I've got to get this proposal video online. In an hour this guy is planning to get his girl to the Web site we made for her. It's on the computer, but it won't link to the site."

"Call Fine Computer Techs. That's what we hire them for."

"Okay. Maybe."

"Don't you need to get to the beach for Clay's proposal?"

"Yes."

A long pause indicates she's hoping not to have to state the obvious. She rubs my back in small circles, then says, "Brooklyn's already there."

"I know."

Malia wraps her arms around my shoulders, leaning over me like a protective mother bird. "Jess, remember what we talked about? What did we nickname him?"

I know exactly what she's talking about, and I'm glad she knows without my saying what is bugging me. "Wet Clay," I say quietly.

"Why?"

"Because he's not formed, not designed right—not for me."

"That's it."

I groan and start composing an e-mail for those Fine Techs. "And I bet you're going to tell me that today is a day worth celebrating."

"Like a graduation from him," she says.

I turn in my chair to face her, and she steps back to give me some space. "Malia, when is this all going to stop?"

"What?" she asks.

"Trying to turn every negative thing in my life into something positive. Every lost love is 'just an opportunity for better love.' Every loser boyfriend is 'just proof I'm too good for him.' It's getting pathetic. People are running out of things to say, excuses for me and my wretched love life."

"You know that book I'm reading?"

"The one where the woman gets her man?"

"Yes. Remember, it takes four hundred five pages to get there. Gracelynn-Danielle Trubeau is falling for all the wrong guys through the whole story. Finally she wakes up to what is right in front of her."

I turn back to my e-mail message. "Yeah, well, with a name like Gracelynn-Danielle, you'd expect her to have some identity crises."

"All I'm saying is that your 'finally'—it's coming, honey. I know it."

"Maybe. But I'm thinking it's going to be more of a *War and Peace* page count, if you know what I mean."

Malia squeezes my arm. "I better let you get back to work."

I shoot off the e-mail to the computer company. I start to grab my things when an alert announces I have a new comment on my blog.

From JessieFan!

I apparently need some help winning a girl's heart...got any advice?

I collect my purse, briefcase, keys, and phone and walk to my car. Do I have any advice? Hahahahaha. More than I'm certain he needs.

But I like this guy. He seems genuine, willing to go the extra mile. I compose a note to him in my head as I drive.

> Dear JessieFan,
>
> In order to win a girl's heart, you need to find out what's in it. Novel concept, isn't it?

No, take out "novel concept." This guy doesn't need sarcasm. I try again.

> Think of her like a treasure. One worth digging through all the muck to get to the beauty.

Too *Pirates of the Caribbean*–ish? I mean, maybe he's the one person on earth who isn't impressed with Jack Sparrow. Okay, let's try an entirely different approach.

> Find out what her little-girl dream is, what she always hoped to do with you once you found her. Did she dream of sitting with you on a porch swing night after night? On your white veranda? Find a way to give it to her.

Yes. I like that. I'm on a roll.

> Does she have a favorite treat? Say, like, dark chocolate M&M's? What's her flower? Don't go standard. For exam-

ple, I'm not a roses girl. Give me daisies. And uncover her favorite song. A guy could melt me with "I Only Have Eyes for You."

And with that, I pull up to the pier, where I'm helping a man propose who *didn't* only have eyes for me. Sometimes my life is so stinking ironic.

Brooklyn is rushing toward me. "Where have you been?"

"Sorry. Had trouble putting up that Web site. How's it going?"

"I think okay. I'm pretty sure I have everything in place." She's looking around, one hand gripping a pencil, the other a clipboard. I study her, and my heart sort of swells with pride. She's being so responsible. I pull her into an unexpected hug.

"Uh…what?" she asks, her words smothered by my shoulder.

I can't stop hugging her.

Finally she pulls away. "What's wrong?"

"Nothing." I smile.

She eyes me as she hands me my walkie-talkie. "Jess, you've got to focus. A lot has to go right here."

"I know." I snap to attention. "Where's the boat guy?"

"He's over there. He's waiting for you. I gave him the hundred-dollar bill."

"Hi, this is Jessie," I say into my walkie-talkie. "Can you hear me?"

The boatman waves to me. "Ten-four, little lady."

I wave back. "Okay, I'm thinking about twenty yards out. Let's try it and see how it looks."

"Gotcha." He pulls away from the dock.

Brooklyn grabs my arm. "I'm going to go get the balloons and tell the camera guy where we want him to hide."

"Perfect." I glance at my watch. "We're about ten minutes out. Clay should be texting me pretty soon. We need to stay in touch, okay?"

"Okay." Brooklyn rushes off.

I'm standing on the small hill near the pier, watching the boat maneuver into place. The sun is setting perfectly behind him. The water sparkles like expensive champagne, and the breeze blows my hair off my face and shoulders. Everything is perfect for this proposal. "Even the *weather* is cooperating," I mumble.

My phone vibrates. It's Clay texting me. R 5 MIN OUT. I put the walkie-talkie to my mouth. "Clay just texted. They'll be here in five. Everyone, stand by."

I turn and gasp. God is back. In my personal space, no less. I take a moment to catch my breath. "Why did You send me to that chapel?" I try not to sound hostile, but I feel that way.

He doesn't answer, but I don't really give Him time, either.

"Besides, of course, to get a chance to prove You do, indeed, control the weather. Like now, for instance. Perfect weather. You and Clay must be tight."

"I was trying to do something for you."

"Really." I study Him. "What?"

"It didn't go according to My plan."

"No? Because I thought the rain shower was so perfectly timed."

He steps even closer, a gentle but serious expression on His face. "So I'm giving you another chance."

"I'm kind of busy right now." I gesture to the water. And the balloons. And the pier.

He doesn't look at any of it. "Go to the twenty-four-hour Laundromat at State Street, and wash your clothes at eight o'clock tonight."

"I have a washer and dryer at my condo." I fold my arms. "Why would I—"

"You wouldn't." He smiles. "But then again, I do have custody of the pen." He turns and begins walking away.

"Hey! When you were *knitting* me in the womb, did it ever occur to You to *knit* me some blond hair?"

"No," He says, without looking back.

"Jessie!" I whirl around and Brooklyn's running up to me. She's out of breath. "Where have you been? I've been looking everywhere for you! I've tried calling you on your walkie-talkie and—"

I hold it up. It's turned off. It can't be said enough—He does like my undivided attention.

"Come on!" Brooklyn says, tugging at my arm. "It's time!"

We race down the hill and take our hiding spots. I can see Clay's car coming toward us, a trail of dust behind him on the gravel road.

"Jess, two o'clock," whispers Brooklyn into the walkie-talkie. "Coming toward ya."

They park and get out of the BMW. Clay and I always thought it was funny that we both drove Beemers. The only difference is that he's the kind of guy that wears his like an emblem.

I haven't seen Gwyne in a long time…except in my nightmares. She's taller than I remember, plus her hair has grown out. It's long, falling down her back in perfect golden waves. She removes her oversized shades and swings her oversized handbag onto her undersized arm. Clay takes her hand, grinning wide enough for a satellite to pick up the glow off his newly whitened teeth.

They are talking as they walk to the pier. A small crowd is there; really, the perfect number of onlookers. Not crowded, but enough to make her the center of attention.

I take a deep breath. Timing is critical. I focus and give the cue for the flare.

A pop and then a whistle causes everyone to look up. The red flare shoots into the sky and reflects against the water.

Clay takes Gwyne's hand and pulls her toward the end of the pier. She hesitates. "Clay, what are we doing here?"

I glance at the cameraman. He's following it all with precision. "Okay, cue banner," I say into the walkie-talkie.

The boat captain raises the banner. In big, black, and—I dare say slightly obnoxious—fancy lettering, it reads, *Marry Me, Gwyne. I Love You. Clay*

As if I've cued the bystanders, they all start oohing and aahing as they watch Clay turn to Gwyne. He reaches for her arms, then squeezes her hands. But she's still looking at the banner.

Maybe she's a slow reader.

"Clay?" she says. But it's not so much what she says as how she looks—like she's a first-hand witness to a tsunami rolling in. "Clay?"

Clay drops to one knee and lets go of her hands to pull out a box from his shirt pocket. Gwyne's eyes are so wide it looks like she's about to put in contact lenses. She's clutching her heart but not in an endearing way. If I didn't know better, I might call for a doctor.

My attention shifts to Clay. He's still grinning, his teeth gleaming in all their glory, but the rest of his face is so strained and tense, the grin looks more like a grimace.

"Marry me?" he squeaks, down on his knee, back straight as a board, one arm extended with the ring, the other behind him like a perfect gentleman.

Gwyne puts her hand to her mouth, shakes her head, cries, looks like she needs a wastebasket.

"Oh no…," I groan.

Then I see the balloons. Brooklyn has released them too soon, and they're gliding upward, twirling in the wind, dancing—but with no occasion.

Gwyne backs away. "No. No. Clay, no. I can't. I—"

Sobbing, she turns and runs. And I mean like a triathlete with something to prove. She's in stilettos, but even that's not stopping her. Neither is her behemoth leather handbag, which nearly knocks over an elderly couple.

She's gone.

Clay is frozen, still on one knee, the ring glinting in the last light of the day. People are shaking their heads and turning away, like they've just witnessed a crime.

Brooklyn is suddenly next to me. "What do we do?"

"I don't know," I say, watching Clay slowly rise and close the ring box. The captain is lowering the banner, and in an unfortunate streak of bad timing, two balloons collide against a light pole and pop, causing a couple of screams and Clay to duck.

"Weirdly symbolic," Brooklyn whispers.

"Wow," I breathe. "I didn't see this coming."

"Well, just make sure you get the check from him. It's not our fault she didn't say yes. He still has to pay for it."

I give Brooklyn a look. "Very businesslike, but let's make sure he's okay."

"I have no idea what to say," Brooklyn says softly.

"Why don't you get everything wrapped up. I'll go help him."

I know a thing or two about being dumped.

sixteen

I order dinner for both of us, though Clay probably won't eat for days. I'm starving but order a salad. I order Clay a thick, twenty-ounce steak, to help him on his way back to manhood.

The restaurant sits over the water and from our table near the glass windows, the ocean rolls and the sun sinks below the horizon. Violins swell through the sound system, and the tiny candlelight between us flickers as waiters breeze by.

I quietly eat, trying to think of something to say. At the pier, I asked if there was anything I could do, and he just said he didn't want to be alone, so I suggested the restaurant where he already had a six o'clock reservation. I think he just wanted to be anywhere but there on that pier. People were still gawking at him when we walked off.

His steak is getting cold and he's on his third beer. The ring in its black box sits alone in the center of the table, next to the candle. He stares at it, like he's in a trance.

"You know, Clay, it was a beautiful proposal. Any girl would love that. And if Gwyne can't see that, it's her problem, you know? I mean, you went all out."

He doesn't agree or disagree. He just stares. I wonder if I should cut up his steak for him. Then he reaches out and opens the box. He shoves it toward me. I look at it and make adoring expressions. "It's beautiful. Wow. Really amazing. Spectacular."

"A month's salary right there. She didn't even look at it."

"Her loss, Clay."

"Yeah? Why does it feel like mine?" He sighs and picks up his fork, stabbing around on his steak. "I can't believe this happened to me."

"Do you think she just got cold feet or something?"

He shakes his head. "No." He pierces a bite of steak, but it doesn't make it to his mouth. "There have been signs. Signs I guess I decided to ignore. When you want something so badly, I guess you tend to just write those off, make excuses for them."

"That's only natural." I cut my salad up, eating slowly.

"We were having a lot of bad days. Lots of fights. Disconnecting."

"It happens sometimes."

"It's just, you know, we've been together for like—"

"Three years and two months."

"Yeah, and that's a hard thing to just turn away from."

"Sure." I take a big bite of bread and study him as he saws away at his meat with a knife that is apparently very dull. Or he's just bad at cutting meat. Either way, the steak is mutilated.

He drops his knife and fork and snaps the box closed. "Has this ever happened to you?"

"What?"

"Rejection in front of a large group of people."

"Clay, of course it has. I've been rejected more times than—"

"I meant with your business. Has this happened with your business?"

"Oh. Um, no. This is a first. But, you know, we've only just opened. It's bound to happen again."

His face turns soft. "I guess you're no stranger to rejection. I'm… I'm sorry about it all, Jess."

I awkwardly dismiss and acknowledge it all at the same time. I think my face is a contorted assortment of frowns, smiles, nods, and lip biting. I would've guessed seeing Clay face the biggest rejection in life might bring some self-satisfaction, but at this moment, I just want the guy to feel better. It's like the past never happened.

He reaches across the table and takes my hand. "Thank you for…I mean, you have no reason to be here for me. Seriously, don't…don't feel like you need to sit with me all night."

His hand feels warm over mine. "It's no problem," I say.

"I'm sure you have better things to do with your time than listen to my sob story."

"No, not at all." I bought him a big steak because I felt sorry for him, but as we sit here and talk, I realize that I feel more than pity.

"I've never talked to anyone like this," he says. "I've never felt I could." Suddenly, as his hand retreats from mine, it knocks over the wine I'm barely drinking. Red liquid splashes all over my shirt. Clay jumps up and grabs his napkin. "I am so sorry! Here, let me…" He starts to dab at my collar.

"It's fine. It's okay." But I lift my arms and let him dab. It's kind of a nice moment, actually.

"Oh boy. I'm making a mess out of everything tonight, aren't I?" He shakes his head and continues to blot.

"Don't worry about it. Please."

He slowly sits back in his seat, shaking his head. "You're going to need to launder that tonight or it will stain."

Clay always was one for domestic knowledge. He taught me how to iron a cotton shirt.

"Nothing a little Spray 'n Wash can't handle," I say. I lean forward and nod toward his steak. "You might want to start on that thing. You'd hate to let a good thing go to waste."

For the first time, Clay smiles.

Somewhere between steak and cheesecake, the conversation shifts from Gwyne to me. He begins telling me about his deep regret that he'd let me go.

"'Let me go'? Come on," I say with a big smile on my face. "How about dumped?"

He grins sheepishly, and instead of going defensive like he used to do, he just nods. "Yeah. That's probably true." I'm not kidding, he gets tears in his eyes.

After cheesecake—and on to my second glass of wine—he tells me that he often dreamed about what our life would've been like together, even while he was with Gwyne. And then by the time the restaurant closes, we are laughing hysterically and remembering old times.

* * *

I slip the key into the door, turn slowly, but it still makes that horrible metal-against-metal grinding noise. And at three o'clock in the morning, it's like it's amplifying off the stars.

I push the door open and realize I'm holding my breath. I kind of feel like a burglar or something. And trust me, I know how that feels. Clasping my keys, I lay them gently down on the table next to the door and push the door shut like it's made of eggshells.

Wow. Things seem darker in the dead of night. I slip off my shoes. My feet are killing me, but nevertheless I tiptoe toward the stairs.

A light clicks on and I whirl around.

Brooklyn sits up from the couch. "Where have you been?"

The question catches me off guard, and I fumble around for some words, accidentally dropping one shoe.

She gets off the couch. "Do you know how worried I've been? Do you know what time it is?"

"Is it late?" I squeak.

She crosses her arms. "Don't give me that." She's scrutinizing me, and I'm certain my expression just ratted me out. "Don't tell me you *just* left Clay."

"Okay. I won't tell you." What am I, channeling Brooklyn here?

"Jessie!" Her mouth is hanging open and her eyes are wide, and I just have to wonder if that's what I look like at three o'clock in the morning, worried sick. It's not an attractive look.

I turn and go to the kitchen for some water. "I know what that brain of yours is saying."

She's right on my heels. "Eight months of mourning that schmuck! That's how long it took. And he's just going to do it to you again."

I fill up the glass and gulp the whole thing back before I answer her. "No. This is different. So totally and completely different."

"You should hear yourself." Brooklyn looks genuinely mortified and worried. "Maybe I should try to explain. This is pathetic. Really. I mean, the guy just got dumped during a proposal. Maybe, just maybe, Jess, this guy has some issues that are wrecking his life."

"Gwyne's the idiot, not him." I pour another glass of water. "Look, there's a reason, okay? There's something more to this, but if I tell you, you're going to look at me like I'm half cracked."

Brooklyn sits *on* the kitchen table, I'm certain just to bug me. "I already think that, so what do you have to lose?"

"You won't believe me anyway."

"You never know."

I slug the water, then slam the glass down on the table like I've just done shots. I wipe my mouth with my sleeve. "Okay," I say carefully. "This time, with Clay. I gotta tell you…it's like…it's like—"

"That stain on your shirt?" Brooklyn says.

"Forget the stain. Listen."

"I'm sorry. I'm listening. I promise. The stain's talking to me, but I'm shutting it out. It's big, though. You know that, right?"

"This thing with Clay, Brooklyn. It's like…God is setting it up."

Silence. Then, "I should call Malia." She reaches for the phone, but I cut her off.

"Please. Just listen."

Brooklyn looks concerned but backs her hand away from the phone.

I sit on a kitchen chair and pull out another, hoping she'll get off the table. "Listen. I know this sounds whacked. More than whacked. I thought so too, at first. Especially when He made me give away proposals—"

"Requested." I hear His footsteps behind me.

"Requested, I mean." I glance at Him. "I thought…I thought it was to hurt me. But now I see it was to get Clay and me back together. He really fooled me." I give Him a quick smile. He doesn't smile back.

Brooklyn is looking into the empty kitchen, then back at me. "He. Fill me in. He who?"

"God."

"God."

"God." I lean back casually. Like this will help it all go down. "Okay, it's like this. God came to visit me the night you moved back in."

"Uh-huh."

"He offered to write my love story." I gesture for God to sit in the chair Brooklyn is not taking. "And I love what He's writing." He remains where He is, leaning against the counter.

Brooklyn hops to the floor and starts pacing. "Okay, God delusions aside, you're saying you and Clay back together is…is…?"

"Perfect. And so ironic." I look at God again, hoping for some help, some affirmation. I get none, of course. "God likes irony. I mean, think of all those Bible stories, Brooklyn. Remember that old couple—they were like ninety and didn't have children—and *bam!* God swung it around and she's pregnant."

Brooklyn quits pacing. "You're pregnant?"

That gets a chuckle from God.

"Brook, stay with me. What I'm saying is that God has a habit of making things that seem impossible possible. Never in a million years would I have guessed Clay and I would be back together. But I've never stopped loving him."

"That's not what you said when you found out he was cheating on you." She finally sits on the chair.

"But Gwyne is out of the picture now. And see, that's how God does things. He takes a situation and flips it around in an unexpected way."

"That's one way of looking at it. Or, Clay's on the rebound and you're available."

God suddenly walks out of the kitchen and around the corner. Part of me wants to follow Him, but Brooklyn's getting red in the face. And so, it seems, am I.

She leans toward me. "Jessie, listen to me. I want you to listen to me, okay? Carefully. God did not visit you and tell you He'd write your love story. I don't know firsthand, but I think He probably has better things to do with His time."

I look toward the doorway where God went. "I'm not lying."

She looks at the doorway too, and then back at me. "That's what scares me. You really think this is happening."

"What? I'm not special enough that God would take the time to do something for me?"

"I'm just saying, it's a convenient excuse for you to get back with a guy who is all wrong for you."

I stand up. "Really? Like you are in a place to give me relationship advice. How many guys have you lived with in the past four years? And each time, 'Oh, Jessie, this is the right one.' How's that been working for you?"

Brooklyn's cheeks are the same color as her lips. "Thank you for

I've prepared myself for this kind of reaction. I knew it would be shocking. But I twirl around and flip my hair like I'm in a shampoo commercial. "What do you think?"

Malia is rushing around the counter like something might be on fire.

I drop my hands. "What?"

"No…no. It's…it's very, um, sunshiny. It's just that I wasn't expecting it." She smiles and combs her fingers through my hair. "When did this happen?"

"Last night." I fluff.

"You didn't want to start off with a few caramel highlights?"

"Nah. Why not just jump in with both feet?"

I see Brooklyn. She's behind the counter, swiveling back and forth in her chair as she hands a customer a business card. "Sounds like fun," she says. "Give me a call." She glances up and does a double take. I'm wondering how much we look alike now that we're both—

"Blonde?" Brooklyn shouts as the customer walks out the door.

Malia squeezes my arm. "Isn't it…breathtaking on your sister, Brooklyn?"

Brooklyn looks genuinely breathless. "She's officially gone insane. Did God tell you to do that too?"

"Why don't you shut up, Brooklyn."

She shrugs. "Hey, I'm just trying to do an intervention before we have to do an intervention, if you know what I mean."

I fluff again. "Good grief. It's not like I shaved my head and joined a cult."

"Really. I'm beginning to wonder."

Malia holds up her hands. "Okay, girls, what's going on?"

that moral judgment." She stands up. "You can go out with Clay. Give your heart to him a second time. Slap a God label on it if that makes you feel better. Just don't come crying to me when he smashes your heart all over again." She turns and stomps out of the kitchen, storming up the stairs.

I throw up my hands. Why even try to convince her? She's narrow-minded and always has been. Well, not really, but in this case, yes. I notice my hands are shaking, and I try to calm myself down. Brooklyn will see, in time, that this is all okay. Besides, I don't have to prove anything to her.

I decide to go find God. I'm about to head upstairs when I notice the laundry room light is on. I smile. He's so into details! Leaving me a little hint to not forget to spray my shirt. I walk in and stop.

He's sorted my laundry. That's nice and everything, but why would He sort my—

I take a step back, staring at the whites and darks in their separate piles.

I was supposed to go to the Laundromat. At eight. An uneasiness sets over me as I back out of the laundry room. I turn off the light and shut the door. Why would God have wanted me to leave Clay right when things were just starting to get good? I'm feeling numb as I climb the stairs. I listen for Brooklyn, but the light is out in her room and all is quiet.

I go to the bathroom and stare into the mirror.

Something is calling me. And it's not His voice. It's under my bathroom sink. It's been there for almost three years, untouched and lonely. It's called me before, but it has never seemed like the right time or for the right reason.

I study myself carefully in the mirror. Is now the right time? Is this the right person? I grin.

Yeah. This is it.

I open the cabinet doors and reach for the box of Nice 'n Easy.

seventeen

I'm whistling, which is odd because I once dated a guy who had this nervous-whistle thing going on and I thought I was going to have to plug his hole. He was a decent whistler but always at the most inappropriate times. I undoubtedly knew he was getting ready to attempt to put his arm around me because he'd start whistling.

The day I broke up with him, I thought the poor guy was goin to run out of air.

But I can't help it, I'm whistling. And bouncing, like my sh have ADHD. It's a good morning. I had no idea one could feel good on so little sleep.

I've been running errands this morning, picking up some fliers and that sort of thing. The weather is nice. Perfect, actu swing the door open to the store.

Malia sets down her book. "May I help y— Oh! Jessie!"

that moral judgment." She stands up. "You can go out with Clay. Give your heart to him a second time. Slap a God label on it if that makes you feel better. Just don't come crying to me when he smashes your heart all over again." She turns and stomps out of the kitchen, storming up the stairs.

I throw up my hands. Why even try to convince her? She's narrow-minded and always has been. Well, not really, but in this case, yes. I notice my hands are shaking, and I try to calm myself down. Brooklyn will see, in time, that this is all okay. Besides, I don't have to prove anything to her.

I decide to go find God. I'm about to head upstairs when I notice the laundry room light is on. I smile. He's so into details! Leaving me a little hint to not forget to spray my shirt. I walk in and stop.

He's sorted my laundry. That's nice and everything, but why would He sort my—

I take a step back, staring at the whites and darks in their separate piles.

I was supposed to go to the Laundromat. At eight. An uneasiness sets over me as I back out of the laundry room. I turn off the light and shut the door. Why would God have wanted me to leave Clay right when things were just starting to get good? I'm feeling numb as I climb the stairs. I listen for Brooklyn, but the light is out in her room and all is quiet.

I go to the bathroom and stare into the mirror.

Something is calling me. And it's not His voice. It's under my bathroom sink. It's been there for almost three years, untouched and lonely. It's called me before, but it has never seemed like the right time or for the right reason.

I study myself carefully in the mirror. Is now the right time? Is this the right person? I grin.

Yeah. This is it.

I open the cabinet doors and reach for the box of Nice 'n Easy.

seventeen

I'm whistling, which is odd because I once dated a guy who had this nervous-whistle thing going on and I thought I was going to have to plug his hole. He was a decent whistler but always at the most inappropriate times. I undoubtedly knew he was getting ready to attempt to put his arm around me because he'd start whistling.

The day I broke up with him, I thought the poor guy was going to run out of air.

But I can't help it, I'm whistling. And bouncing, like my shoes have ADHD. It's a good morning. I had no idea one could feel this good on so little sleep.

I've been running errands this morning, picking up some new fliers and that sort of thing. The weather is nice. Perfect, actually. I swing the door open to the store.

Malia sets down her book. "May I help y— Oh! Jessie!"

I've prepared myself for this kind of reaction. I knew it would be shocking. But I twirl around and flip my hair like I'm in a shampoo commercial. "What do you think?"

Malia is rushing around the counter like something might be on fire.

I drop my hands. "What?"

"No...no. It's...it's very, um, sunshiny. It's just that I wasn't expecting it." She smiles and combs her fingers through my hair. "When did this happen?"

"Last night." I fluff.

"You didn't want to start off with a few caramel highlights?"

"Nah. Why not just jump in with both feet?"

I see Brooklyn. She's behind the counter, swiveling back and forth in her chair as she hands a customer a business card. "Sounds like fun," she says. "Give me a call." She glances up and does a double take. I'm wondering how much we look alike now that we're both—

"Blonde?" Brooklyn shouts as the customer walks out the door.

Malia squeezes my arm. "Isn't it...breathtaking on your sister, Brooklyn?"

Brooklyn looks genuinely breathless. "She's officially gone insane. Did God tell you to do that too?"

"Why don't you shut up, Brooklyn."

She shrugs. "Hey, I'm just trying to do an intervention before we have to do an intervention, if you know what I mean."

I fluff again. "Good grief. It's not like I shaved my head and joined a cult."

"Really. I'm beginning to wonder."

Malia holds up her hands. "Okay, girls, what's going on?"

I start to answer and then gasp. There are daisies on the counter. A whole big bunch of them. "Are those for me?"

Brooklyn rolls her eyes, and even Malia looks less than excited. "Yeah," Malia says. "Came for you this morning."

I gather them into my arms. "Clay must've read my blog."

"Or maybe God sent them to you," Brooklyn says.

"Can somebody please tell me why you two are bickering so much?" Malia asks.

"Sure," Brooklyn says. "It's simple. My sister's crazy. She thinks God has set aside, let's see, little things like world peace, hunger, and global warming to—hold the phone—set her up with her perfect love story. But what really has me worried is that she thinks Clay would spend two seconds trying to figure out what kind of flower she likes."

"Somebody's jealous." Malia winks at me, but my stomach feels funny. Brooklyn has a point. Both of those things *are* highly unlikely.

"No, Malia!" Brooklyn says. "She really thinks God showed up and talked to her!"

Malia looks at me gently. "What you mean is she's having a spiritual awakening."

"*No.*" Brooklyn still hasn't bothered to get up, but she sure doesn't mind staying involved in the conversation. "I mean, she talks to the air as if He's standing right next to her."

I pretend not to be bothered. I lean in to sniff the flowers.

"Okay, let's just calm down here," Malia says. "Brooklyn, hold down the shop for me. Jessie, let's go to the back room." She takes my arm.

"Great," I say, following her. "You always take the crazy one to the back room."

"Not at all," she says as we go in. "Just for some privacy."

"Because we're getting ready to have a conversation you wouldn't want to have out in the open."

Malia sits and offers me a seat. She takes the flowers away from me and goes to the small sink. She takes a vase from under the sink and begins filling it with water. "Sweetie, this does all sound a little strange."

"Of course it does. I know that. Believe me, it took me awhile to believe God was really talking to me. First of all, you should see Him. *Not* what you would expect. He's—"

"Honey, I just wonder. Since this happened when you were younger—"

"Nine, to be exact. That was different."

"Sure. Of course it was." One by one, she begins placing the daisies in the vase. "But maybe the stress of hoping to find someone, and then starting your own business, has maybe…gotten to you?"

I feel myself swinging into a low valley. I was feeling so good, and now even my hair color can't save me. "I appreciate what you're saying. I do. But I'm fine."

She returns to the table, setting the vase down, the flowers perfectly arranged. She takes my hands. "There are so many wonderful men out there. There's one I'd love, love, love to introduce you to."

"Malia. Please. Look, if Clay and I get together, yeah, maybe it has nothing to do with God. But Clay is here, you know? Wanting to see me."

"He said that?"

"In so many words, yes." I touch one of the flowers. "He's changed. So have I, for that matter. I think it'll be different this time." I move the flowers toward me. "I'm not crazy."

"I know that, sweetie."

I'm *not* crazy...am I?

It's a long morning, but we get two more clients. I celebrate by taking myself out to lunch. I try not to hover too much in the bathroom, but I am a little worried about my hair. As the day goes on, a strange tint seems to unfold, especially under fluorescent lighting. Still, it's utterly striking. I just have to stay away from chlorine. A small price to pay.

The rest of the day is spent at my desk working—and trying to ignore Malia and Brooklyn whispering in a corner of the shop. I also try to ignore the weird filmy feel of my hair. I'll need to condition tonight.

"Bye, girls," Malia says, and I wave as she leaves. "Don't forget to lock up!"

"We will!" I say.

Brooklyn is lingering. "Hey, what are you doing tonight?"

I don't even look up. "Clay's coming to pick me up."

"Oh."

The tone of her voice makes me look up. "Why?"

"I don't know. Thought we could hang out. Maybe call Nicole." She smiles. Like that's going to hide it.

I roll my eyes and look back down at my work. "I'm fine."

Brooklyn comes over and sits on my desk. "I didn't say you weren't."

I nudge her until she gets off. I straighten up the items she pushed out of place. "So you want to hang out with me and my married friend

Nicole, who you say oozes so much maternal instinct you're afraid of catching it?"

"No. No, I like Nicole. She's very motherly."

"We're almost the same age."

"I know. But she's just got that quality about her. There's nothing wrong with that."

I lean back in my chair and cross my arms. "You think Nicole can talk some sense into me. Is that it?"

Brooklyn puts on the cute look that hooks so many unsuspecting men but is completely transparent to me. "Just thought we could go out and have some fun," she says. "I need to get out of the house, you know? Go out dancing or something."

"Maybe another night."

She stares at me for just a moment longer, but then realizes she must have run out of ideas. "Yeah. Right. Sure. Have fun." She grabs her purse and is gone. I know she means well. It does seem strange that she's the one trying to talk sense into me. That's never happened before.

I decide to start on some filing. I like to file because it's kind of mindless—and right now I need to think. I go back to last night, after Gwyne dumped Clay, when he and I were having dinner together. There's an episode in *Sex and the City,* season six, where Carrie falls in love with a Russian artist. No one thinks he's right for her, but deep in her heart, Carrie believes he is.

It's a sudden epiphany. Clay's my Russian.

I hear a knock. I walk to the front of the store and open the door. There is my Russian, dressed casually in a cotton button-up, sleeves rolled to the elbow, collar standing perfectly straight. His hair is spiky, like he used to wear it. He smiles when our eyes meet.

"Hi," I say.

"Hi. You ready?"

"Come on in."

"Oh, thanks." He looks around. "Didn't mention it before, but it's a nice shop. Lots of things to look at."

"Yeah. We've been doing good business here." I turn, just in case he can't see the blond. But his eyes are roaming the store. I grab the daisies off the counter. "They're beautiful, by the way."

"What?"

"The daisies."

He looks at the flowers. "Oh. Yeah. Nice. Who are they from?"

I study him. He looks genuinely confused. "I guess I have a secret admirer." I fluff my hair, but still, nothing.

"Hmm. Does that mean I have competition?"

"Maybe," I smile, and run my hand over my head.

His eyes widen. "Oh! Love the hair!"

Finally. But I'm not going to let this one tiny disappointment get in my way of a good relationship. "Yeah?" I ask, putting my flirt in high gear. "Just a little something different."

"No, it looks good on you. Makes you look hot."

Something catches my eye out the window. Oh no. It's Him. I can't make a fool of myself tonight by talking to Him.

Clay takes my hand. "I'm really glad you said yes to this, Jessie. I thought, you know, after what happened..."

Dang, He is so distracting. He puts a hand on the door. It starts to open. Clay turns at the noise, but I turn him back around to face me. I slide my arms around his neck and pull him close. Over his shoulder, God and I look at each other. I expect Him to say something, but instead He quickly backs away and shuts the door.

"It's all in the past, Clay," I say, putting my full attention on him now. The next thing I know, I'm kissing him, full and strong and without any hesitation. I open my eyes, just for a moment, and see God out the window as He walks away.

"Who was that?"

"Huh?"

"That?" Clay says, nodding toward the window.

"You saw Him?"

"Yeah. Is that the daisy man?"

I smile. "He's just a Friend. A protective Friend. Guess that's why He wanted you to see him."

"Hmm." He clasps his hands around my neck. They feel warm. Strong. "You're safe with me."

And before I know it, I'm kissing him again.

I'm just about to shut down the laptop and go to bed when I get a text message from Blake. GET ON CAM.

"Oh brother," I mumble. I'm at my desk on a hard chair, and I'd rather be in my cozy blankets, but somehow I can't ever say no to the guy.

I log on and up pops Blake's dimly lit face. He's moving closer to the cam, and his nose grows long right in front of me, which makes me laugh. However, he's not laughing. He's trying to adjust something on his monitor.

"What's wrong? I can see you fine," I say.

"You can? You look strange. I'm trying to fix the color." He keeps glancing up at the screen and back down at the monitor. "Your hair looks green."

Oh. Yikes. Yeah. Forgot Blake hadn't seen me yet. "Um. It's not your monitor. I, uh, tried something."

He's staring at me. "Tried something? Like a wig?"

"Like a new me."

He opens his mouth wide for a moment. "You dyed your hair?"

"What do you think?" Maybe a big grin will help.

His face contorts. "Are you certifiable?"

"Of all my wonderful traits, that's the one you see?"

Still no laugh. "You hate blondes."

"No, that's not true. I just didn't understand them. This is helping. Truly. I mean, you should see how people look at me."

"I bet."

I bat at the air to shoo away the conversation. "It'll grow on you."

"I doubt it."

I quit the smiling tactic. "Okay, look, I'm tired. Can we discuss my hair color tomorrow?"

"Wait, I'm not finished. What's going on with you and Clay?"

"Your mother. She told you?"

Blake holds up a hand. "She's worried about you."

"No need to worry. Truly. I'm very happy."

"That's what worries me."

I pull my hair back in a ponytail. "I know, it's a lot of change to take in. Blond. Happy. But trust me, this is a good thing."

"No, Jessie, it's not. Clay doesn't love you. He doesn't even care about you. He's rebounding. How can you not see this?"

"What difference does it make to you?" I lean back in my chair, all huffy-like.

"I can't care that my best friend is making the biggest mistake of her life?"

"Please. Aren't you being a little overly dramatic? It'll grow out."

"Stop joking around." Blake tries another adjustment on his monitor. "Clay is bad news. He always has been."

"Look, we've both grown. It's been three years. A lot can change in three years."

"If you never listen to me again, please just—"

I hear a noise behind me. A tapping. I turn and there He is, sitting on my bed with my purple pen in His hand.

I turn back to the monitor. "I gotta go. A man is here to visit me."

"What? Wait!"

"Bye-bye." I turn off the monitor and turn in my chair, ready to thank God for my own personal happily ever after.

eighteen

God is tapping the pen, staring at me as He sits on the corner of my bed. It's the kind of stare that would make a normal person feel uncomfortable—sort of like the guy with no social skills. Except it doesn't make me uncomfortable. In fact, if He weren't looking at me, that's when I'd start getting nervous.

I nod toward the pen and smile pleasantly. "Thank You," I say quietly. It's weird, but suddenly I want to show Him a lot of respect. "Really. And honestly, I would've never seen this coming, which is what's so cool about it."

He doesn't say anything, and I feel kind of awkward. Like I've done something wrong.

"Glad You brought that." I point to the pen. "I need You to write a few adjustments."

"Adjustments?"

"To Clay."

Ding. Like my microwave just sounded, an IM message pops up, and I glance back to see it's from Clay. I briefly wonder if God would stick around if I took a moment to shoot him a quick message. But God is holding the pen out to me. "You can use this pen to jot down candidates from E-Unity, Equally Devoted, and Calvary Café."

Ding. Another reminder that Clay is waiting on me to reply. I try not to worry about it. One thing I've learned: don't be at their beck and call. Except I don't think that rule applies to God.

"Why would I need those sites? I have an appropriately available man IMing me right now." The words sort of stick in my throat for a second. "The one You set me up with."

God doesn't respond. My eyes are drawn to the pen, loosely dangling from His fingers. Why does this have to be so difficult? I turn and jam my thumb into the power button on my computer, and it blinks off. I'm going to pay for that tomorrow, when my computer will demand to know why I didn't shut it down properly.

I stare back at God, who is also, apparently, wondering why I'm not doing things properly. *His* way. I give Him a confused expression, but really, I know… He should keep the pen.

"Keep it," I say, pointing to the pen. "Sorry." My eyes lower.

He is silent.

"You know me by now," I say, looking back up, trying to study His expression. "This comes as no surprise to You."

"Indeed."

Indeed? Why is He being so quiet? Usually He has a lot to say on the subject of me. So I decide to change the subject.

"Why did You make Yourself visible to Clay at the shop?"

No answer.

"But You wouldn't show Yourself to my sister? When I needed You to. Really needed You to."

Again, He just sits.

"She thinks I'm crazy. And she's telling other people that I'm crazy. Doesn't that bother You? It's not just my reputation on the line here. You're involved." I try to say it sweetly. And really, I do care about His reputation.

"I asked you to do something and you didn't do it."

He's talking about the Laundromat. I feel bad, but mostly I'm relieved He's speaking again. "I know. Seriously, I just forgot. I got caught up with—" I look away. It just doesn't seem like He's going to understand this. I feel myself choking up a little. It's confusing me. "He's giving me hope in the 'finally.' *My* 'finally.'" I hope to see some acknowledgment of my pain. "I'm talking about Clay."

"I know who you are talking about."

"Isn't this what You want? Hasn't this been our goal all along?" I'm shocked, but I actually have a tear rolling down my cheek. I swipe it away.

"Seeing what you want tells me a lot."

"What does that mean?"

He moves off the side of the bed and walks a little closer to me, now leaning against my window. "You want to be married so badly that—"

"Yes! What woman doesn't?"

God watches me and then speaks softly. "If I let you get married right now, you'd be divorced in six months."

I stand up. "That's not fair. Why are You saying that? I would never take marriage that lightly. I understand that it's a commitment. A covenant."

"You don't know compromise." His tone is quiet. Serious.

"I can compromise." I fling my arm toward the door. "Brooklyn's living here, isn't she?"

He steps toward me. "Even with us—and there is an *us,* by the way—you don't compromise. You fight Me all the time."

That stings. Hard. It's like He's picking on me. Picking me apart. Seeing all that is bad about Jessie Stone. I fold my arms. "No, I don't. I've done what You've told me to do."

He raises an eyebrow.

"Most of it." I am about to go sit on the bed, but first adjust the chair I was sitting on so it is nicely aligned with the desk.

God comes over and taps the closed laptop so that it is perfectly aligned on the desk. "Not without complaining."

"Yes, well, I'm not Go—" Okay. Better not go there. "I'm not perfect."

God cracks a smile. "Jessie, you're going to marry a flawed human being."

"And I'm okay with that," I say, smiling. I climb on the bed and sit cross-legged in the middle. "Seriously. There was a day that I thought I had to find Mr. Perfect. But now I'm totally fine with flawed and challenged."

He sits on the edge of the bed and looks directly at me. "You're not ready."

I stop at His words. It's *me*? I kind of always imagined that it was the other party involved, that maybe God was doing some work on *him*.

Since a very early age, I've had what I call slow emotional combustion. It starts out with a slight emotive showing. A tease, really, because what comes after it is frightening—and that's putting it kindly. It's never a surprise that it's coming because it honestly feels like it's crawling straight out of my belly, up my esophagus, and using my tongue as a launch pad. However, this rarely happens when people are around. I have enough self-control to keep it directed at a pillow or my mirror or something like that.

But not this time.

"I'm not married to You!" I yell. I squirm away from His hand that is reaching out to me in comfort. "And You know what? I *wouldn't* marry someone who treats me like You do!" I cover my mouth because I can't believe I've said it. Yeah, I'm thinking it, but normally I don't come right out and say what I'm thinking.

God seems relatively unaffected. He's not tense or even shaken. He just looks determined. "No, I don't always do what you want. Welcome to marriage."

I push my wrists up against my cheeks, trying to get the tears to stop. "Oh? So this is marriage boot camp, is it? Without the benefit of the sex part, of course." I clasp my mouth again. This is so weird. Now I'm complaining to God that I'm not having sex? I have seriously lost my mind. I peek through my fingers, which are now covering my eyes.

"I'm aware of your frustrations."

Wow, He's a gentleman. I mean it. At the very least I really opened myself up to some horribly witty joke there. He's so sensitive, but in all the wrong areas. "My frustrations." I sniffle. "You just don't care about them."

"Do you love Me?"

I'm caught off guard for the ninetieth time in this conversation.

"I didn't know that was a requirement for this."

"It's one of those commandment thingies."

That's funny, but I don't show it because once He gets me laughing, I have a hard time standing my ground. "Do You think this is funny?"

"I'd say amusing."

"Glad I could entertain You."

God lies back on the foot of the bed and looks up at the ceiling. "You want to know what I think?"

I pull a pillow onto my lap. "I bet You're going to tell me no matter what."

He turns His head to look at me. "I give wisdom only when it's wanted. Do you want it?"

Okay, see? That's what I mean. It's a trick question because if I say no, then I sound like a know-it-all, but if I say yes, I have to listen to something that will undoubtedly sway my opinion. I sigh. "All right, fine."

"I created marriage, so you could say I'm promarriage." He looks back at the ceiling. "But it's very hard. Not for the weak of heart."

"I'm not weak." My words came out sounding more like a question even though I meant them to be a bold statement.

"I didn't say you were."

Another thing He didn't say, I suddenly realize, is that He wanted me to spend the evening comforting a heartbroken man. He wanted me to go the Laundromat—away from Clay. "I think I know what You're saying."

He looks at me expectantly.

"You're saying You don't want me with Clay." The words are delivered through a soft whisper, all I can manage right at the moment.

He doesn't answer, but I can see it in His eyes.

I flop down beside God on the bed. "But You won't show up with the right guy either."

He holds my hand. "I love you."

"That's all You have to say?" I start bawling. Is He never going to give me what I want? I don't want God's crazy love; I want a real, live, everyone-can-see-him kind of man. Of course He knows what I'm thinking, but He doesn't let go of my hand. But I am frustrated, lonely, hurt—and I take my hand away and turn my back to Him. "Please leave."

He sits up. "You really want Me to leave?"

I throw up a hand in exasperation. "No! I want You to fix this!" I sit up. "I want You to do so many things You just won't do! I want You, just for once, not to tell me to *wait*!"

I reach over, pull back my covers, and pull them over myself. I feel His hand on my foot. I slide it away. I hope He's getting the message.

After a few minutes, the air gets hot and I can't stand it any longer. I peel the covers back.

I'm alone.

Except, the purple pen is back on my nightstand.

★ ★ ★

I have no idea what time of morning it is when I drag myself downstairs, with my robe undone and my teeth regrettably fuzzy due to my inability to get myself out of bed last night to attend to dental obligations.

If I were a smoker, I'd be smoking chocolate right now.

I flip the kitchen light on and swing open the fridge when I hear a noise behind me. It's not actually a noise. It's a voice. "Good morning."

I whip around. "Blake? Malia? Uh…Nicole?" My eyes dart back and forth between them all.

Brooklyn comes around the corner looking very guilty. "Hey, Jess. Good morning. I fixed eggs." She's holding a plate of eggs.

I look at the stove. Sure enough, a pan. A glass of orange juice is poured. I hadn't even noticed it when I walked in.

"What's going on?" I notice I'm the only one in pajamas. I close my robe and squeeze it tightly like it might moonlight as a girdle.

Brooklyn sets the plate on the counter in front of me. "Thought you might like some breakfast." Brooklyn smiles. Everyone else smiles on cue too.

"What is this?" I shove the plate away. "And I don't mean the eggs."

"Honey, Brooklyn invited us all over," says Malia. "Thought you might want to talk about it."

"You know how much we all care for you," Nicole says, reaching out for my hand, which I yank away.

"Look," Blake says casually, "I know this is unimaginably embarrassing for you, but we all love you."

"Love me." I snort. Loudly. It vibrates all the way up my nasal passage. "Really. That seems to be the common theme around here.

Everyone loves Jessie Stone, but nobody's willing to do anything about it."

Malia tilts her head to the side. "That's not true. We're all here for you."

"Because, no doubt, Brooklyn has convinced you that I'm crazy."

"It happens to the best of us," Nicole says. "When I had my third child, I locked myself in the bathroom and cried an entire Sunday."

Brooklyn steps toward me. "They've got great medications these days."

"Okay," I say, backing up with my hands out in front of me. "You all need to leave. This is ridiculous. I'm not talking about this."

"But see," says Brooklyn, stepping closer, "that's the problem. You are talking about it. To imaginary people. That's why we're worried."

"Go home! All of you!"

Blake suddenly stands. I'm backed against the refrigerator but he keeps walking toward me. Now he's close. Real close. He smells like mint and chocolate. I want to know why, but now doesn't seem like a good time to ask because frankly, he looks like he's about to kiss me.

"Jessie?"

"Yeah?"

"You're into me."

"Huh?"

"You're into me."

I glance behind him at Malia, who is nodding enthusiastically.

"Uh. No. No, I'm not. Why would you say—"

"You're into me. But you're chasing Clay. Why?"

I lunge for the eggs and gobble them up, throwing back the orange juice and chugging it in three gulps. "Look, I'm eating. That's what you want, right?"

"Why are you chasing Clay?" Blake asks again, moving in closer. The others step closer too.

I try to back away, "We're here to talk about God! Me and God! And how He's interfering with my life! Right?" I ask. "Right?"

"Maybe you shouldn't leave the house anymore," Brooklyn says.

"That's harsh," Malia says. "She's just confused, that's all."

"I'm voting for the antidepressant," Nicole says, raising a hand.

I look at Blake. He looks at me. Our eyes meet and I am so regretting not brushing my teeth. And then, to my shock, I feel the urge to recite poetry, which is odd, because though I love to write poetry, I never, ever recite it out loud. At least not since third grade when I read a poem to Billy Stuber and my fourth most embarrassing moment was etched in stone. I take a deep breath, like I'm on a stage or something, and begin a poem called "Love Unseen" that I wrote in my blog a couple of nights before.

> "We're all searching for that special love,
> Is love that hard to find?
> Or should we wake the one we know
> So he won't be so blind?
>
> I know I see who you could be
> But your heart won't make the room.
> You're searching for a beginning blossom—
> While I'm the flower already in bloom.

I could be someone that you're kissing.
I have style, beauty, and grace.
You don't even know what you're missing,
And I'm right in front of your face."

I stare hard at Blake. He stares back.

"Jessie?"

"What?" I snap at Brooklyn. She's behind me now, shaking my shoulder.

"Jessie?"

"What? What?" I move her hand away from me.

"Jessie? Wake up!"

My eyes fly open and I sit up, clutching my heart. I swear I have egg taste in my mouth.

"Jessie? You okay?"

My eyes snap upward. Brooklyn is standing over me, her face strained with concern.

"You were having a nightmare. Except it's morning. So maybe it's a morningmare?"

"Oh." I catch my breath. "It was just a dream."

"What were you dreaming about?"

"Killer eggs." I throw back the covers and spot the pen next to my bed. So that wasn't a dream. I wish it had been.

"I came in to wake you up. You overslept. I've got to get to the store." Brooklyn is already dressed. "I'll get everything started. Take your time, okay?"

I raise an eyebrow. Why is she being so nice to me?

"I'll be there in a snap. I can get ready fast."

Brooklyn walks to my door, then turns. "Jess?"

"Yeah?"

"Who were you talking to?"

"Huh?"

"Last night. I heard you. You sounded mad at someone."

I blush. "It was nobody."

"It was Clay, wasn't it?" She looks sympathetic.

I don't answer.

"I'll see you at the shop, okay? And seriously, take some time."

nineteen

I check the address twice. This is it. The house stands smaller in this luxury neighborhood. It's flat-roofed, with modern stucco design, seventies color, and lots of windows facing the street. Bushes are trimmed to perfect box shapes.

I don't turn into the large circle driveway yet. My Beemer idles in front of the house as I wonder just how crazy I really am. First, I'm crazy for showing up here. But the reason I'm here is to find out if I'm crazy. So welcome to my black hole.

I let my foot off the brake. I don't even touch the accelerator but coast into his driveway like a sleuth. I turn the car off and pull the emergency brake. I'd hate to accidentally roll onto this grass, which looks like it costs more than my car.

I've pulled myself together nicely this morning. I learned early on, even as a little girl, you don't want to look disheveled when you're visiting a head doctor. They read every part of your body language. Everything means something in their world. One bad hair day and they're certain you're going to jump off a bridge.

I am seriously doubting myself, even as I emerge from my car. The gentle wind in the hills blows through my hair, and for a moment I think I feel Him behind me. I glance backward but there's nobody.

From inside the house, a dog is barking as I head to the front door, which is tall enough to let Goliath through. I press the doorbell and squeeze my eyes shut. This is such a ridiculous thing to do.

The doorbell chimes out something by Beethoven. The dog is becoming frantic. So am I.

The door opens.

I don't know if I expected to see a butler or a mousy wife or what, but there he stands, dressed down in a cotton shirt and bermuda shorts. That familiar, thin, twitchy mustache is the first thing I notice on his face. My gaze roams to his eyes, still encircled by wire-frame glasses.

"Yes?"

"Hello. Dr. Montrose?"

"How can I help you?" He pushes the little dog behind him, using a gentle foot.

"I'm sorry to bother you. I'm, um…I'm a former patient."

I'm expecting this—eyes widen, face grows concerned—but nevertheless, trying to be helpful.

I blurt out, "I'm not dangerous or anything." I try a laugh but I'm sounding so insidious. "I'm not carrying a gun or anything." That helps. Yeah. My apprenticeship as a raging lunatic is complete. I hold out my hand, and he sort of flinches. "Jessie Stone. Do you remember me?"

His eyes narrow as he studies me. "Yes. Yes, I do remember you. You look…a little different."

"Oh! The hair!" I cackle. Why can't I find the right laugh here? "I'm just experimenting a little with my look. Nothing to be alarmed about. Plus, it has been a couple or three decades. I'm all grown up."

"Um, that's what I meant. You're older. What are you doing here?"

"I was wondering if I could have a few moments of your time. I realize you're very busy." Though he doesn't look it. He looks fully retired, which I'd read about in the newspaper a few years ago.

"Um…"

"Dr. Montrose, you had such a profound effect on my life. I was just hoping you could share some of your knowledge with me on a particular topic."

His demeanor shifts. "Oh. Well, that's kind of you to say. Please, come in."

Huh. That was easy. Flattery does get you places. Yeah, he had an effect on me all right, but I'll leave it at that.

"What a beautiful home," I say.

He smiles for the first time. "Thank you. My wife was responsible for all this," he says, waving his hand around.

I reach down to pet the little dog who is vying for attention. I don't know why, but I was sort of expecting, if Montrose had a dog at all, it would a Chihuahua or a pug or something. This little thing looks like it just arrived from the pound. "Cute dog."

"Thanks. Since retiring, I've been adopting mutts from the pound and rehabilitating them."

"Ah." Not far from what he used to do, I guess.

"Why don't we go to the deck? I was just finishing some breakfast."

"Sure."

I follow him through his house, glimpsing at the décor. Very modern. The living room looks like it all came from some art-museum shop in New York. I'm more of a soft-cushions-and-warm-colors kind of person myself. Then I notice the artwork. All over the house, in black frames, are children's drawings.

His patients. My eyes dart from frame to frame, wondering if one of mine hangs in here.

He opens the door to the deck. I step out and marvel at the view. His home sits high on the hill, and below are lots of other extravagant homes. It does have a king-of-the-world feel to it.

A wrought-iron table with an umbrella sits in the middle of the deck. His plate of french toast is half empty. "Please, have a seat. Can I get you anything?"

"No, thank you. I'm fine. Sorry to interrupt your breakfast."

"Not at all."

I watch as he struggles to pull out his own chair. His hands are shaky, and I notice for the first time the gray at his temples. He's old now. Lines crisscross his face. His ears look like they've grown an inch on either side. Brown spots cover his forehead. But that mustache, as clean and sleek as ever.

"So, Jessie, it is good to see you. I think about you often. Wonder how you and your sister are getting along. Your parents' death was so tragic."

"We're doing fine. Brooklyn has grown into a fine young woman. We live together and own a business."

"Oh? What kind of business?"

"We help men set up the perfect marriage proposal."

"Hmm. Sounds interesting."

Hmm. He used to always say that when something surprised him but he didn't want to let on that it did.

"So," he says, taking a bite of his breakfast and wiping his mouth with a cloth napkin, "what brings you by, Jessie?"

I'd decided not to rehearse what to say. No matter what kind of delivery it came in, this was going to sound weird. "Well…as you remember, I saw you as a child."

"Yes."

"Do you remember what my problem was?"

"I do. You had an imaginary friend."

I smile. "Sounds so innocent."

"It was."

"It was? Then why did I have to come see you?"

He's holding up a forkful of french toast, and his hand is shaking. "Not all children have imaginary friends, and in some instances, it can be a sign of a serious mental illness. Your parents were just being cautious, as they should've been."

"I always felt like a freak for having that boy follow me around."

Dr. Montrose finally takes a bite and chews slowly before answering. "That was part of why you were in therapy. You had to understand how other people were going to perceive your imaginary friend."

"Like I was crazy."

His fork reaches the french toast again. "But we solved the problem, remember?"

I nod. "I think so. I mean, I don't remember exactly when he left, but I know that he eventually did."

"You were a bright young girl, and I knew eventually logic would help you understand that he was going to have to go."

"I did like him."

Dr. Montrose smiles. "Yes. Those are always the hardest cases."

"Was I one of your hardest?"

He seems to be giving this some thought, his fork poised in the air again. "It's hard to recall. But you were definitely one of my successful cases."

"You must've seen a lot of kids through the years."

"Yes. Many. But it's not often I get to see them all grown up." He winks at me. "It's very nice to see you and to know that you're okay." His expression falls. "There were so many I couldn't help. I still regret that." His fork and uneaten bite lowers to just above his plate.

"I'm sure you did the best you could."

"Yes, well. So, tell me why you are here." The fork finally finds his mouth. I claw at my neck like a poison ivy rash has just popped up. There is no other way to say it, no mincing of words that will make this sound any better at all, so I just say it. "God's been visiting me."

Here it comes. The expression. The one that I would imagine psychologists try to never have, but the one that Dr. Montrose couldn't seem to keep hidden. Morbid surprise. He finishes chewing and slowly pushes his plate back, dropping his napkin over what remains. "What you mean, Jessie, is that you've been rethinking spirituality?"

"No. I mean that He is coming to visit me."

"Could you explain further?" His fingers twitch like he's in desperate need of a pen and pad.

I try so hard to sound normal. "Well, it all started with Him appearing to me. He wanted to talk about my love life. Now, I know this sounds strange, but He's really obsessed with me getting the right guy."

"So what you're saying is that God is—"

"Writing my love story. With my own purple pen. It's very symbolic. God is like that. He loves to use things that mean something."

"And when you say 'appear,' do you mean in the clouds? Or with a loud, booming voice? How does that work?"

"He just appears as a man. A good-looking one at that."

"And when He appears, what does He say?"

"He has a lot to say. And don't get me wrong. I was skeptical at first. I mean, until He disappeared into a wall, I was pretty convinced I was being Punk'd."

"Is He…here now?"

I glance around. "I don't think so. It's hard to know, though. Sometimes I can feel Him around but I don't see Him."

"I see."

I feel like a stupid little kid again, but I force myself to take charge and consider all options. "I know this sounds crazy. Believe me. But I mean, it could happen, right?"

"I think you know what I'm going to say."

I lean forward and engage the doctor. "Do you believe in God?"

"I don't know if that's relevant," he says carefully.

"Just play along."

He does his little head-nodding thing. "Yes. I do."

"If He's real, He could do this—appear to a human being. Right? I mean, He's appeared to people before."

The doctor pauses a moment, then says, "Why you?"

"What?"

"Why do you think that God appeared to you, specifically?"

I see his point. I sit all the way back in my chair and look around the doctor's beautiful backyard. "I don't really know," I finally say. "But He has. For some reason, He loves me and He wants me to have a love story." I laugh a little. "Sometimes I kind of get the feeling He wants to be in it. Does that sound weird?"

"What do you think?"

"I hate that question, and I hated it when I was nine too."

"I'm just trying to get you to think through all this." He does a little gesture in the air, like that will help.

"Believe me, I have."

The doctor crosses his fingers on the table. "Has God asked you other questions, perhaps the state of your eternal soul?"

See, this is helping. The guy is thinking of things I hadn't. "No. I mean, He's just very caring. He seems to care deeply for me, but He doesn't have to say it. I sense it. You know what I mean?"

"That's the problem, Jessie. Nobody's going to know what you mean. This is unusual."

"Like UFO-sighting unusual?"

"Exactly."

I put my elbows on my knees and clasp my hands together, staring down at the deck wood under my feet.

"Have you been hearing voices?" he asks gently. "Seeing others, besides God?"

"No."

"And nobody else around you is seeing God, is that right?"

"Right. Wait! No, that's not true. Twice someone else has seen Him."

This gets a little reaction. "Oh? Who?"

"A pastor and a date."

"A date."

"Yes. A former boyfriend I'm seeing again."

"Uh-huh. Interesting. I can see the pastor, perhaps, but an ex-boyfriend?"

"Look. You don't know God. He's very protective. He's kind of… jealous."

Dr. Montrose sits a little straighter. "I do know Him. I go to church every Sunday."

"Oh."

Here Dr. Montrose loses his "I'll save all the lost puppies" look and gets a bit defensive. "I've gone to church since I was a small child, and never once has God spoken to me. He's certainly never appeared to me or to anyone else I know." He adjusts his glasses to look at me better. "You think you're the exception to that rule?"

It stings. No, in fact. I've never thought I was the exception to any rule. Ever. Until God made me feel…exceptional.

"Jessie, you must use some logic here. You must ask yourself why God chose to appear to *you*."

I look up at the doctor. "What you're saying is that I'm nothing special."

"Now…don't read into what I'm saying as something personal," he says in that practiced, predictably kind tone.

"But that's what you're saying, right? That if I understood that

God wouldn't just appear to a nobody like me, maybe this would all seem like nonsense."

The doctor doesn't appear to be a bit flustered, which means the answer to my question is yes. He calmly reaches down and pets his little dog. "Jessie, you came to me, seeking help. People come to their wits' end. They finally decide they need help after things get too hard. Isn't that what happened to you? If you didn't doubt this, why are you here?"

I stare at the deck. "You know, I never questioned that my imaginary friend was weird. It wasn't until someone pointed it out to me that I became self-conscious."

"Sometimes that's what we need to help us get out of something we're not able to get out of ourselves."

"What do you think is wrong with me?" I can't help my shaky voice.

He does sound very sincere. "Jessie, I think you've been through a lot in your life and this is a coping mechanism. Perhaps you're lonely, you miss your parents, you're trying to make sense of it all."

I lean back in my chair, trying to hold back the tears. "It's just that He was so nice. And funny." I look up toward heaven, falling into old habits of randomly talking to God, "I mean, don't get me wrong, aggravating as all get out"—I quickly look back at Dr. Montrose—"but somehow it seemed like He was annoying me for my good. It wasn't all cupcakes and daisies—He wasn't into doing it my way. At all. In any part of it. He's really into His own plan. But we had some good times together."

"Good times together. Hmm." Dr. Montrose is peering at me like

I'm a petri dish. "Yes, well, wouldn't we all want a God like that?" Silence passes between us. "My wife died of cancer four years ago."

I sit up straight. He's never told me anything personal before. I never really considered that he had a life of his own. "I'm so sorry."

The doctor nods. "Do you know how many prayers I prayed? Night after night. All day long. I wept and wept. I cried out. I... begged." His hand goes to his mouth like he's just said something mildly inappropriate. "But she still died." He picks the dog up with shaky hands and holds it in his lap. "So yes, Jessie, I suppose we all would want a God who laughs and plays and writes love stories for us. We all want that. But what we want and what is real isn't the same thing."

"But—"

"If God wants to write your love story, then surely He would want to save the life of a dear woman like Margaret. Don't you think?"

I nod, unable to look him in the eye.

He pets the dog in silence. "You're a smart girl," the doctor finally says. "I always knew that about you. You must apply logic to this situation, and that's when you'll understand the truth."

I'd agree with him in theory, but I remember God too well—the way He smelled and the sound of His voice and the touch of His hand. "But, what about faith? Where does that come in?"

The doctor smiles. "Have faith in yourself, Jessie. You've overcome this once. You can overcome it again." He puts the dog down. "Do you have a piece of paper? A pen?"

"I, uh...yes, I think so." I dig through my purse. "Here."

He jots something down. "This is the name and number of a

colleague of mine. He's superb. He's not quick to go straight to medication either. He really believes in the benefit of cognitive behavioral therapy." He hands it to me.

I stand and he starts to stand too. "No, please. I can see myself out."

He sits back down.

"Thank you for your time."

"Certainly. Jessie, it was good to see you again."

"Thank you, Dr. Montrose." I open the back patio door and let myself into the home, clutching the piece of paper in my sweaty palm. My feet feel light. My head is spinning. I walk slowly through the house toward the front door, and my eyes are drawn to the scribbled, colorful drawings on the walls.

Then I see it.

I remember the day I drew it. I was sitting in his office. He seemed particularly agitated with me that day. I was on the floor, and he asked me to draw a picture of this little boy that was always following me around. I hated Dr. Montrose's crayons. They were all broken, mismatched, the paper torn off. But he insisted I draw anyway.

So I did.

I drew me, drew my little friend—and then scribbled him out.

Dr. Montrose called it a breakthrough. "You see, Jessica? You *do* know that he isn't real. You just have to believe it. Today you believed it."

And now it hangs on his wall as proof that I finally believed that nothing existed.

I glance back and Dr. Montrose is busy clearing his breakfast dishes, so I step closer to the drawing. The color is brilliant and appropriate…peach for the skin, yellow for the hair, aqua blue for the eyes.

The lines are smooth. The coloring flawless. I stare into the large, round blue eyes of the boy who lived in my mind for so long. For months I drew so much comfort from him. Until one day I scribbled him out.

All of my childhood struggles are here. Framed.

Reduced to crayon.

I let myself out and sit in my car for a long time.

Logic. Okay. From now on, logic it is.

twenty

It's been the most intense three weeks of my life, like a constant, unrelenting power ballad. Clay and I talk three or four times a day, see each other every other day. It's like old times, like three years haven't gone by. Well, maybe not the same. I've grown more confident in myself; I've refused to put Clay on a pedestal. I keep reminding him he's lucky I've taken him back, and he always nods enthusiastically, like he is, indeed, the luckiest guy alive.

He texts me more than a guy with a big ego would. He's very gushy, always pouring out his feelings. And I'm an empty cup, ready to be filled with all that gush.

It's a hectic day at the store. We've had three new clients sign up this week, and we're starting to get backlogged, so Brooklyn and I came in early to try to get ahead. We're getting along better, as long as I don't mention God and she doesn't mention Clay.

Speaking of God, He hasn't been around, which makes me realize Shrinkhead was right… He was a figment of my imagination all along. Not that I don't believe in God. I know He's out there somewhere, and He'll look in on me when it's needed. But logic, for once in my life, has prevailed. God isn't *that* into me.

The hardest thing to swallow, besides leaving the idea that God *was* that into me, is the idea that I quit my job and started a new job on the advice of an imaginary sidekick. But, to the credit of my split personality, things are thriving, so maybe I shouldn't worry so much.

I try not to think about any of it, to just focus on my love life—to live in the moment. That's what they say, right? You're not promised tomorrow? So today is all I have, and what I have right now is what I've always wanted. This man adores me. Gwyne was never right for him, but maybe having Gwyne in his life molded him into the right man for me.

Except he's really into my blond hair, and I'm growing kind of bored with it.

For once, though, I try not to overthink it.

Clay texts me, asks me to go to dinner at some place I've never heard of but swears is "the bomb." I tell him I'll meet him there. Brooklyn has left to run some errands for our next proposal. Soon, Malia is nearby, pretending to need something near the counter, but I can tell something is up. She has one of those faces that can't hide eagerness.

"So, I guess you and Clay are doing well?"

"We are."

"Seems like you're having a lot of fun."

"I am."

"He's treating you right?"

"Better than right."

She's nodding and smiling like she's agreeing with it all, but there's a deep crease between her eyebrows that is in obvious disagreement.

"You shouldn't worry so much about me," I say to her. She looks surprised. "Malia, I know you disapprove."

"It's nothing like that. It's just that I want you to be happy."

"I am."

"Your sister is worried sick about you."

I smile a little. "Yes, well, now she knows how I've felt all these years."

Malia laughs. "True enough."

"You know, Blake isn't too happy with me either."

"He'll get over it," Malia says. "We're both protective. Overly protective, I guess."

"It's good to know you care." I check my watch. "I guess I better go. Clay's taking me to some fancy-shmancy place tonight."

"That wining-dining phase can be a lot of fun."

I grab my purse, come around the counter, and put an arm around Malia. "I think he gets me. And that's what I've always wanted...someone who knows me and still likes me and—"

Suddenly, behind Malia, something grabs my attention. I let go of her shoulder and walk over to it. Sitting right on top of her counter is a box of purple pens.

I don't dare reach out and touch. I want to. I want to grab them all and never let go. Don't. *Don't.* But my fingers twitch and tingle. Then I feel a hand on my shoulder.

"Sweetie? You okay?"

"Um…Malia…when did these arrive?"

"What?"

"These pens. These purple feather pens." My hands hover over them without touching.

Malia comes over to look. "I don't know, hon. I think yesterday. This is the first shipment of these weird pens that we've gotten. I don't even remember ordering them." She reaches out to grab one. "Why? You want one?"

"No! No, no. No…" I back away with my hands out. *Smile* so you're not a freak. "Um, just admiring them, that's all."

Malia looks down at the one in her hand. "Really? I think they're kind of junky. Who would pay four bucks for a pen like this?"

"It has character. And flair."

"I need to go put them out on the floor." Malia grabs them and disappears down an aisle.

"No. No." I whisper this to myself as I head out the front door. "It's just a coincidence. Coincidences happen all the time. Now, stop talking to yourself or you're going to look crazy."

I get in my car, turn on music, and drive to Skye Bleu. Its large neon-on-black sign hangs over a dark and brooding building with reflective windows and an enormous glass door. This doesn't look Italian. I was really hoping for manicotti tonight.

I park in back and walk to the front. It's nice to know someone's going to be meeting me here. I so love that I'm not alone or the third wheel or even meeting girlfriends. This feels good.

I round the corner and there he is, leaning casually against a railing.

When he sees me, his face lights up. I approach and lean in for a kiss. He steps back and looks me over. "Stunning."

"Thanks," I say.

And then, from behind his back, pop three roses. Red, no less. "Oh, how kind." I smile and take them into my hand. Okay, so I was sort of expecting him to go with daisies since I've dropped the hint a time…or ten. But you know what? I'm a woman getting flowers from a man who takes the time to buy them for me. Maybe I've misjudged roses. They are the international symbol men use to express their love. I have no room to complain, right?

I shake off my thoughts and gaze up at the building. "This place looks interesting."

"I can't believe you haven't been here," Clay says, taking my hand and pulling me along. "It's the newest place to be. You seriously haven't been here?"

"I've been busy with the business," I say. Shout, actually. The music roars overhead as we enter. A large room with many lights, but few that actually light up the place, greets us. A smoky haze lingers at the ceiling. Strobe lights, all seizure-like, make me blink fast. People are dancing. Bartenders are slinging drinks toward customers. "I thought we were eating!" I shout.

"We are!" he shouts back. "There's a really cool restaurant in the back!" He pulls me along, weaving us through the crowd of moving and swaying bodies. I look around. This is the kind of place where the girls slouch because they're too beautiful otherwise. I don't even have the ability to slouch.

That strobe is about to make me insane.

Soon enough we've made it out of the strobe light and into some decent mood lighting. The music still pulses through the walls, but at least there's room to move. I glance down at my khakis. I am really not fitting in here, but Clay looks comfortable so I pull myself close to him.

"Table for Matthews," he says. The woman nods, glances at me, then offers to guide us to the table. We sit down in a cozy half-circle booth. The menus are already on the table. A candle stands tall, barely flickering, in the center. It's the first time I can hear myself think.

"Wow, Clay, this is quite a place."

"I know." He grins. "They have one of these in New York too. It's where all the celebs hang out. And I swear, you look like the paparazzi should be following you."

I smile a little and forgive the cheesy line. Clay was always one for going over the top while trying to make an impression.

Clay grins at me. "Oh, don't be modest," he says. "You're beautiful. You had me at 'hello.'"

Oh, brother. Not the *Jerry Maguire* line. Ugh. Call me grumpy, but that line irritates me. I smile again like he's just made my day, secretly hoping we can move past cliché, quickly.

I know this place is fancy because all the waitresses look alike and the menu has only five choices. I do love good food, but I can also do a burger or a steak. For Clay, though, I might learn to love the caviar life. Not sure how he's affording all this, but for the time being, it's not my problem.

We both order the halibut, and Clay picks out our wine. Soon enough we are snuggled together as he pours my glass.

"Just a little," I say, holding my hand out.

"Yes, I know," he smiles, pouring way more than a little. "You don't drink much. Weird, but I respect that."

I can get a buzz off cooking wine evaporating from a skillet. I take a small sip, just to be polite, and thread my fingers between his. "This is nice."

"Yeah."

I glance up at him and catch him smiling at me. "What?"

"Nothing."

"No, I can tell. Something." I poke him in the ribs.

"Okay, look." He turns to face me. "Jessie, this might sound, well, you know, really strange."

"Yeah?"

"I don't know. I just get this feeling like…it's timing. This timing. I can't get over how I was there and you were there and…it feels like it means something."

I squeeze his hand. He is looking deeply into my eyes. As deep as a human can look, anyway. "I'm certain it does, Clay. Timing means everything, you know?"

"Yeah. And I really think now would be a great time to just go for it."

My heart flutters, then stops, then restarts at twice the speed. "Really? Clay…really?"

He kisses me on the cheek, then moves his lips to my ear. "Let's move in together."

I drop his hand. Accidentally. I quickly pick it back up from my lap. He moves away from my ear to look at me. He's smiling, sort of that sultry eyelids-half-closed kind of look. Funny, but it's not a good look for him.

"Look," he says. "I know. This is what caused problems for us before. I asked, you sort of freaked out, and things went downhill from there."

"That's putting it mildly."

He asked, I said no, he moved on to Gwyne who moved in with him four weeks later.

"Jess, don't we have something special here?"

I nod.

"And let's face it, we're not getting any younger."

Thanks for the "we."

"Come on," he says, stroking my cheek. "I don't want to be without you."

I'm starting to wonder if it's that Clay doesn't want to be *without*. The guy is striking me as having the inability to be alone. But then he touches my chin. "I love you."

So, this is it? This is my "finally"? Except moving in together is more like a "maybe." Still, I find myself thrilled to hear those three little words.

I look at him and we have this moment. My whole body feels warm. When his fingers touch my skin, it tingles.

"I love you too."

twenty-one

i like shopping at night. Around eleven o'clock, the store is mostly empty and they're restocking the shelves. I want to hum, but I don't, because there's something stuck in my throat.

Hesitation?

Regret?

Pure joy?

Maybe fear.

I don't know. All I know is that next weekend, I'm moving in with Clay Matthews. It feels real and good and—okay, maybe a little bit misguided. But isn't relationship all about compromise? And didn't God tell me I wasn't ready for marriage, anyway?

I'm about to order baloney from the deli when I hear, "Jessie?"

I almost don't turn because I am trying not to react to voices these days. But I recognize it and glance over my shoulder. "Nicole!"

"I didn't recognize you with the, uh, wig?"

"No, it's mine." I tug at it and smile, though it's getting a little annoying having to explain this all the time. "Just trying something new."

She pulls me into a hug. "Where have you been? I've left a couple of messages."

"I'm smack-dab in the middle of a whirlwind romance."

Nicole steps back. "Shut up! Really?"

"Really," I say, beaming and swinging my arms like I'm twelve. "It's been unbelievable!"

She grabs my arm and pulls me toward the cheese. "Tell me all about him."

"Well, you already know him." I pull at my hair and study her face. "It's Clay."

"What?" Expressions don't lie. She's more shocked than when I showed up at the office with my blond hair.

"Yeah. Clay Matthews. You remember him, don't you? We—"

"Remember him? Jessie, I almost plotted a murder against that guy! I have seriously never hated anyone more than him."

I hold my hands. "I know, I know. But Nicole, he's changed. He really has. And so have I. I think we have a good shot this time."

Nicole doesn't look convinced, at least if I'm reading her body language right. Her arms keep crossing tighter and tighter across her chest, like a boa constrictor or something.

"What'd he do with Gwyne? Dump her?"

"Actually…" I lean in. "He got dumped." I'm surprised at how good I feel when I say that. Wasn't it sympathy that brought me to him?

"No!"

I can't help myself. "When he proposed to her in front of a lot of people."

Nicole is gasping with the delight. "Oh! That's beautiful!"

We both stand there smiling like it's our birthday. Then I realize I'm supposed to be on his side now.

"So the jerk came crawling back to you?" Nicole says, and a lady pushing a shopping cart past us smiles.

I wait until she leaves. "Not exactly. It's fate, actually, that brought us together." I explain how I planned the entire proposal.

Nicole still looks skeptical.

"I know, Nic, I know. It sounds crazy. But haven't you noticed the greatest romances are about timing? I mean, I've been on these stupid online sites and dating services, trying to make things work. And what happens? Destiny befalls me and I find happiness."

"But maybe it was just coincidence."

"No. We connected."

Nicole shakes her head. I can tell she's trying very hard to be supportive, but it's killing her. "Okay." She puts a hand on my shoulder and lets a smile emerge. "Just promise me you will take this very, very slow."

I want to listen to my best friend in all the world, except— "We're moving in together next weekend."

Nicole actually yelps.

"Look, Nicole, I appreciate your concern. I really do. And I realize it's ironic that I am back together with a guy who left me because I wouldn't move in with him. But don't you see the complete circle here? The woman who did move in with him broke up with him. And now he wants the woman who wouldn't move in with him. But this time I'm willing to. It's a circle. See?" I draw one in the air.

"You're in some kind of shape, but I don't know that it's a circle." She reaches down and starts inspecting the cheese.

"I've waited my whole life for romance, Nic. Ever since I was a little girl, I wanted what my parents had. When they died, I guess I wanted to carry on their love. I know that sounds stupid, but it meant something to me. Except I failed. I failed to ever find what they had. I searched as hard as I could, you know? You've seen me. Haven't I worked hard?"

Nicole nods reluctantly but doesn't look up at me.

"Yes, I have. Harder than any woman should have to work to find romance. And now here I am, and it's fallen right in my lap. I'm out trying to give my ex a perfect wedding proposal—and I'm doing it even though it's painful—and I'm rewarded. You probably don't understand this, Nicole, because you've been blessed with a beautiful family that came together like you were following some kind of recipe"—she looks up sharply and begins to say something, but I go on—"but for me, luck has been nowhere to be found. I'm as unlucky as it gets when it comes to romance. So this is my moment. It's the moment I've been waiting for my whole life."

I realize I'm giving a monologue in the deli section of a grocery store, but I don't care. This is good stuff.

"And yeah, maybe it's not what I had envisioned. I mean, I've never been a big fan of the test run, but I'm more mature now. Moving in together is a huge step for both of us, and he's willing to make that step. He's been through a terrible ordeal, and I happened to be there to help him out of it."

"Can we say rebound?" Nicole mutters.

I hold my head up high. "Perhaps one would use the word 're-bound,' but we're not a set of basketballs. We're two human beings searching for something, and we've found ourselves on the same court of life."

"Oh brother."

"Okay, maybe that's not a good analogy because it makes it sound like this is a sport and I'm game, but the point here is that life is competitive and if you don't move quickly, you'll lose. Not that I'm moving quickly so I don't lose the game. That would, of course, go against every fiber of my being." I take a breath. "Clay loves me. I love him. We've always had a special connection, and it's time to explore it more deeply. Sure, we had a three-year hiccup. All right, admittedly, 'hiccup' sounds too innocuous. It was more like the superstrain of a virus, but the point is that we've both grown over the years, and even though it seems like we've picked up exactly where we ended, I'm choosing to see this as a new beginning."

Nicole has given up on the cheese and is studying me. She's nodding but not like she's agreeing. More like she's urging me to take another breath.

I do, and what follows shocks both of us. I fall into her arms and sob on her shoulder. "I'm making a terrible mistake, aren't I? What am I doing? I've lost my mind!"

She hugs me tightly. "Yes, you have, but I think you just got it back, honey," she says, stroking my hair.

"What if it never gets any better than this?" I wail.

An older woman grabbing a package of cheddar says, "Dear, it's why they created cheese. Melted cheese will never disappoint you."

I laugh and Nicole lifts me off her shoulder, cupping my face in her hands. "You are worth more. You are worth a guy who is willing to stake everything he has on you, not some guy who wants to give you a test run while he picks up the pieces of his life."

"I know," I say, wiping my tears. "I'm just so tired of being rebounded and dribbled and thrown and shot off the backboard and passed back and forth and—"

"Okay, let's get you off the basketball analogy. You don't even like sports."

"I like swimming." I sniffle. "Except I'm drowning right now."

"Trust me. You're not drowning. Not at all. You're doing great."

I take a deep breath and gather myself. "We need to have lunch. I miss you."

Nicole and I spend another thirty minutes together talking, my pouring out my heart, her reassuring me I'm a complete, whole person. Finally we hug and say our good-byes, and I watch her head to the diaper aisle. I stare at the cheese for a moment. There really is power in feather-shredded cheddar, but it honestly doesn't hold a candle to cocoa. But instead of going for candy, I grab my basket and head for the hair color aisle.

I'm still not sure what sport I'm playing, but whatever it is, it's time to get myself back in the game. On my terms.

I find the towering wall of hair color and am once again amazed at the choices. There's brunette, blond, and red—of a hundred varieties. And I have no idea if I'm color 524. It looks right on the package, but my hand withdraws as I see color 519. And honestly, I'm eying the reds too. Maybe a little fire on the scalp will give me a new perspective.

Suddenly I see a hand. It's holding a box of hair color. Number 548 to be exact.

"Hi," He says. A feeling of complete relief floods over me. I want to hug Him, but I've already made a scene once at the supermarket. And I still don't know if He's real, but right now I don't care. I take the box from Him.

"Thanks." I can't stop smiling at Him.

"Let's walk and talk," God says. "I like spending time with you."

I plug my earpiece in and grab my buggy, pushing it toward the candy aisle.

"I like that too," I say. "It's just that I wish You could do normal things, like dinner. Not that I don't appreciate Your ability to walk through walls."

"Why not dinner?"

I shoot Him a look as I grab a sack of dark chocolate. "You're funny."

"Teriyaki chicken and snow peas. Tomorrow night, 7:24. Your place."

"At 7:24? You're very quirky, You know." I smile and start to glance at Him. "I'm glad You're ba—"

He's gone.

I've pounded the chicken to a quarter of an inch thick, marinated it for two hours, and put it in the pan with olive oil, shallots, and pineapple. I keep an eye on the clock. I don't know if He meant exactly

7:24 or not, but I don't want to overcook the chicken. And I am questioning His food choice. I mean, I love teriyaki, but I figured He'd prefer something like a knish or matzo ball soup. I'm rinsing the snow peas when I hear the doorbell ring. Right on time at 7:24. And that's amazing too, because I set my clocks forward five minutes, so He's actually on time by my time. He really is into the details.

I open the door. He's standing there looking a little shocked.

"What?" I ask.

"I was wondering if…well, we could start over." His hands are stuffed deep into the pockets of his nicely pressed pants.

I laugh and grab His arm, pulling Him in. "Come in. Since when do You ring doorbells?"

"You don't strike me as the kind who likes people to barge in."

"You know me well."

He follows me into the kitchen. "Wow, smells great. What are you cooking?"

I laugh again. "Truly, I wouldn't have figured You for teriyaki. But I love it."

"Me too. But I don't want to impose. That's not true. I really want to impose."

I grin at Him and gesture to the table. "Set for two."

"It's almost like you were expecting Me."

"Well, You are good at dropping hints."

"I didn't think you noticed. I did try being more subtle with you."

"You're a little hard to ignore."

He leans on the counter and watches me cook. "Okay, so you don't mind a little forwardness. So, that other guy you were not ignoring…the one you were kissing?"

I sigh. "Let's not beat down historical figures. Not tonight."

"It's history, then." He smiles. I feel my heart skip a beat. Why is His smile affecting me this way?

I slide the chicken out of the skillet, dividing it equally between the plates. "You're way more flirty than I expected. Not that I'm complaining. I mean, Dr. Montrose would have a thing or two to say about that, but I think it's refreshing. I just think people have the wrong impression of You."

"They do?"

"Yeah. Not everyone, mind You, but I think some people think You're out to get them."

He looks disturbed. "Why would they think that?"

"I know! You've been nothing but kind. I'm sorry for the way I've treated You."

"Water under the bridge."

"So," I say, sliding the snow peas out of their skillet and onto the plates, "are You ready to eat?"

"As long as it's with you."

We sit down at the table. I'm using the good dishes and even have some candlelight going. From what I hear, He's a fan of fire.

I gesture toward His plate. "Please, take a bite. I want to see if You like it."

"Well, it is My favorite, so you have high standards to live up to." He takes a bite. "Wow. *Wow.* I'm not kidding. This is fantastic."

"Thank You."

Suddenly I hear a noise coming from the living room. It's a *thud* sound. Actually several *thud* sounds right in a row. "Excuse me for a second," I say as I stand. "Seriously, stay here, okay? Please?"

I walk into the living room to find Brooklyn coming down the staircase. With suitcases in tow. Anger washes over me. Not again. *Not again!*

She gets to the bottom and glances to the kitchen. "Did I hear a guy's voice?"

"Ah, I don't know. Maybe." I gesture toward the suitcases. "How long this time, Brooklyn?"

"You're one to talk. I don't want to hear it. Besides, if you can make a dumb decision—"

"Brooklyn, I ended it with Clay. Last night. You were right. I was being a moron."

Brooklyn looks relieved and like she's about to hug me, but then she retreats like she remembers we're fighting.

"Brooklyn, this new relationship of yours, it's not going to work either."

Big eye roll. "Don't go melodramatic on me. Please."

"You're just going to move in with a guy you've just met?"

"You want me to try it your way? That's really working for you, Jess."

"But—"

"I don't want to end up your age and alone. This guy really likes me."

Reality comes into clear, stinging focus. Yeah, I'm having teriyaki and snow peas and the company is good. But I'm older. And I'm alone. I plant my hands on my hips.

"Who is it this time?"

She clutches the handle on one of her suitcases. "The one I met at the shop."

"Oh. You mean the customer. The one who was going to hire us to woo someone else. Until he got distracted by *you* and your *blondness*."

Brooklyn drops her bag to the floor and marches straight up to me, her face inches from mine. "Believe it or not, Jessie, some people do like me for reasons beyond my hair color. You think you keep getting rejected because of what you look like. Which, by the way, you looked ridiculous parading as a blonde. Maybe you need to ask yourself what's wrong with *you*."

She steps away from me, her hard stare lingering. Then she grabs her bags and goes through the front door, not even bothering to close it on the way out.

I gasp, probably because I've been holding my breath. My entire body is shaking. How dare she speak to me that way! I walk over and slam the door, rebuttals flooding my mind but with nowhere to deposit them.

Then I remember—He's still there.

I walk in. It's obvious He's been eavesdropping, though I can't blame Him. He probably does have super hearing. "I've raised her better than this." I sigh. He looks at a loss for words. "How do You put up with people? Honestly."

He doesn't answer. I don't blame Him. There's not much to say.

But now I've lost my appetite.

"Look, I'm sorry. I'm just…I'm just not up for this tonight." I take my plate to the kitchen. "But listen, You stay. Eat. Finish up. Take Your time. Really. I cooked this for You." I try a smile. It's really hard to come by right now, though.

I leave Him and walk up to my bedroom. I've got a headache and her name's Brooklyn.

twenty-two

Hopeful Groom, otherwise known as Dave Dewey, is bending one knee, like it's slow motion or something. A little dramatic for my taste, but I think Donna Butler, otherwise known as Perspective Bride, needs the slower version because, frankly, she looks dazed and confused.

This proposal has been unique from the start. Dave is charming and not bad looking, but also a complete control freak, down to every detail. And, it can't be said enough, in my opinion: a little impatient.

He's been planning this proposal for months. They've been together for four years, so he said it wasn't going to be any big surprise when he popped the question. So he decided to go ahead and plan the wedding for the same day, complete with family, friends, decorations. The guy even picked out her *wedding dress.* I raised a concern or two, but Dave assured me he knows her likes and dislikes well enough. And I have to admit, the guy has good taste, all the way down to the flowers and candles.

I stand on one side of the foyer of the Glory Wedding Chapel. Brooklyn is on the other side. I kind of zone out on the big speech he is giving to her, instead focusing on Donna, whose mouth is in a wide circle, like she might belt out opera or something. Surprise. Yes, that's it. Which is good, because this is supposed to be the happiest day of her—

"And we can do it right now!" His voice trumpets, and he gestures toward the lavishly decorated sanctuary. "The chapel is ready! The minister is here!"

"But I need a dress," Donna says quietly.

Brooklyn cues Donna's mother, Eileen, who floats in as she carries the white dress Dave has picked out. Again, the guy has taste. It's soft, billowy, romantic. Eileen grins and lifts the dress a little, like maybe Donna might need a better view. But Donna doesn't.

Donna's eyes are wide. Mine are too, because I would never let someone else pick out my wedding dress, but that's just me. "It's beautiful," she whispers.

"All your family is here," Dave says.

Brooklyn cues family and they begin filing into the small chapel, taking their seats, looking back expectantly, wide grins showing their enthusiasm for what is about to take place.

"Everything is perfect, Donna. Will you marry me?"

Donna is nodding and her mouth is moving, but nothing is coming out.

"Today? Right now?" Dave asks loudly.

"Right now?"

Tears fill her eyes. She glances around, even noticing Brooklyn and me as we try to stand in the shadows. It must be a surreal experience, but I'm wondering…are those tears of joy? Because her chin is quivering in a way that resembles a look of horror, like she's about to be murdered in a slasher movie.

"Yes." It barely comes out and sounds like a rubber-ducky squeak. Or maybe a ducky gasp. "Yes," she repeats. This time slightly better, well, lower. A little foghorn-ish. But dang, the woman has a lot to process here.

Dave looks pleased. He stands and slides a ring on her finger. "Whoa," she breathes. It's a rock. Brooklyn claps like she's a show seal and gives me a knowing glance. We haven't really talked since our big fight, but, like always, things have settled down.

We watch as Eileen, along with three bridesmaids, whisks Donna away to get changed. Dave is high-fiving his groomsmen, looking relieved and over-the-top happy. Brooklyn and I thumbs-up each other. This is probably the biggest proposal we've pulled off to date. A lot of things had to come together.

"So," I say to God, because I can feel Him standing behind me, "that was amazing. We did good, huh?"

"Hmm."

"Hmm?" I glance at Him. He is watching Dave. "Okay. So I get the feeling something's off."

God doesn't answer, just quietly watches.

"She said yes. We all saw it," I say.

"True."

I stare at the wedding party as the groomsmen file to the front. Everyone stands around chatting awkwardly as they wait for the bridal party. I keep quiet, but I can sense that God is waiting for me to say something.

When the bridal party finally enters the foyer, Donna's gleaming smile is doing little to mask her hesitation.

"They don't belong together, do they?" It hurts my heart to even say it. Still, I know what I see in Donna's eyes, and it isn't adoration. I think it might be fear. "Why did she say yes?"

God is watching Donna. "Donna likes to please people. She's been that way since she was a kid."

I watch Donna too. "Why didn't You stop it?"

He turns to me. "Dave went to you for help, not Me."

The words are like a gust of wind, throwing me off balance. "So, am I, um, responsible for this?" He says nothing, and I turn back to watch the wedding-that-shouldn't-happen happen before my eyes. "I pen these romantic moments and if these women fall for them…" Donna stands at the back of the church, watching the bridesmaids walk down the aisle toward Dave. "Are they settling for the wrong guy because he said the right thing? A guy who didn't write a word of this…?" My words trail off as I am suddenly hit with the reality of what I'm seeing. "If she's not supposed to be with him, does that mean she belongs to someone else?"

"She could."

"Then what happens to that guy? Or the girl this groom should be with? I mean, one wrong move and the world is thrown off its axis." Ironically, the world now feels like it's on my shoulders.

God is watching the wedding too. "I never said everything happens the way I want it to."

"But I'm contributing to this!" I gesture toward where the last bridesmaid fluffs Donna's dress and pulls her train into place before turning to walk down the aisle. "You told me to open this business."

He turns to me. "No. I told you to share proposals. The selling part was your idea."

"Yeah, but given that I'm, You know, not *You,* how am I supposed to know who's right for each other and who isn't?"

God smiles at me, one of those smiles that indicates I'm about to be tested and He's sure I'll pass.

"*Great.* I suppose now I have to fix this."

"Fix what?"

I whirl around and Brooklyn is standing beside me. "Nothing."

"I've just been watching you talk to yourself. Seemed like a lively conversation. Thought I'd join in."

"I'm just…" I gesture toward Donna, who is now beginning to step down the aisle. The organ music resounds, filling up every pocket in the chapel. "Brooklyn, did Mom ever tell you about how she and Dad got together?"

Brooklyn's eyes follow the beautiful train flowing down the aisle. "It all sounded whacked to me. I mean, God bringing them together. Mom knowing what Dad was going to look like before she met him." She glances at me. "Hey, they were as weird as you are."

I'm too tense about what I should do to care much about her little attack. "Why are you so skeptical to think God might actually care about one of the most important decisions we can ever make?"

"If He gets credit for writing their love story, then in my book, He also gets the blame for how it ended. Dying together, hang gliding, leaving behind two daughters. Sorry. I just don't subscribe."

I have a sudden urge to protect her. She is standing there with her beautiful blond hair, her perfect-for-the-occasion dress, her canvas-like makeup, and all I see is a little girl. I'm about to ask her to come home…when I hear it.

"If anyone has reason to believe these two should not be together, speak now or forever hold your peace."

"Funny thing," I say as I peer through the small window. Donna is crying. Dave is smiling. "Peace sometimes comes at the expense of unrest."

"Huh?"

"You're just going to have to trust me on this one." I barge through the double doors, causing everyone to turn. I don't know why my legs aren't weak. I feel strong and sustained as I march down the aisle. "Stop!"

Dave's smile slides off his face. "What are you doing?"

"I'm objecting. That is an option, right?"

The justice of the peace looks pasty against his black robe. "Um, yes, but…we're actually already past that part."

"I want my chance to speak or forever hold my peace."

An old woman nearby leans into her husband and whispers loud enough that we can all assume the hearing aids aren't up to par. "Did she say 'hold her pee'?"

I sigh. This is not happening very movie-like. I decide to focus on Donna. "You don't want to get married today, do you?"

She is shaking from her veil all the way down to her fabric shoes. "Uh…uh…no." She falls into my arms. "No. I don't." She turns to Dave. "I'm sorry, Dave. I'm so sorry. But I don't want to marry you."

Chaos erupts.

The justice sits down on the step, wiping his brow and closing his little book. I hand Donna over to her mother who has rushed up. I sit next to the justice. "Bet that's never happened before, has it?" I smile.

"No. No, indeed. Not once." He pats his forehead with a handkerchief. "But it should."

Malia has come back from her lunch break to Brooklyn's roaring explanation of the day's events. She sasses quite a bit about the money we lost, but she ends with, "That was the most intense thing I have ever witnessed. You should've seen Jess. I mean, the woman rocked. She just slapped Dave down. The guy was crying." Brooklyn shrugs at our expressions. "What? I mean, the guy had it coming. Who does he think he is picking out a woman's wedding dress?"

Malia laughs and shakes her head. "You two girls have certainly brought some excitement around here."

"I'll finish the paperwork," Brooklyn says, "and then I'm outta here."

I leave them and go to the break room to check for any Jessie's Corner blog comments. God is waiting, standing next to my bowl of M&M's. I sit down and log in. "You know I just lost ten thousand dollars."

"Uh-huh."

"Paying for someone else's botched wedding."

"A bargain if you ask Me."

"That money wiped out my wedding fund." The words stick in my throat a little.

"You did something good today, Jessie. And you did it for the right reason. *Not* because it was torturing you to watch someone else get what they want."

I grin. "I know, right? If I didn't know any better, I'd think You were becoming a fan."

"Speaking of fans…" He points to the computer screen. "Your blogging continues to attract some attention."

"Ah. JessieFan is back."

Thank you for your post about God-written love stories. They're the only kind worth playing a role in. Hope you get that porch swing.

"JessieFan sounds like a smart dude," God says.

"Dude. I like it. Nobody would believe You talk like that." I look at the screen. "So do I know this guy? Or is he one of those computer geeks who has nothing better to do than post on message boards all the live-long day?"

God pushes my bowl of M&M's to the side and sits on the corner of the desk. "Would you do Me the honor of spending your thirty-fifth birthday with Me?"

"Are You asking me out on a date?"

"That would be highly inappropriate."

I belly-laugh. Seriously witty, I'm telling you.

"So this is Your way of telling me my husband ain't gonna show up by then, is that it?"

"Are you available?"

"Yeah, right. That'll be a joy. I'll sit in a booth talking to You. Spectators will think I'm schizo. *And* I'll have to pay. Some date."

"Well?"

I sigh. "Okay."

"Okay?"

"Yes."

"You'll go?"

"Yes, I'd love to."

I just broke up a wedding in progress. How hard can this be?

twenty-three

I have a ritual on my birthday. I eat white chocolate. It's sort of my protest to the whole birthday thing. White chocolate has no purpose in my life. It tastes like an imposter. It's the perfect way to begin the anticelebration that I'm a year older and still single. I also (attempt to) drink a disgusting cup of coffee, because that's what old people do. And really, not liking coffee is like a social failing too.

I eat the white chocolate for breakfast, when my stomach is empty, so if I gag there's not a whole lot to clean up. White chocolate chased by a beverage that tastes like cigarette butts is far worse than another birthday.

After all, everything has to look up from there.

I walk into work and immediately spot red tinfoil balloons tied to and floating above a tape recorder.

"Are these for me?" I ask Malia.

Her frenetic grin tells me it's so. "Wow!" I say, delighted at the surprise. "Should I press Play? You don't think it's connected to a bomb, do you?"

Malia laughs. "Hurry up! I've been dying all morning for you to come in."

My finger lingers over the Play button as I try to imagine whom this is from.

"Come on already!" says Malia, clapping.

"All right." I push Play. Without the benefit of stereo sound, "I Only Have Eyes for You" plays, sounding tinny and one-dimensional—and absolutely beautiful.

I clutch my chest. "That is my favorite song! Who did these come from?"

"You don't know yet?" asks Malia, just as Brooklyn breezes in.

"Happy birthday," she says, tossing me a card. "Did you make it through your morning ritual?"

"Barely. Check this out!"

Brooklyn gazes at the balloons. "Wow. And it's your favorite song. Invisi-God strikes again."

"Or," I say, stroking the strings on the balloon, "there is one person in my life who said the best way to capture attention is to do something creative. Even secret admirer–ish." I look at Malia, who gives me an agreeing wink.

My cell phone beeps, indicating I have a text message. It's Blake. HAPPY BIRTHDAY! WHAT WOULD YOU LIKE TO DO?

I almost forgot. I have dinner plans with God. And this time, I'm not standing Him up. ALREADY HAVE PLANS.

Blake texts back. WHAT???? I THOUGHT I HAD YOU ON A PERMA-
NENT RESERVE.

I eye the balloons. "That, my friend, can be arranged."

I pull the car into the private parking garage of the restaurant. I have
to laugh.

"Very clever," I say, pointing at the sign. "Noah's."

He shrugs and smiles.

An ocean of cars are wandering through the maze of the garage
ahead of us, but like the parting of the Red Sea, suddenly they move
on and a car backs out, right by the walkway. "You're good." I smile.

I park and before I can even get the keys out of the ignition, He's
on my side, opening the door. I take His hand as He lifts me out. "I
was kind of hoping You'd just pull me right through the thing," I say
as He shuts the door. "Sort of like Superman, when he takes Lois on—
never mind."

He lifts His arm a little, like I should wrap mine around it. I can
only imagine how awkward this must look, but really, I don't care. I
mean, not long ago I was on a perfectly good date with a hot guy and
that turned out to be horrible, so this really can't get any worse.

We walk slowly, like time is on our side. Then He stops and looks
down, which causes me to look down. A fifty-dollar bill, with a ten
next to it, is on the ground to the left of an oil slick. I stoop to pick
them up.

"Can't have you paying for your own birthday dinner, now can I?"

I fold the bills. "Wow. You've thought of everything. Please tell me this dropped out of the pocket of a really wealthy guy who won't miss it."

"On the contrary. His name is George, it's the last money to his name, and he's going to be having a very rough night when he discovers it's missing. He'll be calling on Me for the first time in a long time later tonight."

"Amazing how You work things out," I say as we continue walking. "So, the balloons, the recorder—did Blake send that to me?"

He doesn't answer.

I nudge Him. "It's my birthday. Can't I get one question answered? Just one. I promise. That's it. And I realize I should probably be asking for the cure for cancer or world hunger or something, but...*please.*"

He only smiles and keeps walking. We reach the restaurant. I open the door, just for the sake of keeping this as normal as possible. I catch the hostess watching us. Me. "You could just make yourself seen tonight, you know," I whisper to Him. "I mean, You've done that a time or two."

He's grinning, which translates into, *Absolutely not because you'll learn something this way.*

Yeah. Learn to be humiliated, except I've got that down already. Strangely, though, I'm not too bothered by it tonight.

"Reservations for Jessie Stone. Booth, please."

The waif in black asks, "Will anyone be joining you?"

"Oh yeah. The King of the World. Do you think I'm underdressed for that?"

The woman's prissy expression drops. "One, then. Follow me."

God leans forward. "You're having way too much fun already."

I laugh. "I really am."

The three of us walk to a cozy booth, but the hostess has grabbed only one menu. As I slide in I say, "I'll need another menu."

"Pardon?"

"Another menu."

She sighs and goes to fetch it.

"Can't beat that kind of customer service these days, can you?" I say.

"Hey, no worries. I'm used to people ignoring Me."

I open the menu, and I catch a glimpse of a woman nearby, alone, reading a novel while feasting on an enormous plate of seafood. My eyes sting with tears for her. That's her date tonight—food and a good book. *I've been there!* I want to shout. But tonight's going to bring enough unwanted attention as it is.

I look at God, who is also noticing the woman.

"Ruby. Never been married. Men don't treat her well, going all the way back to her father, Richard."

"She looks sad."

"She is sad."

"Maybe we should invite her over to eat with us."

He gives me a melancholic smile. "She won't speak to Me. She hasn't since her best friend died fourteen years ago."

"Wow. People know how to hold a grudge, don't they?" I lean forward on the table. "Okay, I just have to say… It's just that… I mean, Your eyes… They're sort of, well, amazing."

"Oh?"

"Seriously. In the movies You're always depicted as shriveled and like seventy-two. And sometimes with glasses, which I just think is odd because surely God has twenty-twenty vision, you know?"

"I've been depicted all sorts of ways. Most people don't ever take the time to get to know Me."

"If they only knew," I say softly. The eyes are hard to describe. The color is dynamic, brilliant, like all colors mixed together. They shine with light but are deep with feeling. "How am I supposed to…?"

"What?"

"Notice anyone with You and all Your glory, right in front of me. Who can compete? And that all-knowing thing You've got going. Women would kill to find that in a man."

"It's okay that you're starting to like Me. Even love Me a little."

"But I can't marry You. Don't You see why that's hard for me?" I soften a little and give Him a wry smile. "But why am I surprised? It's the story of my life…wanting what I can't have." I glance over and see a nearby couple staring at me. "I'm going to be talking to myself all night," I say to them, smiling apologetically, "so get used to it."

Suddenly I hear a familiar tune coming from the nearly dead pianist in the corner of the room, playing on a shiny baby grand piano.

"'I Only Have Eyes For You,'" I whisper, looking at Him. "Was this a special request?"

"I've been known to whisper a few suggestions." Suddenly He stands, bows slightly, and holds out His hand.

"What? Here? Now?" A cold sweat puts my deodorant on high alert. I mean, I'm all for shaking inhibitions, but it's more like trying a new dance move, not trying to move with an invisible man while dancing.

"I want to dance with you," God says.

I eye the old couple watching me. I lean in toward God. "Can't we do this somewhere else? I hear the North Pole is deserted. You've got teleporting powers, don't You?" The music swells. The old dude on the piano is doing quite a number with the ivories over there.

And I get caught up in the moment, just like that. I take His hand and He guides me to the dance floor, all Antonio Banderas–like. He's a good dancer, surprisingly. I don't know why, but I sort of expected Him to have big clunky feet or something. But our dance is fluid, graceful. I twirl under His guidance, step out and in, as He leads. Wow, wouldn't we be something spectacular to watch if He wasn't invisible. I laugh. I bet they're all wondering how I'm dipping backward like that without falling on my butt.

I notice the woman who'd been sitting alone. She has put her book down, and she's watching us. Or, I guess, me.

I give her a wink and keep dancing. He's swinging me around like we're auditioning for *Dancing with the Stars* or something.

As I twirl like a kiddie top, and "I Only Have Eyes for You" continues, it seems everyone only has eyes for me. Us. But not for long.

Soon enough the woman has ditched her novel and she's on the dance floor, moving like she's John Travolta. And doggone it if she doesn't pull off disco moves to "I Only Have Eyes for You." Maybe the guy at the piano has picked up the pace or something, but there's electricity on the dance floor.

I swing around, holding His hands, and lo and behold (I speak like this when I'm with Him; I'm harking like there's no tomorrow), the hostess with the mostess is right there with us. She's closing her eyes, dancing round and round like she's being led by a big heart and lots of hope.

We pass near each other and she quips, "Who needs a man, right?"

"Right on, sister."

I glance at God, who is beaming. And I don't mean just happy. He's actually radiating light. I look at all the couples still seated. They wish they were having this much fun.

Soon enough, the has-beens and the have-nots are all on the dance floor. Old Dude Piano Man kicks it into high gear, and we're busting moves that haven't seen the light of day in years.

I have to wonder how long it's been since this waxed-to-the-max dance floor has seen any action. By the surprised and energetic look on the piano man's face, it's been awhile.

God smiles at me. "You really know how to light up a room."

"You're One to talk. You know You're glowing, don't You?"

"I'm feeling the love," He says, then dips me, twirls me—and for this moment, I feel so completely loved that there is nothing else in the world I want.

We're ending the evening on the beach, my favorite place to be. Especially at night, except usually it's not safe for me to be out here alone. Sometimes Blake comes with me, but tonight the God of the Universe is escorting me. I sit comfortably on the sand and watch Him. He stands, bathed by the moonlight at the edge of the water, with His pants rolled just above the ankle, His hands in His pockets, and His white shirt fluttering behind Him in the breeze.

I wonder what it's like to observe all that you've made. To know how to command every wave. To have the attention of everything that swims in the sea. For all the time I've known Him in the recent weeks,

I have not really known Him like this. It's like the water is singing to Him and the moonlight is dancing for Him.

He is majestic and I tremble. For the first time since we met, I feel small, insignificant, unworthy. But then He turns, walks toward me, kicking up sand as He approaches.

Waves crash near where He stood, washing over His footprints. Except when the water recedes, they are still there, untouched. How strange and mysterious and strong He is.

I start to stand as He nears, but He motions for me to sit down.

"I want you to do something for me."

I sit back down. "Sing? Because You know I have the heart but not the ear for it. But since You created me tone deaf, maybe You should be subjected to the torture of it."

He smiles gently, but I can tell something is on His mind. He points to the sand. "Write your initials."

"Huh?"

He tilts His head. "Surely you trust Me by now."

"Well, if you trust somebody enough to lead you on the dance floor, surely this isn't too much to ask, right?" I get on my knees and in large block print I draw J.E.S. I put my fist to my mouth, but shoot, the question pops right out like I have an air gun in my throat. "Why?"

"Couldn't help yourself, could you?" He smiles.

"Sorry."

"It'll make sense one day."

"You are so mysterious."

"All part of My charm." He pushes me and starts running. Oh, how I love a good game of tag!

I start to run, but then I see something in the distance, under the pier. A shadow of a person, lingering. I stand there for a moment but soon enough feel His arm around me. "Come on, let's get you home."

We arrive back at my condo. I let Him drive home. And yeah, we got some looks. It was very funny. Not so funny if Officer Garrety would've driven by, but what can I say? I've become a risk taker of late.

I climb the stairs to the condo and turn, but He's remained at the bottom, the perfect gentleman that He is. "Good night."

"Good night, Jessie."

"This was a really awesome birthday. Thank You. A dream. Really."

"Speaking of dreams," He says, "I want you to let some of yours go."

I stand there. I don't argue, but I'm having a hard time agreeing. Why can't I just throw myself into this relationship and not look back?

"Trust Me with them. I won't disappoint You." He steps back and begins to turn. "Thanks for dancing with Me."

I watch Him walk away, vanishing into the dark shadows of the trees hanging over the sidewalk. The shadows seem to disappear along with Him.

twenty-four

i can still smell the salt water from the night before and hear the sounds of the ocean as I drive up into the hills, to the neighborhood that Blake had shown me before. I'd reflected on this place a lot last night. This symbolized so many of my dreams—to settle down, have a family, live in my dream house. So giving this up had some sacrifice attached. It meant no more daydreaming about all that I wanted out of life.

I park the car and stare at one of Blake's unfinished houses, the one he let me tour. Then I notice something. A white veranda…and a porch swing!

I lean against my steering wheel. "God, this is hard. I mean, why does there have to be a porch swing? I know, I know. Because the porch swing means so much to me. And I know that's stupid, but it's—" My gaze focuses on something moving in the window.

It's Blake. I can see him putting on a door.

"Wait! What the—" It's God, right there next to Blake, helping him put the door on! They're talking to each another.

I throw myself backward into my seat. "Whoa. Whoa!" Could it be? I mean, I can hardly let myself dream that big, but…"Is this really— Are You giving me what I asked for? Are You telling Blake now?" I laugh. It's almost a cry. I cover my mouth. "You're telling him Yourself."

I put the car in reverse. "Okay, do Your thing. I won't interrupt this one."

I drive home, slowly, with the windows down. I feel free. I sing to the radio and punch a hand in the air as I hit a hill. So this is what happens when you give God your dreams. Everything works out. It's just that you have to have the courage to do it.

Of course, what if Blake says no? I've known God long enough to know that He is persistent, but He doesn't ever force anyone to do anything. So it all sort of hinges on whether or not this is what Blake wants.

Before fear can clutch me, I remind myself that He is very persuasive. He tends to put things in very convincing terms.

Trust Him, I tell myself.

I drive to work and meet with a client for two hours, making sure the man really loves and cares for this woman. I'm fairly convinced they would marry even if I wasn't providing a dream proposal, so I'm at peace with it.

Brooklyn doesn't come in, and Malia tells me she decided to take the day off. I try not to worry too much. She's been working hard, and if she needs a day off, then she deserves it.

I finish up with the client and check my voice mail. Blake has left a message!

I sit down as I hear his voice. "Jess, listen, I know this is last minute and everything, but can you meet me for dinner tonight? I have your birthday gift, and plus, I want to...well, I want to tell you something. Something really cool. Okay. Call me."

I quickly text him, and we arrange to meet at our favorite seaside seafood restaurant. I work the rest of the day, humming to the point that I'm certain Malia is annoyed, except she keeps giving me this knowing look. Without saying a word, we seem to be on the same ecstatic page.

After work I rush home to shower and get ready. I know exactly which shirt to wear—a Chanel lightweight sweater that Blake got me for one of my birthdays. It's a favorite and easy to accessorize. I decide to borrow a few bangles that Brooklyn has left behind. The woman has more jewelry than the queen of England. I blow-dry my hair straight and take the time to apply my makeup. I step back from the mirror and take me in.

This is the night that is going to change my life. My dreams are coming true. I swipe my lips with red and then go into my bedroom. It's not quite time to leave yet. Normally I would be journaling, but what's strange is that I'm not sure how to journal real life. All I've put down in those heaps of paper are dreams and fantasies. Now that it's all coming true, what am I to write? Besides, I don't have possession of my purple pen.

And I'm better for it.

I decide this would be an appropriate time to pray. On my knees.

Haven't done that since I was a kid. I remember praying like this as a child, with my mom next to me, holding my hand. I remember not always knowing what to say. It seemed greedy to just ask for toys, but that's all I wanted. Mom would remind me of hurting people in the world, and I would try my best to care about them.

Now it seems a little hard to pray too. It's hard to find the right words to the One who has given you your dream. But I bow my head anyway. "God, I want to thank You. You're amazing, and I'm sorry I've doubted Your love for me. You're kind and You really care about me. I'm so—"

"Thank God!"

I jump to my feet, startled. Standing there in my doorway is Brooklyn, holding her suitcases.

She shakes her head. "At least this time you're not talking to yourself." She drops her suitcases. "Guess your prayers have been answered. Here I am."

I rush to her. "You're home?"

"I'm home."

I hug her. She pats me on the back and tries her best to enjoy it. When I release her, she's staring at my wrist. "Are those my bangles?"

"Um…yes."

She steps back and gives me a once-over. "Wow. You really pulled that outfit together well. The bangles are perfect. And am I seeing things or are you wearing red?"

I pucker my lips. "Yep."

"What's the occasion?"

"I'll give you details later. You'll be around? I gotta go."

"I'll be here, eating trans-fat food and watching something with Julia Roberts."

I give her one more hug and then rush out of the house and into my car. I check my watch. I do *not* want to be late!

I'm flying down the boulevard when I see the flashing lights behind me. "No. Oh man. No! God, help!"

But He doesn't appear. I pull to the shoulder and watch in my driver's side mirror as the officer gets out of his car.

Garrety. Of course.

I roll down my window and try to look peaceful and normal. "Hello, Officer."

"Well, hello there. Fancy meeting you here."

"I'm sorry. I know I was speeding, but I—"

"Were you? Because I pulled you over for failing to yield."

"I, uh…"

"I'm just messing with you. You were speeding."

"Oh." I try a smile and hand over my driver's license and registration.

He is checking it over. "So, how is life going, Ms. Stone?"

"Wonderful. Couldn't be better."

"Oh? Why is that?"

"I'm at this very moment driving to the destiny that awaits me."

"Oh boy. I might've let you off the hook if you'd just said you were running late for a meeting."

"Officer, you don't understand. I've been through a lot, you know? And finally, tonight, it's all coming together for me. I'm finding my 'finally.'"

"You do look much happier. And, um, saner."

"Please, can you let me off the hook? Let me go so I'm not late?" I sort of lean out the window and express desperation.

"How do you know?" he asks.

"Know what?"

"That this is the thing that you've been waiting for?"

"All the signs are pointing to it, and I'm learning to read the signs."

"Except speed-limit signs."

"Uh, yes. Except those."

He hands me back my license and registration. "Well, I don't know what kind of destiny you're headed to, but let's make sure you get there alive, all right? Drive carefully."

"Yes sir. I sure will, sir. Thank you."

I roll up the window and in my enthusiasm accidentally peel out, but I slow it down and drive the speed limit all the rest of the way there.

I'm only five minutes late, but I'm trembling all over with anticipation, hoping and praying he is still here.

I walk in and immediately spot him, already seated at a booth. A cozy booth, actually. The kind that is a little half circle and no matter what, you have to sit next to the person.

"You're late." He smiles.

I sidle up next to him. "Sorry. Little run-in with the law."

"Again?"

"I don't know, I seem to attract trouble these days."

"Speaking of attract, you look outstanding. Really. I can't remember ever seeing you this…dressed up."

I shrug coyly. "What can I say? I'm excited."

"Wait! Did my mother tell you? I told her I wanted to."

"I knew she knew! She wouldn't say anything, but she kept giving me these looks all day."

Blake settles comfortably into his seat. "I never thought it would happen, you know?"

"Believe me, Blake, I do know."

He is looking at me as he sips his drink. "I didn't think you were going to be this excited, to tell you the truth."

"Are you kidding? I've been waiting forever."

Something strange flickers across his face. I can't imagine it, but maybe the guy didn't have a clue all these years that I had the biggest crush on him.

"Why?" he asks.

"What?"

"I'm sorry, I'm just a little nervous. It's just…" He stares into his drink. Poor guy, his nerves are shot. I take his hand.

"Blake, I didn't think this would ever happen either. You're my best friend. And there were times that I questioned whether or not this would be the right thing, but I think we've proven to each other how much we care, and we have this amazing foundation to build off, and—"

"Um, Jess, I—"

"Can you believe we won't need to IM late at night anymore because you'll, like, be there. Right there. Right there with me and—"

His hand retreats. "Ah, Jessie…I…"

"What?" I shake my head. "I know. I'm sorry. I should have let you do this. I'm the queen of proposals and I totally just screwed this up."

I smile at him, but the guy is going pale, like he's just been whipped into buttermilk. "Blake, it's okay. It's me. We're best friends. I mean, there's not too much we can embarrass ourselves with, you know?" I chuckle. He tries very hard to smile, but it doesn't come through.

I look into his eyes, searching for that excitement that was there just moments ago. I panic a little because I feel like I'm bungling his moment. But what I'm seeing in his eyes is not fear or hesitation. It's raw pain.

"Blake, what's the—"

"Jessie, I wanted to see you tonight to tell you I met someone."

I suddenly can't breathe. "You met someone?"

He nods, watching me carefully, sadly. "That's what I wanted to tell you. I wanted to tell you in person because you are my best friend and you mean so much to me. Her name is Denise, and I think you two would really hit it off—"

"What are you talking about? I saw you!"

"What—"

"I saw you. Today. At the house. *Our* house! Talking to Him. Didn't He tell you? Didn't He?"

"What are you talking about, Jessie? What house?"

"With, with, with...our porch swing."

Blake's eyes are wide, searching. "Jess, I didn't build that for me. It belongs to somebody else. I'm just doing some work for—"

Suddenly a pin-thin, gorgeous brunette approaches. I'm expecting her to ask what I want to drink, but she slides into the booth, on the other side, next to Blake, who says to her, "Um, listen, maybe you should...could you just wait for a sec to—"

I stare at both of them and then shove myself out of the booth. "I gotta go." I bolt, and I mean in a full run, out of the restaurant. I feel like I'm going to puke. Holding my stomach, I manage to get to my car. I slam it into reverse, not even looking behind me, and peel out of the parking lot. I catch a glimpse of Blake, standing at the door of the restaurant.

I punch my hand into my dashboard and scream at the top of my lungs.

twenty-five

If I could bury myself in sand, I would. Instead, I stomp across it, kicking it as I go, punching the air. But nothing I do is taking away what just happened. I hardly got a glimpse of the woman that Blake has fallen in love with, but I got enough of one.

Brunette, for one thing. *Brunette.* The guy doesn't even like brunettes…right? Otherwise, what's wrong with me? Her hair was long and straight, layered around her face. Wide brown eyes, perfect olive skin, a grin that evokes instant jealousy.

How could I have been so stupid? "I am such an idiot!" I scream to the water. "To think Someone out there was writing me a love story! Who does that?"

"One with faith."

I don't even turn around. I don't want to see Him. "Shut up! Just *shut up*! You are not real. You are some whacked-out figment of my

whacked-out imagination that I made up because I'm whacked out."
I wipe my eyes. "Because I'm pathetic."

"You are not."

"I have to write imaginary guys into my life. Dance with them
alone on my birthday while everyone around me can see me for what
I am. A freak. A freak and never anybody's choice." I turn around,
walking backward, and look at Him. "Never anybody's choice but
Yours. So stay away from me. I don't want to be Your choice anymore.
I want You to leave me alone."

"Jessie, what happened with Blake…I know, it was upsetting. But
you are not a freak."

"Oh? Then what am I? No, don't answer that. Get away from me."
I turn back around and march forward.

"I wish you could see yourself through My eyes."

"I think that's the problem. Go away."

"Did you know your name means 'God sees'?"

"No kidding. I thought it meant 'Old Maid.'"

"I whispered your name in your mother's ear when you were born."

I stop and whip around to face Him. "Fantastic. Is that supposed
to give me some kind of hope? God sees? No, God doesn't see. Because
if God sees, He would've seen a lonely and scared little girl who has
lived all of her adult life alone and who just wants somebody—"

He's got an expression on His face that I haven't seen before. He
actually looks like He wants to cry.

I point a finger at Him. "You are no more real than that boy who
used to follow me around when I was nine. I can't believe You anymore."

"Why?" His tone is calm and self-assured, which makes me want
to scream.

"Why? Do You know how much it hurts to be standing here with the one person who has the power to fix this—and everything that's wrong in my life—but He won't? He just keeps alluding to the idea that something is out there waiting for me, but there's not! You, of all the great loves in my life, have led me on worse than anyone."

God steps forward, gently, His eyes intense. "I need you to do something."

"No," I say. "No! I'm not doing anything for You anymore. Everything You ask me to do leads me to nothing. Writing my initials in the sand? Yeah, that was my favorite. Very mysterious. Made me believe that it was possible, that something good was possible for me. But it all leads to my heart getting ripped out." I stare hard at Him. "Whatever You have in mind for me, I don't want it."

"It's not just yourself you'd be hurting, Jessie, if you give this up. You have someone else to consider. Someone who's been waiting for you. Just you."

I laugh harshly. "Oh, *come on*. We're still there? At the one-true-love thing? Why should I believe a word You say? Every day starts the same and ends the same. I need to just accept it, stop hoping for something more. It's not worth all this pain."

His eyes shimmer with tears. "Love is the one thing worth pain."

I stand there for a moment, my heart pounding, out of breath, the hairs on my body standing at attention. I stare at Him, and for a brief moment my heart starts to soften; I want to be held by Him. The feeling flees quickly though. I make it flee. Anger returns. I pull my cell phone out of my pocket and hit speed dial, never taking my eyes off Him.

"Hello?"

"Brooklyn, it's me. Meet me at that karaoke bar. I want to see how your half lives."

"Jess? What? Jessie—"

I snap the phone closed and walk away from Him toward my car. For once, He doesn't follow me.

"Woo hoo!" I pump my arm up and down and cheer the fat lady on. "It ain't over till the fat lady sings!" I holler. Brooklyn grabs my sleeve and yanks me back onto the bar stool.

"Shut up. What are you doing?"

"Can't a girl have—" I glance up and see the bartender. "Another one! Pour away, kind sir!"

The bartender glances at Brooklyn, then pours me another shot. I swallow it in one gulp. It burns all the way down my throat. At least I think it does. I'm not really feeling pain right now.

What I am feeling is the urge to dance. I bounce around on my bar stool. Yeah, karaoke is way cooler than hitting the dance floor with an imaginary partner.

Brooklyn doesn't seem to be having the fun I am. "Come on," I yell over the music. "Why aren't you drinking? Isn't this what you do? Drink, dance, sing? That should be a Coke commercial or something."

"Maybe we should go home."

"Home? Come on! We're just getting started here." I signal for the bartender as I talk to Brooklyn. "So, the test drive on the new guy didn't work, huh?"

"Jessie, what is your problem?"

"Can't a girl have some fun? I think those were your exact words a year ago at that beach party." My cell phone vibrates a few inches across the bar. "Maybe I shouldn't answer that."

"Why?"

"Could be God."

Brooklyn rolls her eyes. "You are really scaring me."

"I'm not kidding. The guy is kind of stalker-like. Very nice. Quite the gentleman. But doesn't take hints, you know?"

Brooklyn grabs the phone and looks at the screen. "It's Malia."

"Terrific. It's my never-to-be mother-in-law." I pick up the phone and without answering it put it in front of my face. "Nobody's there. Here, I mean." I laugh, put the phone down, and am feeling an urge to sing. And none of that old-fart stuff either. I want to jam up there on stage, rock the house. *American Idol*ize myself. "Woo hoo!" I hop off the bar stool and dance toward the line for karaoke. Yeah, this feels sooo right. I'm way more loser. Looser, I mean. "Lookie, Brookie!" She's not. She's ducking her head. Some people are so uptight.

My wait in line is a little long. I've struck up a convo with Denver, Susan, Charlotte, and London. Add Brooklyn, and we've practically got a world map. But we're having a good time.

Charlotte is next and she sings "Sweet Home Alabama," which Denver and I are cracking up at since she's Charlotte. It's a funny thing what alcohol can do. It can make imaginary friends completely disappear.

It's almost my turn when I feel an arm grab me. Uh-oh. He's back. Nope. It's Malia. Thank God.

"Come on, honey."

"But I'm next."

"They'll save your spot. Come on."

Malia's got me by the arm. I trail her, dancing all the way to a rounded booth she insists I slide into. It's just like the one I sat in with Blake. *Perrrfect.*

I fumble my way in, and the next thing I know, Brooklyn's on one side of me and Malia's on the other. I put an arm around each of them. "Good times. Good times."

Malia peels me off her. "Blake called and told me what happened."

"Fantastic!"

"Jessie—"

"No, seriously. It's fine. The humiliation is spreading like a rash, but I've got cream, alcohol, I mean. Maybe he can post the story on a billboard tomorrow. Better yet, tell him to drop by my blog and share."

"Honey, I love my son. I do. But—"

"Me too. Cheers." Except I don't have a drink. I grab Brooklyn's and sip it. "Water? You are such a drag."

"Jessie, listen to me. I know what Blake did was kind of stupid. He didn't think through how to tell you, and he doesn't really know what a hard time you're going through. It was just bad timing and…" Malia takes my hand. "You're a treasure. You really are, sweetheart—"

"Oh yeah. Treasure. Gotta dig so deep, it's hard to find. Jack Sparrow, call me!"

Over the speakers, my name is called. "Jessie Wessie, you're up!"

"Saaweeeet!"

"Jessie Wessie?" Brooklyn says. "She is soooo drunk."

But I'm gone, slipping underneath the table, across the floor, and up on stage. Singing my new favorite song. The only song that makes sense to me right now: "Don't Want to Know You."

> *"You seemed the kind of person*
> *I'd really like to know*
> *But now I'm not entirely sure*
> *That's where I want to go*
> *The hurt that you unleashed on me*
> *It cuts me like a knife*
> *And now my broken heart cries out*
> *Why won't you save my life?"*

The crowd is feeling it. Several of my new buddies are clapping loudly for me. I'm not actually singing to the ceiling. But they don't know that. But maybe He's not even listening.

> *"So I ain't listening anymore*
> *You can walk straight through that door*
> *I'm tired and mad to the core*
> *And I don't want to know you"*

Hey! Alcohol also cures tone deafness. I think.

And then I see Him. He's at the door, watching me. I didn't see Him come in. I sing to Him. He loves to hear me sing, right?

> *"I've gotta dig down deep within*
> *If I'm to take this stance*

I'll bottom line it for you, dude
I'm over this whole dance"

Whew! I hop right off the stage like I'm Kenny Chesney or something, swinging my hips. Lots of claps for that one. I tip my mike to the crowd. They are *loving it*!

God isn't. His face drops at the sight of me. That's a first.

"I'll take this lonely road
Because I know it to be true
Your chance has come and gone
And I don't want to know you
I don't want to know you
I don't want to know you"

Before I get another stanza out, He starts to leave.

Oh well. "Bye! Buh-bye. See ya later. Bye-eeee."

He's gone.

Somebody's got my elbow. I twirl around, hoping it's a hot guy with an empty lap.

Nope. Malia. Again.

"Jessie, you know I love you, which is why you have to stop this." Malia takes my mike and hands it off.

"Awww, come on, Malia. I was just getting snarted."

"*Started* doesn't have an *n* unless you've been doing shots." Her tone is harsh, a little motherly-like. "Now come on. Let's get you some fresh air." Malia guides me outside.

Brooklyn is right behind me, shaking her head. "Dude, I didn't think you had it in you."

"Brook, shush," Malia says.

"What? I'm just saying, I didn't think—"

"Okay, we get your point. She's having a rough night, aren't you, honey?" Malia says, rubbing my arm. We're standing near the wall of the club, a few feet away from the entrance.

"Look, I know I'm wasted, but I swear the buzz is making everything come into focus. I'm getting it, all right? Really, this time. You guys don't even have to tell me. I already know. I'm like *Sixth Sense* crazy. Seeing people where they aren't. Talking to people who aren't—uh-oh."

I have the clarity of mind to vomit in the other direction.

"Whoa. Sorry. That came up fast."

Brooklyn is making a face. "Jess, good grief. If you can't hold it down, don't drink it!"

I wipe my mouth and lean against the brick. "The guy at the door, He took my purple pen. I'm not kidding."

"What is she talking about?" Brooklyn whispers to Malia.

"I can hear you. I'm only *tone* deaf. I'm talking about my pen! My pen with the feather. You know the one. No matter. By now it's probably back in my bedroom. 'Cause He doesn't need it, see? It's over. I'm cutting Him off. Zip. Goner. Not that I won't miss Him, mind you."

Malia stops me. "Wait. You said the guy at the door?"

"That's what I said. Mr. Invisible."

"You mean the one you were singing to so rudely that he bolted?" Brooklyn asked.

"Yeppers. And it's a real shame you can't see Him, either, because honestly, He's cute. But only I can see Him. Well, except ministers. The minister at the chapel saw Him, but that's because he's very spiritual. Don't ask me why I can see Him and you can't. I ain't spiritual."

"You never say 'ain't,'" Brooklyn says.

Malia holds out a hand. "Wait. Jess, we did see him."

The sidewalk is spinning but I manage to focus. "What?"

"We saw him."

Brooklyn nods. "Yeah. He was there, standing at the door, watching you make a fool of yourself."

Malia takes my shoulders. "I'm the one who called and told him to come here."

I steady myself against the brick wall and blink. "God has a phone number?"

"Jessie, that's not God! It's Jonathan. The guy I've been telling you about? The one I've been wanting to introduce you to?"

"The computer geek?"

"Jonathan, yes."

"He's not a geek."

"That's what I've been trying to tell you. Jonathan."

A memory flashes through my swimming mind. I'm at the gift shop. There is a pregnant woman. *We consider this little guy to be a gift of God. That's what Jonathan means.*

"Gift of God," I whisper.

"I don't get this," Malia says, folding her arms. "Don't you already know him? I told him to go see you at your condo the other night, after you ended it with Clay. He said you invited him in and you were cooking his favorite meal, teriyaki chicken or something like that."

Since when do You ring doorbells?

"Yeah," Brooklyn says. "I remember hearing a guy's voice."

"He thought that was cool," Malia continues, "except then you left him to eat by himself. He didn't quite know how to interpret that, but he thought he'd give you some room. He knew you were going through a hard time."

The sidewalk is steady, but now my mind is spinning.

"What is going on?" I ask.

"What is going on is that I met Jonathan through work. He owns Fine Computer Techs. Ever since I met him I felt like you two would hit it off. And tonight, well, after everything that happened with Blake, I called him and asked him if he would come. I thought it might encourage you to see this guy who's been wanting to get to know you. And, I should add, being very patient about it too."

"But, I—"

"I mean, the guy even sent you a singing telegram with balloons and a tape recorder. How creative was that?"

"I thought— I'm so— I gotta find somebody!"

I take off north. Brooklyn and Malia are right behind me.

"Where are you going?" Brooklyn asks.

"Five blocks this way."

"Shouldn't we stop her?" Brooklyn is asking Malia. "I mean, what if she does something stupid?"

"I think we've already passed that point," Malia replies.

"I can hear you!" I say, marching forward. Well, maybe weaving. But I have to say, the buzz is wearing off fast.

"Jessie, where are you going?"

"Just trust me on this one."

They follow the rest of the way in silence until I get to the community church. I walk to the dark side of the church where the A/C unit is.

"Um, Jessie. You can't—"

"Trust me. I'm a pro. I've only gone to jail once."

"Malia, we've got to stop her!" Brooklyn says as I attempt to pry open the window.

"Dang, I wish I could walk through walls."

"Hold on," Malia says softly. "Let's let her do what she needs to do."

"Aren't we accomplices?" Brooklyn asks.

Hello, melodrama.

I finally shove the window open. "You two gotta stay here."

As I crawl in I hear Malia say, "Let her go."

I hurry myself to the sanctuary. It's dark and quiet, just like I like it.

"Okay," I yell into the darkness. "I'm an idiot. And not just because I got drunk tonight. But to my credit, I only had three shots of alcohol."

"Four."

I turn and there He is, sitting in the front pew. I can't help but grin at Him. I step forward a little. "I'm sorry."

"I know."

"I'm so confused. Who did they see tonight? Who is Malia talking about?"

"Someone I've been wanting to introduce you to. And so has she. You just wouldn't hear us."

I need to grab something. The lectern is nearby. "You mean he's real? Human real?"

"Yes."

"And...he looks like You?" I rub my temples where a slight head-ache is coming on. "What'd You do? Borrow his face while You were writing my story?"

"Sometimes I can be unconventional. People don't give me enough credit. I parted the Red Sea, you know? This was nothing."

I make my way to carpeted stairs that lead up to the platform. I sit so I'm facing Him. "But...I saw You with Blake. At the house. Talking to him...about me."

"That wasn't Me you saw through the window. That will make sense later. But I needed you to find out about Blake so I could move you on. Blake was never as captivated by you as I am."

I feel the blood rush through my body. "You're...captivated by me?"

"Yeah."

I sit on the highest step of the stage, overwhelmed by it all. Over-whelmed by Him. And before I know it, I'm crumpled against the carpeted stairs, crying. "I'm so sorry, for everything, for everything I said. I guess I could never really believe, with the seven billion people on the planet, that You also cared for me."

"I care about all of you."

"I see that now. I do. I'm sor—"

I hear faint commotion outside. "They have a silent alarm. It takes the police about—" I glance at my watch. "Yeah, they're probably here by now."

God hands me a piece of paper that I don't remember seeing in His hand before. "Get there. Right away."

Without even looking at the paper, I stuff it in my pocket and start to run out of the sanctuary. "Wait. Will I see You again?"

He only smiles, that gentle reassuring smile that is low on information but high on assuredness. "You better get going."

I hurry back down the hallway and to the office. The window is still open and I rush to it, sliding my body through. My feet hit the A/C unit. That's when I see red and blue lights flashing off the metal.

Slowly I turn around, planting a grin on my face. It's Officers Garrety and Lakeland, standing behind Malia and Brooklyn. "Hi."

"Hi."

Malia is chewing a fingernail. Brooklyn has a slightly amused look on her face. Officer Garrety steps between them. "Hello, Speedy."

"Hello, Officer Garrety."

"I can see you've returned to your old ways."

I take a deep breath and offer the most innocent-by-reason-of-insanity expression I can muster. I hop off the air-conditioning unit. "Listen, I need a police escort. You available?"

twenty-six

I feel awful leaving Malia and Brooklyn behind. They've had quite a night keeping me out of trouble, only to watch me be taken away in a police car with flashing lights. But Garrety and I have an understanding. I hope. I'm pretty sure he's not taking me to jail.

He's looking at the address on the piece of paper I gave him. "I'm not sure where this is. Hold on, let me call Dispatch."

I stare out the window as the world passes by in a blur. It seems surreal, yet it's like a puzzle coming together. All this time I doubted Him, doubted His love for me, doubted that He had my best interest at heart. Doubt almost wrecked it all for me. Why couldn't I have just believed, right from the start? He did nothing but show me love.

I feel wretched and humiliated by my humanness, except that that seems to be exactly what He liked about me. He knew everything about me, except He always seemed surprised by and in wonder at the very thing He created.

I close my eyes and tip my head back against the seat. The alcohol, like the devil, made life fun for a little while. Now it's betraying me with a headache made worse by strobe lights.

I feel the car slow and open my eyes. We're turning into—

"Oh…my…G—"

Officer Garrety cuts me off. "Huh-uh. Not in my car, young lady. I'm a religious man, and I won't take any of that, especially from a woman who keeps breaking into a church. At least have some respect for the Almighty."

I smile. "Believe me, I do." I figure now's not the time to explain I was actually calling upon God. As we drive up the hill, I see the house with the porch swing. And there He is. Wait…there *he* is. "Jonathan."

Officer Garrety pulls to a stop near the driveway. "This is the guy, huh?"

"I think so."

"He looks nice enough."

"He's been very patient with me. I'm just hoping it's not too late."

"A guy, if he's worth his weight in denim, will find patience, will dig deep." Garrety gets out and opens the back door of the cruiser.

I step out, staring at Jonathan. He stands and walks to the edge of the porch. I turn to Garrety. "I feel like I should tip you or something."

"Just donate to the Retired Officers' Fund, ma'am."

I laugh. "Okay. Thank you." I hold out a hand for him to shake. He takes it firmly and we have a moment. He looks like a proud dad and my heart melts a little. Garrety returns to his cruiser and drives off. I'm having a hard time turning back around, but I manage to. My feet still feel a little sloshy from the alcohol. Or maybe it's just that I'm swooning just looking at this guy.

I make it to the bottom of the veranda. "Hi."

"Hi."

I stare up at him. I can't help it. "Hi."

"You said that. Come on up."

I take the few steps up. "I said a lot of 'byes' when I saw you last. So, I owe you a few hi's. So, hi. I'm Jessie."

He blushes. "I know. More than I should. What are you doing here?"

"Looking for you."

"How did you know I'd be here?"

"Had a feeling." I hold out a nervous hand. "So, you're Jonathan."

He takes it, gently holds it for a moment longer than it takes to shake a hand. "Yeah. Jonathan Fine. Or…JF…JessieFan. Whatever you want to call me. Or not."

I cover my mouth. Wasn't expecting that.

He shakes his head. "I'm sorry. I know I should've—"

"No, please. Please. Don't apologize. I think it's cool."

He gestures toward the bench where he had been sitting. "Not stalker-like? Pumping you for information about you to use for my benefit?"

I walk over to the bench and sit down. "Love it."

He sits beside me, on the edge, as if ready to jump up. "I figured you were, you know, a reliable source."

"Often, yes." I look at my feet. "Except tonight, you know, I'm so sorry about…at the bar. I never drink. Ever. So it's kinda, yeah…but no worries. I left most of it back at the sidewalk outside the bar. It's a great sobering technique, and I am talking way too much."

He laughs. "I like that."

My gaze follows the outside of the unfinished house. "So…this house. Is it…?"

"Mine? Yeah. I've been working with Malia's son, Blake, to make some modifications."

"The porch?"

"There's that. Not done yet, but we're making good time on it."

I get up and walk to a window, peering in, trying to hide my grin. "So. You're my number one blog reader."

He joins me. "Guilty. You must think I'm kind of strange, huh?"

"Not at all. My standard of strange is very low in order to take into account myself."

He laughs.

"Did you have a favorite?"

"A favorite what?"

"Post?"

"I liked the one you wrote about guys never seeing you because you're not a blonde. Oh, and the one about the allergy risks you take just to eat chocolate." He looks down. A self-aware smile emerges. "I kind of liked all of them. You were very…vulnerable. Especially when you wrote that poem "Love Unseen." It was beautiful, raw, real. I, um, understood your pain of not being seen. I felt like that's where I met the real Jessie."

I step toward him. I can smell his cologne. Wow. Smells a little like the ocean. "Why didn't you say something to me sooner? About who you were?"

"I tried. A few times. But you weren't always very welcoming."

"When?"

"At the wedding chapel. I work two blocks away. I stepped inside because I was walking nearby. I didn't know you were going to be in there, but I felt this weird urge to go in. Didn't know why, but I—"

"Wait. That was you?"

"*Well, hello, you two.*"

"*You two? You can see Him?*"

Jonathan gives me a wry smile. "Is my face that forgettable?"

"No! No, not at all. But I was so…not nice to you."

"I noticed. When I tried to come meet you again at your shop, you were in there kissing this guy—and, like, kissing him so I would see you kissing him."

I bite my lip. "Um…yeah. That was Clay. And that explains why Clay saw you."

"Huh?"

"Nothing. Look, I am such an idiot."

"A cute idiot."

I walk over to the porch swing. "May I?"

"Sure." He sits with me.

"All this time, He was trying to get us to meet, and I—"

"Who?"

I turn to Jonathan. "Why didn't you give up on me?"

"I wanted to. Believe me. But then something would happen, like the night I felt like taking a walk on the beach and found your initials carved in the sand."

I smile, shaking my head. "Wow."

"I took it as a kind of signpost, to not give up. And I wanted to. I mean, I'd get these feelings, you know? Like I went to the Laundromat one night, hoping you'd be there. Of course you weren't, and I felt stupid for thinking you would be there."

"Oh boy."

"I know, totally ridiculous, right?"

"No, no. Trust me. It's not."

"And that blog of yours. Every time I read it, I felt like I wanted to know more of you." Suddenly he stands. "Hey, can I give you a tour? I'd love to show you the rest of the house."

"I would love that."

I follow him in. The smell of cut wood lingers around a faint smell of new paint. I get that new-car feeling as I follow him. He points out the living room—big, round, a see-through fireplace. A bay window. Perfection.

But what I notice as he is showing me from one magnificent room to the next is that as beautiful and dreamy as this house is, it's this guy who has me captivated. He's gentle and humble. I suspect a deep heart guides him.

We get to the kitchen, and we both immediately notice a puddle on the floor. "Oh no. Not again. Sorry about this. I told Blake we might need a plumber. I just can't seem to get this water to stop leaking." He gets down on his knees and ducks under the sink. "Hey, can you hand me that wrench sitting up there?" I do and I hear him clanking around. "Ahhh!" He backs out from underneath the sink, drenched. Then we both hear a popping sound, and before we know it, water is erupting from the pipe and pouring into the kitchen. Jonathan freezes, wrench in hand.

I grab it and quickly crawl under the sink, reaching for the valve. It's a hard turn, but I finally get the water to shut off. I emerge like I've just gone swimming.

I start laughing and his mortified expression retreats. He helps me up. "Welcome to my home."

"It's lovely. Truly." I smile.

"Wow. That was some kind of maneuver with that wrench."

"I can change tires too."

Time has drifted by like a lazy log on a river or superlong karaoke song. We're eating the last of delivery pizza when a soft light begins glowing from the horizon. "It's morning?"

Jonathan turns to look out the window. "Wow. I had no idea."

"Nice view of the sunrise out there."

"I know. It's great, isn't it?" He stands. "More Coke?"

"Yeah. I think I'm going to need some major caffeine." Although the adrenaline is doing a fine job of keeping me alert.

He pours more into my cup. "The first time I heard about you was when your parents died."

"No kidding. That was a long time ago."

"My mom went to school with your mom. She read that article about you losing your parents and becoming a guardian to your twelve-year-old sister. Because there wasn't anyone else."

"I remember being so mad they printed that story. Like for them, it was news for all of a day. I didn't want people's pity."

"You know, I was the same age as you. And I kept thinking what that must have been like. I have this huge family. Too huge, sometimes. I wondered what it must be like to be you."

"What it must be like to be me?" I laugh. "Oh, it's quite a ride. So, you have a large family?"

"Oh, it's horrendous. In a good way. I mean, at holidays it's mass chaos. Kids running everywhere. People talking nonstop. I'm a little terrified to take you home to meet—"

"What?"

"I'm sorry. I'm being so presumptuous."

I grin. "Please. Presume away."

"You know," he says, sitting back down, "this whole thing, it kind of came about from these strange feelings I'd get. Malia called me one day and asked if I was seeing anyone, and from then on, I would feel an urge to go do laundry or an urge to step into a chapel. It was so confusing. I mean, I'd prayed for a long time to find the right woman, but sometimes I wished God would just come down here, appear to me, tell me exactly what to do, you know? The 'feelings' seemed so ambiguous."

I nearly spew Coke out my nostrils.

"What's so funny?" he asks, looking slightly wounded.

"Nothing, I promise, nothing," I say, trying to swallow. I wipe my mouth with a napkin. "It's just—well, I don't know that God appearing by our sides would help much."

"No?"

"We're stubborn creatures, certain we're able to direct our own lives, certain we know better. Maybe God speaks quietly because we don't always respond to the direct approach."

"Maybe. I don't know."

"But we're here, aren't we?" I smile.

"Yeah. I think it took a minor miracle to get us here, though."

I take a big bite of pizza. "'Minor' is an understatement."

I'm not sure what time I finally arrived home. I didn't want to leave, but I couldn't keep my eyes open any longer. He drove me home, taking the long route, I noticed.

"So," he said, taking my hand. "I want to see you again, if you haven't already figured that out."

I grin. "Me too."

"I want to see you tonight."

"You want to wait that long?" I tease.

"Let me walk you up." He gets out, hurrying around to my side, and opens the door.

"Guys don't do that much anymore," I say, taking his hand as he helps me out.

"What can I say? I'm a throwback."

We walk toward my condo. The stairs are hard to climb—I'm so tired—but I finally reach the top. I turn, but to my surprise he isn't there, and for a split second I sort of panic and wonder if he's walked through a wall or something.

But, no. There he is, standing at the bottom, being all chivalrous. I'm not kidding, I nearly burst into tears.

"I'll see you later, then?"

"Definitely."

I don't walk through a wall, but I definitely float into my condo. If I weren't so tired, I'd do some crazy dance or something. But I figure all I've got left is enough energy to climb the stairs and crawl into bed.

I reach my room and immediately spot a gift sitting on the edge of my bed. It's wrapped in gold with a sparkling, expensive ribbon around it and tied into a larger-than-life bow.

"Brooklyn?" I call, but she's not home.

I take the gift into my hands and dare myself to wonder who might be responsible. I untie the bow and it falls gracefully to the ground. After I lift the top off the box, a surprised gasp escapes.

There it is. A purple pen, feather and all.

Underneath is a brand-new journal, and not one of those cheap kinds, either. It's leather, with heavy paper. I crack it open. On the first line, where it says *To,* fancy calligraphy takes up nearly the entire first line. It is my name, *Jessica,* and next to it: *God Sees.* Underneath is written *Jonathan,* with the meaning of his name: *Gift of God.*

I laugh and hug the journal to my chest. This is one journal I can't wait to fill. In fact, maybe I should start writing now, before I take my nap. I flip the top off the pen and smooth my hand over the first page.

Then I hesitate.

I slowly close the journal, put the lid back on the pen, and put them both into the box. I take the bow and wrap it around, tying it simply. I set it on my chest of drawers, then crawl under my covers. It feels good to rest.

"I think I'll give that back to You," I whisper. "I want You to write the rest of my story."

twenty-seven

He wasn't joking when he said he came from a large family. I am standing in the middle of a nicely decorated living room. It's modern and warm all at once. I see where Jonathan gets his love for architecture and home design.

Swarming around me are people and children and pets. A parrot actually flies by. I feel like I'm the eye of the tornado as I watch it all. Coming toward me, like she is in complete command of this storm, is Jonathan's mother. She is the picture of elegance, with perfectly bobbed hair, oversized earrings that offset her tiny frame, and a smile that is all tooth and gleam.

"You must be Jessie," she says, reaching toward me with a hand. I take it. It is smooth and soft, like she is much younger than she is, and it smells like cherries and almonds. That's the same lotion my mother used to wear. "I am so delighted to finally meet you! Oh, you're just a dream!"

A more excitable and younger version of Jonathan's mother is bouncing toward me, her shoulders lifting up and down. "I'm so excited to meet you! Jonathan's told us a lot about you! We were all beginning to wonder if you really existed!" She pulls me into a hug. "I'm Laura, one of his sisters."

"And I'm Ruth, his mother. And this is our family. I hope we don't scare you off!"

"I love big families." I smile, choking a little on my own emotion.

"Come to the kitchen with me. I'll pour you a drink and we can chat where it's a little less noisy." Ruth takes my hand and pulls me away from Jonathan, who smiles and nods.

The kitchen is separated by two double doors, and strangely, it is very quiet. "Sweet tea? Seltzer water? Cola?"

"Tea is fine. Thank you."

"Only adults are allowed in the kitchen. Love all those munchkins, but they can be a wild group. We had to set some boundaries when they all came along, so they're not allowed in here. This is our quiet spot."

"Your kitchen is lovely," I say, taking in the large center island, the enormous stove and fridge, and the window that looks out onto an acre of gardens and fountains. Right over the sink, I spot a framed picture, and it takes my breath away.

Ruth looks at me. "Are you all right?"

"Yes, yes. Fine." I pick up the frame. It's him. It's him! It's my imaginary friend who used to follow me around when I was a kid.

Ruth looks over my shoulder. "That's my Jonathan. Isn't he a doll?"

I clutch the frame. "I feel like I've known him my whole life."

"That's what he said about you."

I carefully set the picture down. "How old was he in that picture?"

"Nine."

The kitchen doors burst open, and kids flood in like a levee broke.

Ruth smiles tolerantly. "Well, sometimes boundaries are meant to be broken."

The little ones tug at my hand. "Jessie! Jessie! Come out here!" The big ones are jumping up and down.

"What is it?" I ask them as they guide me out of the kitchen.

"You'll see," says a little girl with her hair tied up in ponytails. "We have something for you!"

"Maddie, hush. Don't say anything else," an older boy says, catching my eye. "She sometimes talks too much."

I look down at Maddie. "I have that problem too." She smiles, and she's missing two front teeth.

I have now been guided to the center of the living room. Jonathan is leaning casually against a bookcase, seemingly having fun watching all this chaos. A wall of children are standing in front of the coffee table, their hands clasped behind their backs, all wearing mischievous smiles.

"What's going on, you cuties?" I ask them. They all look at Jonathan.

"Just a little gift to make you feel welcome," he says.

The kids part, and sitting on the glass table are two large glass containers of M&M's. I can't help but laugh. "Oh my! What is this, the twelve-pound bag?"

Maddie says, "Jonathan says you love chocolate! Except he says you swell up like a—"

Jonathan holds up a hand. "Juuusst trying to paint a complete picture of you to my family." He smiles and shrugs.

I laugh and pick up one of the containers. "So these are for me? I am going to bloom into ten cows!"

Jonathan approaches me and puts a hand around my waist. "Do you know what today is?"

"Obviously it's my lucky day!" I say, eying the M&M's. I'm drooling.

"We've been dating three months."

"Oh. Yeah. That." I laugh. "It's actually been three months and eleven hours."

"Exactly."

"So, is chocolate the gift for that kind of anniversary? Seems so extravagant."

He pulls me near. "You can't help it, can you?"

"What?"

"You can't keep your eyes off the chocolate."

I kiss his cheek. "But you're a very close second, babe."

"Well, I suppose it's not nice to give you the chocolate and then not let you eat it."

The little boy with glasses looks transfixed. "If you swell real big, can we call you Puff Daddy?"

"Sounds a little masculine," I say, scooping a few. "How about Powder Puff?"

"Oooh! Yes!" says the little girl with the pixie cut. "That sounds like a cool superhero name too."

I start to throw a few in my mouth when a little hand grabs my arm. "Wait!"

"What?" I ask, looking at her cherub face.

"You should read it first."

"Read what?"

"The M&M. It has instructions on it."

"Melts in my mouth, not in my—" It's teeny, tiny writing. White block letters. I hold it up, hoping for better light. "No!"

"No?" Jonathan asks, his face dropping.

"No, not no! Not no! No, I just can't believe it! That kind of no!" I stare at the two words on the M&M's: MARRY ME

"So…is that a yes?"

I throw the M&M's in my mouth and jump into his arms. "Yews! Yews!" I manage to swallow. "Yes!"

He kisses me on the cheek, then on the lips, and everyone in the living room applauds. Everyone except two little guys who are apparently very grossed out by the idea of kissing. I give them a quick wink. "Grab some M&M's. It'll help."

Jonathan slides a ring onto my finger. It is simple, delicate, with three tiny diamonds.

"Perfection." I wipe my tears.

"Really?" He looks relieved. "It's a little intimidating asking a woman to marry you who dreams up these amazing marriage proposals for a living."

I hug him tightly. "At the end of the day, it's all about heart. You've just made me the happiest woman on earth."

"Your ears are, um…"

"They're turning bright red, aren't they?"

"Very Rudolph-like."

"What can I say? They're happy too. Mostly about the chocolate, but they like you also."

Jonathan holds my hand tightly. "I have one more surprise for you."

"I don't know if my histamines can take it."

He laughs. "You are so hilarious. Come on." He guides me through the house with the entire family following us. We end up on the back porch. And I spot her immediately. She is walking through the grass toward us. I look at Jonathan, tears spilling from my eyes. "I knew you'd want her here," he says.

I run down the steps of the deck and wrap my arms around Brooklyn. We hold each other for a long moment. She whispers, "I am so happy for you. You deserve all of this."

"I love you, Sis."

"I love you too." She takes my hand. "Come on. I hear there's fine chocolate somewhere!"

It is late at night. Brooklyn and I are finally home after spending the entire day at Jonathan's family's house. My cheeks suffer one spasm after another because I can't stop smiling. In the dim light of the kitchen, I can't take my eyes off my ring. I try to imagine what Mom and Dad would've thought of it.

"Here." Brooklyn has come back into the kitchen. I didn't even hear her. She slides a piece of paper toward me.

"What's this?" I look at it. It's a check for ten thousand dollars. "Brook!"

"For your wedding. I'm the last person on God's green earth who's ready to get married."

"I can't take your—"

"Shut up. Let me do this. There's gotta be some benefit to giving up your entire young life to raise a blond, bratty sister."

"You are not a brat. Most of the time. And there's a lot more to you than just hair. I'm sorry I—"

"It's all right. And let me do this. I mean, I do get the condo, because you, my sis, are finally getting a real house with your own master bedroom."

I squeal with excitement. I'm a squealer now. "I know. I know!"

"With a queen bed and a hot guy in it. But first, you gotta let me tweeze your eyebrows."

twenty-eight

i have imagined this day for nearly my entire life. It's better than anything I ever could've written. I swear harp music is playing through my head. And seriously, I feel a light breeze through the chapel, like a heavenly wind. I've spent the morning with Brooklyn, Malia, and Nicole, getting ready. Brooklyn has the magic touch. My hair is stunning. And I never knew makeup could do so much good.

We are all standing around in the room used for changing, waiting for the wedding planner to tell us it's time. "Hey," I tell the girls, "can I have a moment alone?"

Brooklyn eyes me. "You're not going to sneak chocolate, are you? It's too risky right now. Wait, you're not having cold feet, are you?"

"Not at all. Are you kidding me? I just want some time to reflect. To settle. This is my last moment as a single woman."

"You gonna miss any of it?" Nicole asks me.

"No. I don't think so. But it's a strange feeling to work toward something your whole life and then achieve it. There's sort of a blank slate in front of me now. I've never dared to dream beyond this day."

Brooklyn smirks. "You're too deep for me, Sis. But yeah, take some time. We'll be spying on the men."

Brooklyn and Nicole walk out, but Malia stays for a moment. "Hey. I just want to make sure you're okay, that you haven't changed your mind about walking alone down the aisle. You know Blake would be more than happy to do that for you."

"I know. He's a sweetheart for volunteering. But no. I've been doing this on my own for so long, it's okay. I can get there myself. Besides, I don't want a stand-in. I want the real thing."

Malia squeezes my hand. "What are you going to do, having someone to take care of you from now on?"

"Weird, huh?"

"Good."

"Yeah. Good."

"Okay. I'll leave you to your thoughts. You look stunning."

She walks out, quietly shutting the door behind her. I turn, staring into the long oval mirror before me. Organza drapes over the beaded lace. I wasn't sure I could wear an empire waist, but it creates a perfect line around me. The chapel train is drawn up beautifully.

Petite daisies seem to bloom from my hair. And they're layered throughout my dress too. The designer created a masterpiece. Somehow I've managed to not look like a walking garden. I pick up my bouquet and practice holding it at the exact right level. I smile into the mirror and try to remember that I need to smile at my guests as

I walk down the aisle. But I have a feeling I'm only going to have eyes for him.

Something catches my attention in the mirror. I whirl around, grabbing my dress like I might need to protect it. Behind me stands an old man. I feel frightened until I look into His bright blue eyes. Underneath the slightly crusty, very old appearance, two eyes dazzle and dance with life. Peace engulfs me. I would recognize Him anywhere now.

"Hi," I say.

"Hi."

"You're not borrowing Jonathan's face anymore, I guess?"

"No."

"Nice face you got there."

"I am an artisan."

I step closer. "And you're dressed in a formal white tuxedo. Now that's more like the God we all imagine, you know?"

"I know."

I feel kind of shy, for some reason. "So I wasn't sure I'd be seeing You around anymore."

"I'm always near. Remember that."

"I will."

He comes over and touches my hand. "I thought maybe you'd like someone to walk you down the aisle. A father, perhaps?"

"You want to give me away today?"

"Like a father should." He grins. "You don't want a stand-in, do you? You want the real thing."

I feel emotion tickling my insides. "It would mean the world to me."

"Just remember, I'm *sharing* you. Don't forget about Me."

"I don't know how to thank You. There's not even a way to thank You. I could never have written this for myself."

"I know that too."

"When my parents died, a part of me died too. I didn't know if I could ever find happiness." I wink at Him. "You're a great writer."

"I have good material to work with."

"So," I say, wiping a tear that is threatening to drop down and ruin my makeup, "any last tidbits of wisdom?"

"Yeah." I see sadness in His eyes.

"What's the matter?"

"These are not the last words I'm going to speak to you, but they are the last ones I will speak to you like this. Do you understand?"

I don't know if I understand.

"You're the bride. He's the groom. You represent a lot to me. More than you know. You see, I have this dream. A dream a lot like yours, about a day when My Bride will come to Me. The day I will be the beloved Groom. A day when everything that is set right in heaven will be set right on earth."

The tears drop. I can't help it. I never imagined *Him* having a dream, a dream that hasn't been fulfilled. "You make a great groom."

God holds my hand and covers it with His other. "My voice will be quiet, like a breeze inside your soul. You will have to listen hard. You will have to shut out all the other voices."

I nod.

"Today is a great day for you. But not all your days ahead will be great. There will be times Jonathan's going to make you angry."

I open my eyes wide. "But You picked him for me."

"Yes, but you'll wonder what in the world I was thinking. Jonathan never wipes off countertops, you know."

I smile.

"There will be times you won't understand his choices, what he's doing, why he's doing it."

I stare at the floor, shaking my head. "Like You. That's what you were teaching me, huh?"

"You'll wonder why you fell in love with him to begin with. But you'll stay because you'll know it's right and you'll know it's real. And you will have learned to love unconditionally."

"That's why You were so annoying!" I give Him a wry grin. "And I mean that in the most affectionate way possible."

God lets go of my hand and opens the door for me. "I like to think of it as engaging. Pun intended."

I walk through the doorway. "You know, it doesn't escape my notice that this could have happened a lot sooner had I not gotten in Your way."

"I know."

"You're gloating."

"I'm not. I just enjoy being right. It happens a lot."

I feel that breeze again, the one I felt in the chapel. "You were there, weren't You, when Mom and Dad met. Did You do the borrowing-of-the-whole-face thing?"

"Things never happen the same way twice."

I shake my head, wondering if I'll ever get this down. "One last question: can You at least tell me if they're okay?"

"They're more than okay." He looks at his watch. "It's almost time for Me to walk you down that aisle."

"Will they see You?"

"Yes. They will see Me in you and Jonathan and your love for each other and others."

The girls see me and rush over. "It's time! It's time!" says Brooklyn.

"All of you look so beautiful," I say. "Thank you for being here with me on this day. And all the days leading up to this. I don't know where I would be without all of you." I glance behind me and don't see Him.

Malia takes my hand. "Let's get you married."

We trail into the small foyer that leads into the sanctuary. The doors are closed. Two men in tuxedos, Jonathan's friends, stand by each door, ready to open on cue. I hear the music play. My eyes swell with tears. I can't believe, after all this time, it's *my* time and *my* day and *my* life.

I watch Malia, the first bridesmaid, walk down the aisle in a deep purple bridesmaid dress. Okay, yes, and matching shoes. I couldn't resist. Then Nicole. Brooklyn takes her place and looks back at me, grinning. "You are beautiful." Tears stream down her face. "And I don't mean just on the outside." She then turns and walks, her head held high, proud to be my maid of honor.

The doors close so the crowd can't see me yet. Jonathan's two friends smile admiringly at me. I look to my right. I know He will be there. And He is, standing stoic in His white tuxedo. "This is it."

He nods. "This is it."

I feel His gentle arm at my elbow, guiding me as the two men open the doors for me. I step forward, right into the doorway. Most everyone is still watching Brooklyn as she makes her way to the front, but near the back is Blake. Alone? I smile brightly at him, and he smiles back, but with a hint of sadness. Perhaps he knows that I have a new best friend and new person to fill my heart. I want to rush to him, hug him, tell him to trust God. But I feel a nudge.

"Well? What are you waiting for?"

He knows that I never intended to run down this aisle. Nope. I was going to walk, take my time, make the guy wait.

I laugh and then grab my dress, hike it up a foot, and start running down the aisle toward Jonathan, whose face lights up with surprise. The guests roar with laughter as I pass. What it must look like to see a bride flying by! My veil has to be flapping behind me like a cape.

I reach the altar, a little out of breath. Jonathan is nearly belly-laughing at me as he pulls me next to him. The pastor looks horribly confused but is nevertheless stretching a smile across his face.

"Okay. This bride's in a hurry, isn't she?" He offers me a grin.

"Yes to everything. Yes, yes. Yes!"

The pastor looks baffled again.

Jonathan laughs, shakes his head, and sort of nods apologetically to the pastor. He puts an arm around me and pulls me close. "You're awesome."

Pastor Landry opens his little black book and puts an authoritative tone into his voice as he begins. "We are gathered here today to see this man and this woman wedded in holy matrimo—"

Gosh, I'm impatient. I turn, grab Jonathan's face and kiss him. And kiss him again. And before I know it, I've melted into his arms, and the world around me has vanished.

Until the pastor clears his throat.

I slowly release Jonathan, and he releases me. We laugh and so do the guests.

Pastor Landry raises an eyebrow.

"What do you expect?" I declare. "I'm *finally* the bride!"

I couldn't have asked for more perfect weather. We decided to hold the reception at our new home, out back on the grassy hillside that overlooks the ocean. The breeze from the water washes over all of us.

Jonathan holds me tightly as we dance to "I Only Have Eyes for You." He dances just like God, or maybe God dances just like him. Whatever the case, the moves are familiar and I let him guide me. It's nice to be directed.

"I love you," I say. "I hope you like greeting cards."

"Huh?"

"I've got a sack of about fifty that I've been saving my whole life to give to you."

"Somehow that doesn't surprise me," he says.

We finish the dance, and I feel a tap on my shoulder. I turn. It's Officer Garrety and his partner Lakeland.

"Hello, Officers."

"I should arrest you," Garrety says to me.

My heart skips. "Huh?"

"It should be illegal to be this happy." He smiles.

Lakeland gives a goofy smile. "Of all the criminals I met, I was hoping you'd be the one that ended up turning out okay."

I laugh. Me, a criminal. That's funny.

Jonathan squeezes me. "I'm going to go mingle with guests."

"All right. I'll be right there," I say, leaning to the side for a better view of something that catches my eye. Brooklyn is chatting with the old man in the white tuxedo. God, my *Father.* My hand finds my heart as I watch the two interact. She's engaged and at ease with Him. I stand there for I don't know how long, just watching them, longing a little to be with Him again like that.

Two arms wrap around me. "Come on. It's time for us to go."

My body tingles with excitement as I take Jonathan's hand. He leads me through the house and to the front. The guests are lining the sidewalk that leads to the veranda, ready to throw—I laugh as I see it—miniature M&M's.

A horse-drawn carriage awaits us. The driver stands at attention. Everyone is smiling and cheering.

"You ready?" Jonathan asks.

"Almost. Just a second." I walk forward a little to where Brooklyn is standing, clutching her bag of M&M's. "Thank you for standing up for me today."

"You're welcome."

"I saw that guy you were talking to during the entire reception."

Brooklyn's face lights up. "I know! Wasn't he hot?"

"Hot? The old guy?"

"Come on, he's not *that* old, for heaven's sake. I mean, if thirty's old then you're ancient, Sis. *Loved* the spiky blond hair. And his eyes. Can't even describe his eyes." She looks at me. "Don't look so worried. Goodness. It's not like he proposed. I mean, we were just getting to know each other. He was very respectful. You just don't find that quality in a lot of men these days." She pulls me into a hug. "I love you, Sis. My whole life I thought we were so different. But you know what?" she whispers. "I want what you have."

"Somehow, I think you might just get it."

I step back next to Jonathan. He looks down at me. "So are we going to walk like two civilized people, or should we bolt like crazed, in-love maniacs?"

"I vote for maniacs."

"Then let's do it!"

Hand in hand, we race past the M&M's and our family and friends. We climb into the carriage and wave as it pulls away. I notice the sunset over the water.

"Look at that," I say to Jonathan, leaning in to him.

"It's like it was designed just for us, just for our day."

"I think it might've just been."

acknowledgments

From Cheryl McKay:

Whenever I tell anyone about this project, they look at me with intrigue: "Your screenplay is being adapted into a novel? Isn't that the opposite of the normal order?" Yes, indeed it is. Rene and I are happy to blaze this unusual trail together.

First, I must thank God for inspiring me to write this story. He definitely took charge of the "purple pen" I used to develop this idea. He also let me live some of its angst. God is the master at turning pain into humor; my life is no exception. I am so thankful to know God as my matchmaker, my best friend, my counselor, my Father, and my true husband, just as the character in my story comes to know Him.

I must thank Rene for taking over the purple pen in translating this from script into novel, for being so faithful to the story while adding her own incredibly talented and comical flair. (I loved watching her get inside my head!) I'm truly grateful to our agent, Janet Kobobel Grant, for her support of this project.

I also appreciate my writing mentors who believed in this story when I first started writing the script: Susan Rohrer, Dean Batali, Key Payton, and Gil Elvgren, as well as those who've invested in my development as a writer: Regent, Act One, and Art Within. Grateful acknowledgment goes out to Producer Cecil Chambers of Triumphant Pictures. I'd also like to thank Rick Eldridge for hiring me to write the screen adaptation of *The Ultimate Gift*. Rick was instrumental in introducing me to Rene when he hired her to novelize my screenplay for *The Ultimate Gift*.

Many thanks to my incredible friends and family who supported me in this process: Darin, Denise and Mark, Ashley, Peggy, Dawn, Coach Mahr, Louis, John, Kendal, Sheri, Lisa, Lana, Caroline, Ali, Laura, Connie, my parents—Tom and Denise—and .my sister, Heather. To all of you: your encouragement and prayers mean the world to me.

Finally, I am so grateful to the team at WaterBrook Multnomah for believing this was a story worth telling and for doing the unconventional by adapting a script into a book. Special thanks to Shannon Hill Marchese, Heather Gemmen Wilson, Laura Wright, Sandra Holcombe, and the rest of our amazing team.

Please visit www.cherylmckay.net

From Rene Gutteridge:

I was first introduced to Cheryl McKay through her writing after I was hired to write the novelization for *The Ultimate Gift*. I remember reading and rereading her screenplay and being completely taken by the story, the characters, the words, the dialogue. I knew before I ever wrote the novelization that I was blessed to be a small part of the much bigger picture of *The Ultimate Gift*.

As I got to know Cheryl better and better, I found a passionate, intelligent, highly creative, and immensely warm woman. We became instant friends and knew we'd work together again.

When Cheryl told me about her screenplay *Never the Bride,* I had to read it. I loved every moment of it and knew I had in my hands not only a terrific and entertaining story but also a message of God's love, devotion, and delight in His children. *Never the Bride* tested my ideas of God's love for me, and I had to dig deep in myself to find the courage to understand how much God really loves me. Jessie Stone challenged me to get to know my God in a deeper and more intimate way.

I am thoroughly blessed to bring this story and the character of Jessie Stone to you in novel form. It was fun to dive into the inner life of one of the most delightful characters I've ever had the chance to get to know. I hope you have enjoyed her as much.

So much goes into the writing and production of a novel, and doubly so in a collaboration. I'd like to thank Cheryl McKay for her wise and passionate voice and true storyteller's heart. Also thanks to Shannon Marchese, Laura Wright, Heather Gemmen Wilson, Sandra Holcombe, the entire staff at WaterBrook Multnomah, and Janet Kobobel Grant—it's always a delight to work with all of you.

And with great love and appreciation, I offer thanks to my husband, Sean, my children, John and Cate, and my friends and family who continue to support what I do. Thanks also to ChiLibris, to my beloved Kansas Eight, and to the Flock that Rocks. My final thanks to God my Father, whose sacrificial love continues to beckon me.

Please visit www.renegutteridge.com.

Wacky characters, sincere faith, and surprising plot twists in one hilariously addictive series!

With unexpected and delightful humor, *Scoop* offers a behind-the-scenes look at a local TV news team's desperate grab for ratings—and the hazards of taking one's faith into the workplace.

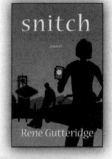

When an inexperienced clown-turned-cop with outspoken faith joins an undercover team in Las Vegas and tries to shine a little light around Sin City, the criminal justice system may never be the same.

Pack your bags for high-flying fun with a quirky flight crew and a cabin full of zany passengers, including a corporate spy sent to test the limits of customer service.

Available in bookstores and from online retailers.

WATERBROOK PRESS
www.waterbrookmultnomah.com

Experience quirky fun and suspense in Skary, Indiana

Available in bookstores and from online retailers.